After Genevieve

The Pathway Home

by
Rachel Menin

Visit Rachel Menin's Author Page at
www.ArdentWriterPress.com

For general information about publishing with The Ardent Writer
Press contact *steve@ardentwriterpress.com* or forward mail to:
The Ardent Writer Press,
Box 25
Brownsboro, Alabama 35741

This is a first edition novel, *After Genevieve: The Pathway Home*, by Rachel Menin. Excerpts of text may be posted online only for a noncommercial use, provided quotations do not exceed a total of over three hundred (300) words.

Cover art and composition are by Laurie Powers Going, Austin, Texas. Composition and cover are covered by the same grant for noncommercial use as noted above.

Library of Congress Cataloging-in-Publication Data

After Genevieve: The Pathway Home by Rachel Menin.

p. cm. - (Ardent Writer Press-2021) ISBN 978-1-64066-133-2 (pbk.); 978-1-64066-134-9 (eBook epub)

Library of Congress Control Number 2021950031

Library of Congress Subject Headings
- Fiction/General
- Fiction and reality

BISAC Subject Headings
- FIC045000 FICTION/Family Life/General

First Edition (Copyright Rachel Menin © 2020)

Contents

Acknowledgment

I thank Jesus Christ my Savior for making anything done here on earth worth doing. Scott Menin, you are the best husband ever; your love keeps me going. Rachel Luann Strayer and Justin Kassab, thank you for paving the way for me and supporting my insanity. I have THE best friends and family in the world; just try to prove me wrong. I may not have named you all here, but you are reflected in the story. Let me know when you find your quirks and habits—wink, wink. Thank you to my students who encouraged me with their dreams and aspirations.

Thank you to those who helped me understand my manuscript settings and answered all my simple questions: the proprietors, Joe and Becky, of *Aunt Rebecca's Bed and Breakfast* in Baltimore, Jeff Landis from the Mennonite Visitors Information Center, and Esther from the *Antique Village* of Strasburg. Penny Jackson, thank you for giving me courage to talk with strangers and helping me commandeer tobacco leaves.

I am grateful to the Wilkes University community, especially Lenore Hart, who works harder than any writer I know. Thank you, Dr. Nancy McKinley, for boosting my confidence when I wanted to concede to my inner critic. Thank you, Laurie Powers Going for your creative ideas and excitement. Thanks, Mobies, for the unquestionable support; we were blessed to find each other.

To Doyle and Steve at Ardent Writer Press, thank you for this unfathomable opportunity. I am grateful for your care and treatment of not only my manuscript but of me as well.

Dedication

To my father, Raymond Michael Wiren, Jr.,
who always dreamed more for me
than I ever dreamed for myself.

From my front porch in heaven, I watch through a window of clouds.
                                                                -Genevieve

Chapter 1

LAINEY BLACKED OUT her father's eyes using the sharpie she kept wedged under the crack on the front porch steps. Her secret project had been to sift through Grandma Tessie's photo albums to destroy every visual proof she had of Jeremiah Traynor. Only the first week of summer break and this was the last one as far as she could tell, except for the gallery of family pictures that lined the walls of the stairway. At eleven years old, she did have a plan. When she was old enough to leave for college, she would cover her father's face with a picture of a donkey's head and take a selfie with it because she would finally be old enough to have a cell phone, according to Grandma Tessie's rules.

Lainey stuffed the marker and album under the porch swing cushion when she saw Grandpa Jude's pickup truck turn onto the lane. He was two hours earlier than expected. Lainey jumped off the farmhouse porch and raced across the grass to greet him. If her timing was right, he might let her drive down the gravel road to get last night's mail, even though she still had to prop a toolbox behind her back to reach the gas pedal. He'd made all four of his daughters wait to practice driving until they were thirteen, but if he was in a really good mood, he would try to sneak her by the main authority— Grandma Tessie. They'd gotten away with it five times in the last two weeks.

Lainey stood to the right of the split-rail fence separating a long lane from the house's driveway. Across the fields of the Virginian farm, the tobacco leaves were fat and ripe like overgrown spinach. She loved living here more than anything. She could roam through rows and rows of green, pretending to be in a giant ogre's dinner salad. It was her favorite spot to daydream about owning her own horse. Her mother Genevieve had loved horses, and Lainey wanted to be just like her someday, even though she couldn't remember her very well. Lainey would name her own horse Genny and feed her carrots and sugar cubes.

According to Grandpa Jude, many of the tobacco farmers from Florida to Pennsylvania were selling out due to government regulations and anti-smoking campaigns. But not him. While he understood the pressure of societal concerns, he wasn't about to give up just yet.

Lainey didn't understand what the fuss was about. All she knew was the tobacco plant was beautiful, and this farm was the only place in the world she ever wanted to live.

Grandpa was definitely in a hurry, and he'd turned the headlights on despite their being drowned out by the morning sun. Lainey wiped splotches of mud from her khaki walking shorts while waving to get his attention, but the rusty Chevy truck was barreling straight toward her and Grandma Tessie's ever-blooming rose bushes.

Lainey stepped to the side of the fence, but Grandpa wasn't slowing down. An avalanche of fear rushed through her stomach. Instinct forced her to sprint back to the front porch seconds before the truck smashed the fence.

Grandpa Jude slid out of the driver's seat; his mouth was moving, but Lainey could not hear the words.

She sprinted back to the scene of impact and rested her arms and hands on the hood of the truck, attempting to stop them from shaking. "Are you okay, Grandpa?" The heat from the engine was coloring pink marks onto the underbelly of her forearms.

"Get behind the wheel and put the truck in reverse."

"But Grandpa, look at my hands—" She held one out and watched her fingers twitch. "Plus, I'm not good driving backwards yet."

"Do as I say," he said then spoke under his breath with incoherent syllables.

Lainey reached for the gray and black toolbox in the corner of the truck bed and lodged it snug on the driver's seat.

"What's taking so long? Get in the damn truck!" Sweat beads poured down his red face.

Shocked at the anger in Grandpa's voice, Lainey jumped behind the steering wheel and slammed the door shut. Her hands shaking, she supported her lower back with the metal of the toolbox. She wrenched the old gear into reverse and made sure she had a firm step on the brake. "I'm ready," she yelled out the window.

"Back up slowly," he said.

To press the gas pedal with her toe, Lainey let go of the brake and straightened her knee as far as it would go. She looked over her shoulder and pressed a little harder. The truck didn't want to move. She pushed harder, gunning the gas. Stones, dirt, and grass spun through the wheel well as the truck jolted away from the roses. The truck accelerated backwards, sped across the fifteen-foot-wide driveway, and smashed its back bumper into a two-hundred-year-old oak tree.

On impact, Lainey's head slammed back onto the headrest then bounced forward onto the steering wheel. She could feel hot tears streaming while she tried to control the quiver of her lower lip. A bump was already growing on her forehead, and the back of her head didn't feel so hot either.

Grandpa Jude jumped out of the truck, rushed to the fence, pulled the white-washed rail out from the dirt, then jammed it back into place. He slammed his palm against the side of the post three times.

Brushing the wet off her face and biting her lip, Lainey put the truck into drive and parked the Chevy parallel to the fence. She took a deep breath then jumped out to help Grandpa Jude cover the damage with any unharmed roses left.

"Don't be mad at me, Grandpa. For hitting the tree." She stroked the knot on her head which felt hot as a log on fire.

The old man kept fiddling with the flowers, filling in the holes that still showed the broken rail.

"Grandpa!"

"Hey there, Lainey girl." Grandpa Jude pointed a shaky, bent finger toward the magenta petals mixed with white paint chips that covered the dirt. "Think ole Tessie'll notice? Almost ran the bush clean over."

"Uh, yeah. Grandma sees everything. Plus, you almost hit me. And I just crashed the pickup into the tree."

Grandpa snapped off a ripe bloom. "Wouldn't ever hurt my little Pumpkinhead." He bopped her on the head with the flower; three petals floated past the bumper.

Lainey folded her arms on the fence post and rested her chin on the crook of an elbow. The shaking she had felt in her whole body relaxed to a slow simmer.

"What is going on out there?" The screech came from the front porch.

Both Grandpa Jude and Lainey turned to see Grandma Tessie walking toward them with no shoes on, hobbling over loose rocks and bumps in the ground.

Lainey held out her arms to let Grandma Tessie enfold her in an embrace.

"I ate a bug trying to run out of the way, and my head really, really hurts." She caressed the massive bump on her head. "I can feel it growing."

"Let me get a look at this." Grandma Tessie grabbed Lainey's chin to inspect the growing bump.

"When you hear my little tale, you won't even notice the damage to the roses or her head. I guarantee it." Grandpa stood by the fence grinning, looking at the sky.

"Don't you care what I did to the truck, Grandpa? Or the tree?" Lainey laid her head on her grandmother's shoulder.

"You've only been gone a half hour, Jude," Grandma Tessie said.

Lainey felt Grandma's hand putting slight pressure on her head to keep it tight to her shoulder.

"I missed breakfast." Grandpa Jude's voice sounded shaky.

"Okay, then." Grandma Tessie patted Lainey's head three times. "Why not go ask Evelyn to fix Grandpa something to eat, Lainey?"

"It's Friday. You never let us break the Friday rule—don't ask Evelyn for anything extra so she can get her work done and get out of here for the weekend."

"Today can be an exception. Jude, take Lainey with you to the kitchen for some frozen peas to put on that nasty bump."

Grandpa's farm-worn hand reached to grab Lainey's. They walked a snail's pace around the side of the house, leaving Grandma Tessie fussing with the rose bushes. "Don't go frettin' about the truck or the flowers, Lainey," he said.

"And the fence." Lainey raised both eyebrows. She could feel her forehead getting tighter from the swelling. "Just saying."

He swatted her shoulder one last time with the flower, finishing off the luscious petals. The naked stem drooped in his thick grip. "I can handle the stern hand of Grandma Tessie."

He swung the kitchen screen door open wide. "Evelyn. I'm needin' me some good old home cooking! Think bacon and eggs and grits," he yelled.

Evelyn stood scrubbing the week's grime off the six-burner gas stove, with her back toward the unwelcome guests. Only five-foot one, her blue apron hung three inches below her knees, the same apron she'd used for twenty years cooking for the Westons. Evelyn had joined the family right out of high school and never thought twice about leaving.

After tossing his hat on a peg, Grandpa Jude settled into his favorite dining chair, the one facing the picture window. "Look at that view, ladies. Miles of green, almost a century of Weston pride. Our sell-out neighbors just don't understand the beauty of tradition!"

Evelyn blinked her eyes and bit the inside of her cheek. Pointing to Grandpa Jude behind his back, she glanced at Lainey and mouthed, "What's he doing here?"

Lainey shrugged.

"What happened to your head?" Evelyn threw a whisk into the sink and rushed to examine Lainey's bump.

"I sort of bounced my head on the steering wheel and it feels like my head is growing another head. I'm thinking of calling her Charlotte. Grandma Tessie sent me in for a bag of frozen peas, please."

Evelyn nodded and fetched the vegetables before turning toward Grandpa. "Sure is a splendid view, Mr. Weston. How 'bout some coffee?" Evelyn poured the last drops from the carafe into a wide-rimmed mug and set it down in front of him. The liquid was muddy brown from sitting all morning. "I just need a few minutes to make the rest."

He grabbed her wrist, tapping her left hand. "We must get a ring on that finger, Evie. What're you doing wasting all this time working for me, when you could be feedin' a man of your own?"

Lips pressed together, she removed his hand with a gentle touch. "We've been through this, Mr. Weston. You walked me down the aisle three years ago since my own daddy had already passed on. Just don't like wearing my ring while I work, sir."

"Well, let me tell you, Evelyn old girl, when I got down on one knee for Miss Teresa Susannah Green, all the mothers and single ladies of Sussex County cried for weeks."

"Must've been the saddest of days, when *you* went off the market, sir." Evelyn patted his shoulder. "Why not take that coffee onto the porch? I'll give a shout when breakfast is ready."

She turned toward Lainey. "As soon as those peas thaw a little, come back in for a bag of corn."

"The porch! A mighty fine idea." Grandpa lifted his mug in cheers. "Give me a chance to rehearse my story on little missy here."

"I'm not little, Grandpa," she said with a tired voice.

"Always be little to me, Lainey girl." He motioned for her to follow him to the porch. The button on his cuff had popped off, and the thin cotton sleeve flapped with each swing of his arm.

Lainey waved at Evelyn then trailed behind her grandfather, matching him stride for stride, holding the bag of peas tight to her forehead. Grandma Tessie called him duck-toed. It hurt Lainey's hips to turn her feet out so far. As Grandpa settled himself into the double seated lounger, she plopped onto the front porch swing and pushed off, flip flops scraping the floorboards. "Okay, let's hear your story. But remember, I'm almost twelve and I have a life. And after the truck incident, I'm extremely happy about that."

"It was *extraooordinary*, Lainey girl," he began.

Wasn't it always? Grandpa Jude liked to daydream. He would use his deep Virginian drawl to spin what he called 'fantastic tales'. In the last eight years of living with her grandparents, Lainey had visited tropical islands, sailed pirate ships, and wandered in fairy woodlands, all with Grandpa Jude at the helm.

But lately Grandpa was changing. Like his driving so crazy this morning. Plus, he hadn't even reacted to the massive dent in his pickup truck's bumper. Or her cracking her head on the steering wheel. This wasn't the Grandpa Jude she knew.

In the past Grandpa had never been a yeller, but no one wanted to debate the evils of tobacco with him anymore. He'd once told his three, grown daughters that he understood the world was changing, but the Weston farm would have to change after he was gone and not one day sooner. His face had been calm, his eyes glassy with a layer of tears.

That was years ago. Now instead of discussing it, Grandpa would just stomp out of the room like a child who wasn't getting his way. Seemed like no one could tell him anything without his getting angry.

His finely concocted stories were changing, too, and now-a-days it sounded like he believed them. He'd yell or sulk when people doubted him, so his audience had to take cues from Grandma Tessie, who listened behind his back. If she offered a slight nod, it was the truth. If her ears went side to side, he was telling a whopper.

Grandpa Jude was changing all right, but stranger still— Grandma Tessie had stopped getting testy, or as the family always joked, "getting Tessie" with him. Just yesterday, when they were bickering about not drinking sweet tea since he had diabetes, Grandpa Jude had slammed down the pitcher, splashing sticky puddles onto the counter.

Lainey had been about to ask why they bothered making it at all if he wasn't allowed to drink it, when Grandma calmly pushed the chair back from the kitchen table, walked to the sink, and ripped off a paper towel to clean the mess. Then she walked away—paper towel still in hand—without having the last word. Or cleaning the sugary spill. Grandma Tessie had broken a very important house rule: proactive cleaning prevents ants and pesky vermin.

Sitting here on the front porch, though, Grandpa seemed more like his old self. His eyes were bright blue. Lainey watched him as he stared off again in another dream. Despite the pounding in her head, she reminded him of his extraordinary story.

"Right. Well now, this here young boy named Jorgé was riding a ten-speed bicycle."

Her eyes closed as the continuous motion of the swing synchronized with the cadence of Grandpa's sing-songy lilt.

"It was red, you see, with silver pin stripes. Can you picture it, darlin'?"

Lainey peaked with one eye. Both of Grandpa's hands flew above his head and shook with excitement about this bike. "Yes, Grandpa. Red with silver stripes." She closed her eye again, waiting for the story to continue.

"I hit that boy with my truck."

"What?" Lainey's eyes bugged. Her feet screeched the swing to a halt so fast the dangling chain smacked her nose. It was not a good day for her head. The bag of peas flew to the porch and burst open spewing tiny green pellets all over.

"Jorgé flew fifteen feet. I knocked him clean off that purty red bike!"

She grabbed the chain with both fists. "Is he ... dead?"

"Hear me out, now." Grandpa's eyes welled up, drowning the brightness. "Jorgé jumps up off the asphalt like he's landed on a trampoline. Dang bike's got nary a scratch. The boy turns to me and says, 'Mister, God protected me from getting hurt. No reason to tell my papa about this.'"

"But—"

Grandpa shrugged. "Of course, I don't even know his daddy. So, I dusted off the bike and sent him on his way. That's why I missed breakfast at the gun club."

"Did you call the police?" Lainey felt prickly stings run through her veins. "What if the kid's hurt?"

"Aww, he's fine, Pumpkinhead. Pedaled off like mad. I'm the one all shook up."

She grabbed his thick hand and felt it trembling.

"That's what made me take out the rose bushes. Got all flustered."

Maybe Grandpa wasn't quite back to normal after all. She yanked at his arm. "Let's see if Evelyn's finished with breakfast. And after that, we can go examine the damage I did with the truck."

He nodded and let her lead him to the kitchen still holding his hand. "Think we could sneak some sweet tea?" he whispered.

"It's nine in the morning," Lainey whispered back.

"And?" Grandpa nudged her forward.

"Fine. I'll pour some when Evelyn's not looking. But if Grandma Tessie catches you, I'm gonna lie myself out of that one real quick." Lainey popped her head through a rip in the screen door for reconnaissance. Grandma Tessie had this door repair on the top of the to-do list for the week, but Lainey would take advantage while she could. She turned toward Grandpa Jude with the plan. "Evelyn is whistling back in the laundry room, but she's already laid out the grits. Go now, and she might not catch us."

Minutes later as Evelyn placed eggs and toast on his plate, Grandpa Jude swilled the last of the forbidden nectar, wiped his mouth with a plain white napkin from the lazy Susan, slapped both palms onto the table, and smiled. His top dentures were a soft white, but his bottom teeth were the real deal, a muted yellow. He picked up a fork and pointed at her. "Lainey, I got a story you just won't believe. Extraooordinary. I met a young boy named Jorgé riding a red bike with silver stripes. Can you picture it, Pumpkinhead?"

೭ೞ

ONE WEEK AFTER the accident, Tessie was throwing sweaters, boots, and dresses out from her master bedroom closet to distribute into piles. The Weston clan had been supporting the Hopewell Evangelical Presbyterian Church of Waverly and its local causes for eighty years, and she'd promised Pastor Tim enough donations to clothe fifty homeless people.

Tessie was dressed in her bright red, self-imposed cleaning uniform, head to toe. "Purging closet space is a red-letter day," she had said to Lainey who leaned against the bedpost. Bright colors always lifted Tessie's spirits, and she really could use a lift. She had wrapped her hair in a red bandanna, put on red and white checkered tennis shoes, a tomato red t-shirt with sequins in the shape of a parrot, and faded red pedal-pushers bought over forty years ago. "Because I still fit in them, confound it," she pointed out. And the rule was, whatever she was wearing, she didn't have to donate.

"Grandma, it was so weird," Lainey said. "The boy flies fifteen feet, then just up and walks away? What's even creepier is ten minutes later Grandpa tells me the same story all over again. Then every day since he—"

"Didn't we go through all this already?" Tessie chucked a boot over one shoulder, right out the door.

"Hey!" Lainey ducked. "You almost crushed my head and that's the last thing it needs!"

"Sorry!" Tessie yelled from the closet. "Get on the bed and you won't be in any danger. You're supposed to be taking a low profile for a whole month."

"Don't you think it's kind of strange that Grandpa hit some kid on a bike and didn't even call an ambulance?"

Tessie stuck her head out of the closet doorway, four black neckties dangling from her shoulders. She met her granddaughter's eyes. "Not particularly, no." Back she went to throwing clothes and hiding from Lainey.

"Grandma, he almost hit me, too, remember!"

Tessie sighed. She stepped out of the closet, rolling up Jude's leather belt, the one with a large brass Smith and Wesson buckle. His favorite out of a total of twenty-two, which is why she never felt guilty for buying shoes. "Get comfy, honey." She pointed to the king-sized bed. "I need a minute to think."

Lainey hopped up, wrinkling the yellow, gingham quilt. Tessie winced as the solid oak headboard knocked the wall. She could see her granddaughter in the oval-shaped mirror hanging over the center of the matching bureau. Lainey grabbed a square pillow for her lap, nibbling on a thumbnail. Tessie held back her standard lecture on the evils of nail biting.

She laid the belt down on the bureau, letting it loosen around one finger. The buckle fell limp against the oil-stained leather. She glanced at the bump on the girl's head which had flattened a bit and turned a light shade of green.

Tessie started pacing from the bed frame to the lounger she used for reading, then back to the bureau, where she fought to rewind the belt. Once again, it unraveled. Tighten, unravel. This was not going to be easy. Tessie tossed the belt onto the shoe pile. "I've got to just spit this out, Lainey, but you have to promise not to get worked up." She could tell her voice was too loud, like she was talking over a hairdryer. She took a deep breath to lower her tone. "Grandpa's sick."

Lainey's brow crinkled. "I told him not to drink any more sweet tea."

"Not the diabetes." Tessie went to the foot board and leaned her knees against it. "He's got what doctors call Lewy Body Dementia. Notice how he's quick and strong one minute, then shuffles like he's ninety just walking to the bathroom?"

Lainey shrugged and continued chewing at the nail.

"Proteins are shooting onto his brain." Tessie flinched as Lainey's nail ripped from one side of the thumb to the other. "Soon enough, it'll be much worse than just slow walking and a bit of forgetting. No one can tell me for sure how long it's going to take."

Lainey's eyes shifted left and right as if she was thinking. "But what's that got to do with hitting a bike? Or almost running me over last week?" She reached over the nightstand and dropped the bit of nail in the tiny plastic trashcan. "Why do you let him drive?"

Tessie wasn't quite sure how to stop him. Or maybe she just wasn't brave enough. Dementia had turned a kind, pleasantly stubborn man to just plain obstinate—even ugly at times. Stranger still was the new selfishness the disease had conjured up. Jude's generous spirit had been the main reason Tessie had fallen in love with him. Fifty-two years ago, he'd traveled all the way to Greenville, South Carolina, where her family vacationed every year, just to present her birthday gift in person.

His first thought had always been for her well-being, next for his daughters'. After his family, anyone in town could count on Jude Weston. At church, he'd been re-elected deacon for twenty years in a row—a church record—because he was wise, calm, and good at business. Now, all he focused on were guns and the farm, and he stopped attending worship services altogether. A disease was taking Tessie's husband away, leaving in his place an argumentative, overgrown ten-year-old trapped in an old man's body.

Tessie faced Lainey again. "He never drives real far, and he knows these roads like the back of his hand, but listen ..." She inspected the faded white ceiling, noticing cobwebs in the corner. "There are spiders up there. I need a broom." Tessie drew in a deep breath as she left the room and prayed for divine intervention in dealing with this whole mess. Strength and composure. That's what she needed right now. Thirty short seconds she was back, attacking the cobwebs.

"You're acting weird, Grandma. If shooting proteins makes Grandpa not be able to drive—"

"Listen." Tessie stopped mid-sweep with the broom's fibers on the ceiling. "Another symptom of Lewy Body is hallucinations."

Lainey scrunched her nose, like she smelled a skunk.

"There was no boy on a red bike with silver stripes. I called the sheriff." Tessie let the broom head fall from the air onto the carpet.

"Grandpa just thinks he hit the kid?" Lainey munched on the other thumbnail.

Tessie leaned the broom against the bed and gripped the edge of the foot board. "Grandpa's had a persistent cold as of late, and those types of things make the hallucinations more prevalent." She glanced at Lainey then bounded back into the closet to finish the collections. To hide once again.

"You're scaring me, Grandma." Lainey slipped off the bed and followed behind her.

The closet was tight with them both in there. Tessie wondered if cedar was a good scent to have inside a coffin. She kept her back to her granddaughter, whose breath sounded quick and shallow. She felt a tug on her sleeve.

"Is Grandpa going to die?"

Tessie turned and stared down at the crooked part in the young pink scalp, amazed how this girl could be like an adult one second and then still a child the next. "Not right away." Juices churned deep in Tessie's stomach. "The problem is his mind. He's forgetting so many things. Last week he couldn't remember what kind of crop we grew on the farm."

Lainey leaned her back against the wall.

"Soon the hallucinations will get worse. I once heard of a man who saw gigantic black spiders crawling all over the living room. Started digging holes in the drywall to exterminate them. His wife couldn't convince him they weren't real, and he—"

Lainey shut her eyes so tight the lashes brushed her cheeks.

Tessie wanted to protect her like she had for the last eight years since her father Jeremiah had dropped her off on the doorstep. Tessie reached out to touch the young girl's hair.

"Dementia's a scary disease, which is why I called a family meeting. Your aunts will all be here the beginning of August. We'll do our best to help Grandpa during the next six weeks until we can make some plans for the future, right?" Tessie licked her thumb and patted the loose hairs down then lightly squeezed Lainey's head and kissed Charlotte.

"I would like you to finish tying these bags closed for me and get them into the car to take to the church, although where Pastor Tim plans to find fifty homeless people in Waverly, I just don't know. And put real shoes on; those flip-flops are not conducive to walking down steps. I'm not convinced you don't have a concussion from that bump."

Tessie turned away from Lainey and left the room without another word between them. When she reached the hall bathroom, she locked the door in slow motion to keep from making noise. She turned the faux crystal knobs full blast, filling the sink. Then she turned the shower on. Next, she slammed the toilet lid shut and flushed. In that house, it was the only way to cry in peace.

LAINEY DRAGGED the bags of donations to the car. Thoughts of Grandpa dying made her head and stomach feel like she'd just got off the Tilt-a-Whirl at the county fair. At any moment she could chuck her lunch, so she kept swallowing and taking deep breaths as she stuffed the bags into the trunk. She slammed the door with all the strength she had left then gave a swift kick to the bumper of the old Pontiac.

Once Grandma Tessie was off to clothe the homeless, it was the perfect chance to spy on Grandpa Jude roaming around by the barns. Lainey wanted to see if she could tell he was sick, now that she knew it wasn't just diabetes. She tried to shake the queasy feeling of sadness when she noticed Grandpa Jude's pickup parked in front of the stick barn.

In olden days on a tobacco farm, field hands would stab the tobacco leaves with a spear and lath, then hang them from the ceiling in the stick barn for curing. The Weston's stick barn was the size of two outhouses, and no one ever used it anymore. It leaned so far left, Lainey imagined it was trying to lie down to sleep after a hard day's work. Grandma Tessie wanted it gone, but Grandpa Jude wouldn't let go of the past. After the farm expanded in the early 1950s, Great-Granddad Weston had built an industrial-sized storehouse with gray corrugated siding. It offered sections for curing, storage, sales, and equipment. He'd even put an air-conditioned office on the second floor for both him and the foreman, which had been Grandpa Jude at the time. Today, Amos Lowry was running the whole show, and Lainey felt like she was in the way when she went in there.

Her favorite barn was the traditional structure painted red and white. Upstairs was a loft where she had set up her own hideaway. Using a cherry picker, Grandpa had hoisted her mama's old roll-top desk up there so Lainey could do homework or draw. Grandma Tessie liked taking Lainey to those starving-artist sales held in hotel lobbies, buying up every picture with a horse in it. To date, there were almost twenty paintings covering the back wall. Lainey had an antique Tiffany glass hurricane lamp with a Virginia rose pattern of purple and teal. Grandpa Jude had taken one look and said, "I refuse to inhabit this place now that you've girled it all up!" But he came to visit all the time. Or he used to anyway.

Lainey ran past the stick barn straight to her red barn standing tall and unassuming. The door was old and thick, so she yanked it open with two hands adding strength from bracing her legs. That's one thing you learned growing up on a farm—lift with your legs. When she heard the click of the latch behind her, she slumped back against the door, happy to find the building empty. The earthy smell of dirt and tobacco plants filled her nostrils.

Before she could climb the sturdy mahogany ladder to begin her spy mission, she heard a massive thump like a sack of potatoes hitting the hard dirt. Curious, Lainey went back out the front door and ran around the wood walls of the edifice to investigate.

Fifty yards in the distance, Amos Lowry was running full speed toward her and the barn. He was yelling at the top of his lungs, but she couldn't quite hear what he was saying. He was a tall, chubby man, and his work boots had come untied, the string snapping against his jeans. As he closed the distance between him and her, Lainey noticed a man-sized lump lying next to the back side of the barn. Plaid shirt and jeans, a head of curly gray hair, the tip of a cowboy boot pointing straight to the sky. The body was still.

"Mr. Weston!" Amos reached Grandpa and knelt to shake his shoulder. No answer.

Lainey froze to her spot, halfway hidden behind the side wall of the barn. She could smell tar paper heating up from the late afternoon sun.

"Lainey, he needs an ambulance," Amos shouted over his shoulder.

She retreated even farther behind the wall. Never having seen a dead body before, she didn't want her first one to be Grandpa Jude.

"I left my phone in the truck," Amos yelled.

She took three steps toward Grandpa then stopped. As still as Grandpa. She couldn't tell if he was breathing.

"Lainey! Move it!" Amos kept shaking Grandpa Jude's shoulders, but nothing would wake him up. He started pumping on his chest with both hands, one on top of the other.

Lainey felt her legs start moving, then running toward the house. In the kitchen, Evelyn was leaning over the sink, sniffing a package of meat.

"Grandpa fell. Amos said call an ambulance."

Evelyn rushed to the phone. Lainey stood as if she was posing for a portrait; her head felt like it was in a fishbowl. Evelyn's lips were moving fast, and her free hand was waving about in the air, but Lainey couldn't comprehend any of the words. Grandpa Jude was dead, and Lainey couldn't stop the shaking she felt in her chest.

Evelyn slammed down the receiver and walked toward Lainey who was an inch taller than she already. They stood face to face. "Ambulance is on the way. I also called Mrs. Weston. Tell me what happened, my little one."

Lainey let Evelyn scoop her into her arms as she started to cry, glad she didn't have to pretend to be brave anymore.

෴

HOURS LATER, Tessie left Jude's hospital bed to find Lainey and Evelyn in the waiting room of the ER. "He's finally stopped screaming about battlefields and submarines. He thinks the Navy is holding him hostage." She put her arm around Lainey and guided her toward the electric doors.

"Then he's not going to die?" Lainey asked with her eyes as wide as walnuts.

"Not anytime soon. We'll get you and Evelyn home before they put him in his own room. We've completely missed dinner."

Evelyn dabbed her eyes with a tissue.

Tessie wanted to ease the tension she felt in her bones, but she couldn't really think of any good way. "The doctor said his cold has turned to pneumonia," she said. "He's so disoriented, they aren't sure he's going to return to us."

"What do you mean 'return,' Mrs. Weston?" Evelyn asked.

"Mentally. This episode accelerated the dementia, which means severe hallucinations. More often." Tessie could feel the tears stuck in her throat.

"The doctors told me that in cases of dementia, routine is key. So being at home might help him keep his bearings longer. I meant it when I said for better or worse. Jude is my priority."

But he had almost killed Lainey with the truck. Tessie couldn't leave him alone anymore. At this point she had no choice but to find a safer place for her granddaughter. She wished the family meeting could be moved up. August was just too far away, and she needed help now. How could she follow through with sending Lainey away? How could she not?

"Mrs. Weston, you know I'll help you with everything. You and Mr. Weston have been my family for twenty years, now. My James will understand if I have to work longer hours."

"Thank you, dearest Evelyn. This could get ugly." Tessie turned toward Lainey, wanting to be straight-forward and honest. Her granddaughter's blonde hair was shooting every which way but down; her blue eyes were large with confusion.

Tessie took a deep breath. It was time. "Lainey, I've decided I can't let you stay with us anymore."

❦

AS SOON AS THE PONTIAC changed gears from drive to park, Lainey was out the door, running to her loft.

"Come back here so we can talk this out," Grandma Tessie yelled after her. "It's going to be dark in an hour!"

Lainey ignored her grandmother's plea. Leaning back on the old, thick door, she couldn't catch her breath. *I can't let you stay.*

Her lungs felt tight; her eyes burned. She lifted her face toward the ceiling. "What do you mean I can't stay here anymore?" she screamed. The words echoed through the empty barn and bounced off the tin roof, as if she'd bellowed into an oil drum.

Lainey slid off her Sketchers—which Grandma Tessie instructed her never to do in the barn—and climbed barefoot up the ladder, holding the tennis shoes in her right hand.

I can't let you stay with us anymore.

Lainey could feel the fear bubbling from what Grandma Tessie wasn't saying; she was going to make her live with Jeremiah. She hurled both shoes at the side wall. A wallet-size of her mother's senior class picture tumbled from the tobacco sizer she now used as a shelf. It still had a faint smell like sweet hay from when farmers used it to sort the leaves. She snatched up the photo and plopped into the desk chair. She stared at Genevieve's smiling, eighteen-year-old face then felt something sliding on her shin.

A thin red ribbon of blood was trickling down where she'd scraped it on the ladder. Lainey reached into the top drawer for a tissue, rummaging through the yellowed drawing paper, ballpoint pens, notebooks, beat up troll dolls, and her mother's monogrammed stationery. The letters *G R W* were fancy, like on menus in expensive restaurants. *Genevieve Rose Weston.*

Whenever anyone told a Genevieve story, Lainey would run to her loft and capture it in writing as best she could, then lock the precious notebook under the roll top. Last year she'd finished her fourth full book. She wore the key to the desk around her neck, on the same chain her mama had used when she was a little girl. According to Grandma Tessie, Genevieve had been teased by her older sisters, so she too had to hide her private thoughts in this desk.

Lainey could remember a few things about life before she came to live on the farm: her mother's light blonde hair, soft hands with nail polish that matched her toes, the same blue eyes she saw in her own mirror every morning. There was one ancient image she put out of her mind every time it crept back—wearing a puffy blue dress, holding on tight to a brown pants leg, her lip moist with snot. She knew deep down it was her earliest memory of her now absentee father, but she pretended it was Grandpa Jude's leg she had been clinging to.

She opened to page three of the notebook: *Grandma Tessie told me today that Mama loved lemonade rather than drinking milk. Me too, cause milk tastes like chalk on my tongue. Then Grandma explained how Aunt Faith was twelve years older than Mama, Beth nine years older, and Madeline seven. She says the older sisters spoiled and bossed her around all in the same breath. Basically, Grandma Tessie says my mother grew up with four mothers of her own.* Lainey traced her mother's name with her finger.

She had only a few memories of her father. Fine by her. Sometimes Grandma Tessie tried to talk about Jeremiah, but Lainey refused to write any of those stories down. "I'm not wasting ink on him," she replied every time. She'd even tried to convince her grandparents she should change her last name from Traynor to Weston, but that's when Grandma Tessie got really mad, so she dropped the subject. She could do that when she turned eighteen. Lainey Weston had such a great ring to it.

I can't let you stay with us anymore.

Her cheeks burned so hot, the tears felt cool sliding over them. Her fingers and toes prickled when she pictured Grandma packing a suitcase to send her away.

As she bent over to wipe her shin, she noticed the blood had dried. Grandma Tessie would've licked her thumb to wipe it down with spit.

"Tattoo made of blood," she said, leaving the marks in rebellion.

Glancing over the desk, she studied her painting collection. On the back of each painting, she'd taped a photo. She spun one frame around, twisting the wire. As she pulled on the tape, the backing peeled off in a thin brown layer. This was the only snapshot with her father in it that she'd kept, from the Christmas back when she was three. They all were in red pajamas on Christmas morning. Jeremiah had on a Santa hat with a bell dangling from the tip. Mama was wearing brown felt reindeer antlers. She was smiling down at Lainey, who was cradling her new doll named Lulu.

I can't let you stay with us anymore. Lainey reached behind another painting. The photo of Grandma Tessie and Grandpa Jude sitting on their favorite rockers came off with ease. They'd just bought her an old-fashioned Polaroid camera, and she had made them pose for pictures everywhere. This one was her favorite. Lainey traced a finger over Grandpa's face. Then she took a black pen to poke Grandma's eyes out. She couldn't color in the teeth cause Grandma never showed them when she smiled.

Lainey taped both pictures back in place and spun the paintings to face front. "I wish you were still alive, Mama," she said looking straight at the ceiling. "And if they make me go live with Jeremiah, I'm gonna fight. Or else just run away."

A plan started to form. She rushed to the old sizer and picked out three more photos: Aunt Faith with her short brown hair and brocade scarf, Aunt Beth at a pig roast, and Aunt Madeline with a cheesy smile that made it look like she had forty teeth stuffed in her small mouth. If she couldn't stay at the farm, maybe she could live with the aunts. Her mother's sisters. On rotation so she wouldn't become a burden to any of them. A family circuit.

She could spend the first two years with Uncle David and Aunt Madeline. They lived in the mountains of West Virginia but close enough Grandma Tessie might be able to visit sometimes. Then, when ninth grade came around, she'd go on up to Boston. Aunt Faith had no one left in the house besides Uncle Barry. Going to school in a big city could be an adventure, and who really cared if Aunt Faith sort of believed she was British, kept an 8 x 10 portrait of the Queen on the mantle, and sat down to tea each day at four o'clock?

Next, Lainey would move to Iowa, where she'd have the most fun. Uncle Chase and Aunt Beth had three boys who teased her like she was their own sister. They always made up fun games like 'tackle whoever has the ball' and 'how many times can we swat a beehive before getting stung?' They'd got in trouble for that one, since a neighbor kid had to be taken to the hospital after his EpiPen refused to work.

Then, when Lainey graduated, she'd go off to college, and none of them would have to worry about her ever again. She would change her last name to Weston and get herself a good job. Grandma Tessie had told her once that Jeremiah set money aside in the bank every month for her college tuition. Okay then. She'd let his money be useful as long as he didn't try to see her. After college Lainey could move back to the farm. Home again.

Satisfied, she made detailed notes and locked them up with her Genevieve notebooks until she needed them. Her aunts wouldn't get there till August. That was a month away. She could explain the plan while they were all together because Grandma Tessie wouldn't listen, otherwise. Lainey toyed with the key around her neck. "If Grandma Tessie's going to send me away" she said, "then I've got to go with the next best thing."

The Sisters Tour was it.

Chapter 2

BROOKE NELSON BORROWED her boss's dog for a walk in Patterson Park, the oldest public park in Baltimore. Brooke hoped to get another glimpse of the man who had smiled at her two days in a row. In the right hand, she held the leash. In the other she held an open coffee cup with steam wafting out the top. Before she had a chance to get some caffeine into her system, a fruit fly dive-bombed into the sixteen-ounce cup and drowned itself. Then she saw the man on a bench past the large oak tree, and her heart jumped into her throat. The dead fly left her mind in an instant.

He wasn't as fashionable as she would have liked with his navy-blue pants and navy-blue tie. His white shirt was too big for him and wrinkled like he hadn't even bothered to shake and snap the shirt before letting it hang to dry. Or worse yet, he had let it sit in the dryer until he was ready to wear it. He was a bit older, but that could mean stability, right?

The dog was dragging her left and right across the pathway. "Stop yanking the chain," she raised her voice through a gritted, toothy smile. The tiny dog almost jerked her arm out of its socket, spilling brown liquid all over her hand. The fly remained in the cup. "Brownie!"

The man made a coughing noise that came out more like a growl as she slowed her pace in front of the bench. "I can't believe such a small dog has that much strength," he said.

Brooke flashed a smile, and with a smooth turn of her chin, she tossed her straightened brunette hair for effect. "I know, right?" She lightly yanked the leash to keep Brownie out of a discarded chip bag. "She just doesn't like to walk with me."

"Oh, I doubt that very much."

He looked away, but Brooke noticed his cheeks turned red. Brownie started sniffing at his brown dress shoes, and Brooke didn't bother to stop her. As the man reached down to pet the tiny ball of brown and gray fluff, Brownie latched her teeth onto his ankle.

Brooke yanked harder on the chain while trying to keep the coffee cup level. "Bad girl. Bad doggie," she cried. Nothing she said worked on the dog's grip. Sharp teeth ripped right through his acrylic sock.

Finally, the man grabbed Brownie's collar and extracted the dog from his leg. "You might want to get your dog some obedience lessons."

Brooke laughed. "To be honest, she's not my dog. That's why she won't listen." She sat down next to the man, placed the cup between them, and stuck out her right hand. "My name's Brooke. I borrowed the dog in hopes of meeting up with you. Now, I owe you some new socks."

The man's eyes sparkled as soon as his grin turned into a full smile. "My name's Jeremiah. It's very nice to meet both of you."

Once they finished inspecting his flesh wound, Brooke showed Jeremiah the dead fly in her now empty coffee and asked if he would like to buy her some more.

BROOKE WAS NERVOUS. For the short time they'd been seeing each other, Jeremiah insisted on taking her out or going back to her place rather than letting her see his apartment. She was fine with keeping things light and fun as long as he stayed attentive. It was fun dating a man who knew how to treat a lady. But since he was at least ten years older, Brooke felt it was time to see if they had anything else in common. Or if he was hiding anything.

So yesterday, Brooke placed a hand on his knee and told him she wanted more of a commitment from him, and that he should start by having her over for dinner. She didn't like being demanding, but she wanted to keep things moving. Her main goal was to find out what he did for a living since it had yet to come up in conversation.

When Jeremiah opened his apartment door, Brooke took in the bachelor scene. Every white wall held a slight yellow dinge.

Each room just the bare essentials. Kitchen: a table for four with two chairs. Living room: a brown plaid couch and a TV on an old microwave stand. Bedroom: a bed. "I like how simple you keep it," she said with a smile.

"Well, that's a nice way of putting it. Go ahead and look around," Jeremiah said heading toward the kitchen. "I don't really have an eye for décor, but you can use the bathroom because I cleaned it an hour ago."

"I'm flattered." And Brooke really was. Not many guys had bothered to treat her well in the past.

"It's good you like things simple. I hope that goes for food, too. I haven't ever really cooked much. Do you like spaghetti?"

"I love it." Brooke flashed an amused smile.

"How about store-bought sauce?"

"Perfect. I've never been able to notice the difference."

"I even bought some garlic bread, but I am pretty sure the vegetables are overcooked and need to be reheated. If it gets really bad, we can order a pizza or stick with the salad."

"I'm sure it will be great, Jeremiah." There wasn't anything left to look at, so it didn't take long for her to end up on the couch, staring at a black TV.

Jeremiah opened a bag of lettuce and dumped it into a shiny salad bowl. "Having you here is making me nervous. Like it's a first date. I bought a 40-piece dish set for the occasion."

"Once we begin eating, we'll find our comfort zone again. Do you need any help in there?"

Jeremiah slammed a loaf of garlic bread onto the counter. "Um, Brooke, would you be okay here by yourself if I ran to the store?"

"I'm sure the meal will be fine. Don't make a special trip to the store just for me." Brooke thought he looked so cute standing there all vulnerable and sheepish.

"This is so embarrassing. I wanted to wait until you got here to start the pasta, and well, I seemed to have forgotten to actually buy the pasta. There's a convenience store around the corner; I'll be back in ten minutes, I promise." Jeremiah grabbed his wallet and keys from the battered, make-shift TV stand and slammed the door behind him.

Brooke took note that he needed a side table by the door. Not sure what to do with herself, she went to the kitchen. She searched through drawers for salad tongs but found nothing except wooden stirring spoons. They would do. She wanted more choices for salad dressing, but the refrigerator was empty except for the half used 24-pack of Natty Bohbeer on the bottom shelf. She finally found some napkins from the Shake Shack that she folded in triangles then placed under the forks and knives Jeremiah had already put by the plates.

Brooke heard a buzzing from the counter. Jeremiah had left his phone behind. It rang three times, then stopped abruptly. She leaned over the screen to watch for a voice mail notification, but one never came. Ten seconds later, it rang again. No name was displayed, just two letters T W. Again, no voice mail. The third time, curiosity grabbed her, and Brooke swiped up to answer the phone. She left it lying on the counter and pushed speaker phone.

"Hello?" Brooke felt a rush of adrenaline, realizing how inappropriate this was. What if T W told him she had answered?

"Jeremiah?" a female voice asked.

"Uh, he's not available right now. May I take a message?" Why had she answered his phone?

"When will he be available?"

The voice sounded irritated and maybe a little old. Definitely southern. "My guess is any minute," Brooke replied.

"Dangflab it. Just tell him, 'It may be time;' he'll know what that means."

Before Brooke could ask the caller's name, the connection ended. Brooke picked up the phone to swipe the screen, removing any visual record of the call, just as Jeremiah walked through the door with two boxes in his hands.

Brooke laid Jeremiah's phone back onto the counter, hoping he hadn't seen it in her hands.

"I wanted to call you to tell you I was on the way and realized I left my phone here. I promise I'll get better at all this."

"You're doing great, Jeremiah. Really. But you did have a few missed calls while you were gone. Someone named T W." Brooke wanted to be open with Jeremiah.

Jeremiah's neck stiffened.

"I'm sorry I looked at your phone. It buzzed a couple different times, and I was standing right there. I didn't realize I was being nosy until I had already seen—"

"Brooke. T W is just someone I knew from a long time ago. No worries." Jeremiah opened the cabinet above the refrigerator. "I could use a drink. What kind of wine goes best with Ragu?"

"I believe that would be red," Brooke said, relieved Jeremiah wasn't going to question her about the phone call.

"So, Jeremiah. That day we met. What made you go get coffee with me?"

Jeremiah smiled. It was the most genuine look she'd seen on his face these last few weeks. "When I saw you, a shiver rushed down my spine."

Brooke stuck her fork into a wad of pasta, turning it slowly. She winked at Jeremiah in approval.

"For three days, I found myself walking a little faster during my break, trying to catch another sight of the brunette and her Pomeranian."

He was being flirty, and she liked it. "On break? From what?" Please have a job, please have a job, please have a job.

"I work at Harrison Mortgage down in the harbor."

"Interesting. I don't know very much about that world."

"Well, the owner Phil, an old college buddy, hired me as a broker. It's partly how I ended up in Baltimore. But I switched to management; I run the office now."

"So you've been there for a while?"

"Yeah, Phil's a good friend." Jeremiah drained his glass of wine then walked to the kitchen for another bottle.

Brooke didn't want to pry too much further. She had to be content with the information he was sharing, or he'd run like all the others. She smiled then bit into a left-over croûton from her salad bowl as he refilled her glass.

$\approx$

A MONTH LATER, Jeremiah was late returning to his apartment. He had left immediately after letting her inside, and Brooke was irritated. She stood in the bedroom packing his clothes for a trip to Philadelphia and had questions about what he needed to take along for their weekend. He had ignored her last five texts and two phone calls on the subject, and she did not care to be ignored.

Finally, a car door slammed right outside the building. Brooke looked out the window to see his car parked halfway onto the flattened macadam. She picked up Jeremiah's toothbrush holder while he thumped up the steps to the door of his apartment. Out of breath, he made his way to the bathroom, and stood in the doorway. He was lucky he was cute.

"There's mold in here." Brooke held the plastic tube an inch from his eye for him to inspect his lack of cleaning skills. "You really need help. When we get back from Philadelphia on Sunday, I am going to clean—"

Jeremiah ripped the container from her hand. "We need to talk."

Brooke's heart dropped to her stomach. He'd come to his senses and was going to break up with her. She'd have to tell all her friends that he bolted. Brooke tossed the toothbrush into a sandwich baggy, avoiding eye contact.

"I thought you'd be finished with this and onto making dinner already," he said.

"Well, I had questions about where you keep things, and you didn't answer my calls." She looked up then pursed her lips in a pout, a maneuver she employed to keep men around just a little longer. "My bags are in my trunk still. Why don't you go switch them to your car now, so we don't have to worry about them tomorrow?"

"We can't go."

Her lips protruded further; her jaw locked. This time she was not trying to be attractive; neither was she being manipulative. She was furious that he could dismiss their plans so easily.

"Those phone calls from T W. I missed another one." Jeremiah took a seat on the edge of the bathtub and covered his face with his hands.

Was he breaking up with her or not? Where had he been the last three hours? Brooke took a deep breath. "Jeremiah, did something happen?"

"Not today," he spoke behind his hands.

His refusal to communicate was so frustrating, but she wasn't going to let him get away with it tonight. "I told Karen we'd be there by nine tomorrow night. We're going to meet her fiancé and make plans for her wedding. We were supposed to get ready tonight. Together."

"Shhh. Just stop talking and let me think."

"Don't shush me. We had plans, and my friends want to meet you. Plus, I don't appreciate you stopping for a drink when you told me you'd be home for dinner. I can smell it on you."

"I only had one."

She stared into his eyes to verify.

"I have a daughter."

Brooke felt her eyes glaze over, hearing her mother's voice in the back of her head saying, *There are no good ones left. You're not pretty enough or smart enough or interesting enough to keep the bad ones either.*

"Did you hear me?" Jeremiah said.

Brooke focused her gaze down and rummaged through his overnight bag. "I knew better than to go away with a guy so soon." She picked up random objects and chucked them back into the bag. "Even my mother told me not to do it, and she has *no* judgment when it comes to men." She glanced at him in the mirror.

"I'm sorry. I should've mentioned—"

She snorted. "You think?"

"Fourteen years ago, I married my college sweetheart."

"You're married?"

"Yes. No. We had a little girl ... Alaina Rose. One night, Genevieve wasn't feeling well. She had a headache, wanted to get out of the house. Gen always loved to hear the rain hitting the roof of the car; said the pitter-patter soothed her."

"So that's the T W who called you a month ago? *The Wife*?" Brooke felt like someone was pressing an anvil on her heart. She focused her eyes on the thin, gritty grout stuck between the black tiles. The fan in the ceiling squeaked every five seconds.

Jeremiah shook his head and closed his eyes. "Genevieve couldn't see so well in the dark, especially not in the rain. I never should've let her drive with those old glasses on. She kept meaning to get new ones. Alaina was asleep, so I stayed behind. Then she ..." He held his breath and pushed his knuckles deep into his chest. "... hydroplaned into a tree."

Brooke felt sick to her stomach for being so angry with him. She reached out, placing a hand on his forearm.

"Genevieve left Alaina and me behind eight years ago this month. I was ... broken. I ... left Alaina with Gen's parents. T W is Gen's mother." He stretched his chin toward the ceiling and blinked back tears.

"Jeremiah, breathe." With tears in her own eyes, she turned to kneel in front of him.

Jeremiah grabbed her hand but would not look into her eyes. "I feel guilty for leaving my daughter, ignoring all those calls from Genevieve's mother, and I promise you, I only had one drink to help me relax."

Brooke covered his hand with her free one.

"Keep going." She hoped her voice sounded normal.

"I let Gen's parents raise Alaina all these years, and now I'm afraid they want me to come get her. I don't know what to do. I can't raise a girl by myself. I can't face her after all these years. Alaina hates me."

"You don't know that, Jeremiah."

"Hell, I hate me. I need another drink."

Brooke gently forced him to look at her. Tears fell down her face, smearing her mascara. She was partially sad for the broken man in front of her and partially relieved that he wasn't done with her. "Jeremiah, where does Alaina live?"

"Virginia."

"Then forget Philadelphia this weekend. Virginia is where you are going."

He pulled her toward him, setting her sideways on his lap. He wrapped his arms around her waist. "I can't just show up on their doorstep."

"Not everyone gets a second chance. You can fix this…" Brooke brushed her hands through his hair "…but only in person. You're essentially packed, so here's the plan. Tonight you sleep, then tomorrow night after work you get in the car, drive to Virginia, and make this right."

"I'm scared to face Genevieve's family alone." He looked her in the eyes for the first time. "Would you come with me?"

"Of course." Brooke hugged his neck.

"Then, what would you say if I asked you to marry me?"

Brooke closed her eyes and held her breath. She'd never heard those words before, at least not directed to her. Usually by the second month she was getting the "it's-not-you-it's-me" excuse.

"You're too fragile right now." Brooke's voice came out in a shaken whisper.

"How about if I said you were the only certainty that I've felt in eight years?"

Brooke's ears tingled. "Then I'd say yes. I'll be with you the whole way, Jeremiah. It's going to be all right."

Chapter 3

OVER A MONTH SINCE he fell at the farm, and Jude was still not home. He had been moved to a geriatric, psychiatric hospital where they were struggling to regulate his meds to control his confusion. Until that happened, Tessie would not be able to care for her husband by herself.

But the family meeting could finally commence Friday morning, and she was impatient for her girls to get there. Tessie begged Evelyn for a list of supplies from the grocery to keep her occupied that morning. She'd left Jude sleeping at the hospital, and just couldn't sit still in the house any longer. "I'll head to Hattie's Supermarket after I drop Lainey off at the church." Pastor Tim had asked the youth group to help paint the vestibule as a summer service project.

Tessie wanted to keep life as normal as possible for Lainey, but the young girl started in on her as soon as the car hit asphalt.

"Why can't I be home when the aunts come?"

"I need time to explain the extent of Grandpa's condition. I didn't want them rushing back homelike he was dying, so I didn't quite reveal the situation in depth as I should have. You're old enough to understand that, so stop whining like you're eight years old."

"Fine." Lainey crossed her arms and rolled her eyes.

Tessie disliked one-word answers; they were dismissive and disrespectful, but she kept her peace for the time being. The ride was quiet until she spotted the steeple up the hill. "Work hard," she said. "It's for the Lord, you know."

Lainey slammed the car door and ran up the sidewalk to the white-washed church building.

"Goodbye to you, too." Tessie gave a little wave toward the back of Lainey's head.

Wandering the aisles of Hattie Rae's Market, Tessie thought over the last few weeks. It was hard skirting the "you can't live here anymore" conversations and just plain keeping peace around the house, all while visiting Jude and fielding questions from friends and extended family. In between all that, she tried her best to figure out how to approach Jeremiah. Was he even capable of taking care of Lainey? Who was that girl who had answered his phone?

Crunchy peanut butter.

The sisters were not going to take this well since Tessie had taken great pains to keep Jude's deterioration from them before he collapsed. When they saw Jude, his condition was going to devastate them.

Dish detergent.

Tessie had started noticing things more than a year ago. Thank the Lord Lainey had been at school when Jude had lost his balance that first time, just walking to the kitchen. Once on his back, his mind couldn't figure out how to get his legs working again. Tessie had to call some work hands to pull him up, but it took cracking his head on the tub before he'd agreed to see a doctor.

Flour.

Her first fear had been a brain tumor. You hear stories like that. How a healthy man falls over and in an instant there's a tumor the size of a tennis ball on his brain. A week later he's dead. But no. This was an even more cruel and slow disease.

Mustard.

Shielding her daughters from the dementia had taken some creative storytelling and—well, just plain old lying. God forgive her, she was getting as good as Jude at telling tales.

Crunchy peanut butter. Wait. Tessie shrugged and stuck a second jar in the cart, walking back down the same aisle once again.

Her mind wandered back to Jeremiah at the funeral: shoulders slumped, blue circles shadowing his eyes, jaw so clenched the cheek muscles rippled. There wouldn't have been a funeral at all if the Westons hadn't shipped Genevieve's body home to Virginia. Late that evening, after the interment and small reception at the church, he'd climbed the front steps of the Weston house, face wet with tears. "Just take her, Ma," he'd whispered.

There stood Alaina, in serious need of a tissue. She looked so much like her mother with that blonde hair and blue eyes. Her face was round like Genevieve's, her laugh lilting an octave at the very end. Just like Genevieve's. The nail-biting was all her mother, too. Genevieve used to polish her nails every week to keep from ruining them. That trick didn't work with Lainey. She would scratch off the enamel with her teeth, then start in on bare nail.

Lainey clung to Jeremiah's pants leg in the pale blue dress Tessie had bought the night before. He hadn't packed enough clothes for the trip and certainly nothing appropriate for a funeral. The sweet little girl was holding Lulu close to her chest, whispering into the doll's ear. With one hand, Jeremiah pushed Alaina toward Tessie. "I can't do this right now."

So, she had agreed to look after Lainey until he was ready. She'd wanted to give him some room the first month and didn't contact him. In some sense, it was a relief to have someone else to care for after losing her youngest daughter. After the first month of silence, she'd called Jeremiah every week through the first year. Another year went by, and Jeremiah finally showed up to get his girl. Lainey was six by then and had moved on from missing him. Despite Tessie's efforts of keeping their memory alive, Lainey had a young child's bitterness rooted deep in her heart. He got scared of her tantrum when he tried to kiss her cheek, and they all decided the poor thing needed more time.

Time got away from them all.

Even now, Lainey had the Weston fight. At any mention of her father, anger would flip the on-switch, her eyes shooting darts at the target. Tessie had once made the mistake of pointing out how she crinkled her nose when she was thinking really hard. "Just like Jeremiah."

"Don't tell me about some man who didn't love me enough to stick around," she'd snapped.

Jeremiah had no other family to help him. He'd only just met Genevieve at a college football game when his parents' deaths brought them closer together. Maybe too close. Once, Tessie had tried to warn him. "You rely too much on my daughter, Jeremiah. You need to turn to God."

"I appreciate what you're saying, Mrs. Weston," he had said. "But without Genevieve, I have no faith in anything."

Tessie could picture their wedding like it was yesterday, when they bought their townhouse, and the day Lainey was born. Her heart beat faster as she recalled the night of the accident. After a while, it had been easy for the whole Weston family to just let Jeremiah keep his distance.

She smacked the grocery cart. "Enough thinking, Tessie." She paid the bill, rushed to the car, and sped back toward the farm to meet her girls.

❧

PASTOR TIM'S WIFE dropped Lainey back at the house at four o'clock that afternoon. "Thanks for the ride, Mrs. Bartle." Lainey's pink shorts looked like they'd lost a paintball war. Most of her ponytail had escaped, curls tickling her face.

"Say hi to Tessie for me."

Lainey waited as the car drove back down the dirt road then waved one last time before heading onto the back porch. She could hear the aunts talking, the clinking of ice on glass. Curious, she leaned against the white siding and listened through the screen door.

"We're not in London, Faith. Drink the tea cold like the rest of us. It is August for pity's sake." That was Aunt Madeline talking. Her southern accent was more distinct compared to her sisters who'd moved away.

"All I asked for was boiled water. What's the big—?"

"Girls." Grandma Tessie sighed. "Focus. If we're going to get to Jude before visiting hours are over, we have to discuss the Lainey issue."

Great. Now I'm an issue, Lainey thought.

"Daddy looked so normal at Christmas," Aunt Madeline said.

"Dementia doesn't change a person's appearance, really. Not yet, anyway. And up until June he was coherent most of the time," Tessie explained.

"This still seems too fast," Beth said.

Lainey laid one hand on her stomach and one on her heart. She didn't like to think about Grandpa being sick in the head.

"Live with it every day and you'll be more likely to say how slow this disease creeps in." Grandma Tessie sounded tired. "But you're right. The pneumonia accelerated this illness, and we've got a problem that is not going away. We're two months into this, and it's time to make decisions."

"We should sell the farm. With all the controversy in tobacco these days, it's time to do the right thing," Faith said. "Buy yourself a nice rancher closer to town. It would be so much easier to take care of Daddy there. A place for you to grow old, peacefully."

"We're already old." Grandma Tessie cleared her throat loudly. "And the thought of the farm is the only thing keeping your daddy together. He'll be safe here once we get him out of that hospital. I've already prepared the first-floor bedroom and bath."

Lainey could hear clicking like a baby woodpecker. Aunt Beth had long nails and liked to make noise with them. Such as when they played board games, she insisted on tapping each space with a freshly painted acrylic tip. "If you think it best for Lainey to leave, we have to start with Jeremiah. Ma, you should call him again."

Lainey reached for the doorknob.

"I just don't know if he's ready." It was Grandma Tessie again. "Lainey'll be a teenager in a year."

Lainey felt her anger soften a bit toward her grandmother. Maybe she really did understand.

"But, you also have a good point, Bethy."

Uh-oh.

"He's a good man that got lost in grief," Grandma Tessie said. "What worries me most...I think she hates him."

Lainey's anger was boiling so hot she felt a ringing blast in her ears. Her arm lowered toward the door handle. *Hell yeah, I hate him.* Good thing Grandma Tessie couldn't hear her swearing in her head.

"I don't blame her."

Nice. Aunt Faith was on her side. Maybe the Sister's Tour would work.

A loud clang sounded, like metal on metal. Aunt Madeline must be at the sink, her usual post. Sometimes she'd clean up so quick you didn't have time to finish food before she swiped your plate.

"Blaming Jeremiah isn't going to help. Neither is cracking all the dishes," Aunt Faith said with a hint of anger. "All I'm saying is Lainey has every right to hate him. She doesn't even know him. Why should she want him now?"

Go, Aunt Faith!

Everyone went silent for a full thirty seconds.

"Maddy, sit down over here with us."

Crap. Grandma Tessie had lowered her voice an octave. A clear sign of taking control.

"It's not as simple as who wanted who. He did want her; he just couldn't handle his pain. But, it's been eight years. I'm figuring there's no time for judgment on our part. We have to help Lainey forgive Jeremiah."

Hell no, Grandma.

"That means forgiving him ourselves. And getting him to forgive us for not trying harder."

Lainey reached for the knob again.

"I think Maddy and Beth agree with me that you'll just have to lay down the law with her, Ma. Just outright tell her: 'Lainey, you're going to have to live with your father.'"

"Oh, no, I'm not!" Lainey screamed out on the porch and whipped the screen door open.

"Oh, honey." Madeline walked across the kitchen and hugged her before she could get the rest of her protest out. She grabbed Lainey's shoulders and steered her to the table. "Why don't you sit and have some tea? Evelyn's added mint. You like that, I hope?"

Lainey shrugged Madeline's hands off and shook her head. "I won't go. You can't make me." She darted under Madeline's arms. The screen bounced twice on the frame as she ran out the door.

From a tree limb behind the house, Lainey heard the kitchen screen door swing open, then squeak shut. She jumped down then raced up the steps to her room. From her window, she watched Aunt Beth and Aunt Madeline head out to check the barn. Good. Their little hunt to find her would buy enough time to sneak out of the house. The Westons knew everyone in town, so she had to get to town by dark, to catch a bus to Suffolk. There was enough money saved from Jeremiah's birthday cards for a ticket. For once her so-called father would actually be useful. Seven hundred dollars could get her far enough away.

She'd have to leave her Genevieve books behind for now. It wasn't like she wanted to run away, only pull something drastic to make them listen. Once they heard her plan—the Sister's Tour—they'd…

"That's it," she whispered. "Reverse the plan!" She pushed off the window frame and slid her left arm under the bed, searching for her stash of money and neon yellow backpack.

She was sure everyone would listen to her if she could just get to Iowa. It was simple. Lainey could take a Greyhound to Des Moines. It was baseball season for Aunt Beth's kids; that's why Uncle Chase had stayed home. When she knocked on the door, he wouldn't know what to do with her. He'd have to wait till Aunt Beth got home. Everyone would realize how serious she was about not living with Jeremiah. They'd just have to give in.

She stuffed two pairs of shorts, five tank tops, and some underwear in the backpack. She could use the tanks for bedtime, too. The front zipper pocket of the bag was large enough for her hair bands, money, and address book. Grandma Tessie was so old school she wouldn't let Lainey have a cell phone which forced Lainey to go old school to keep contact information. The only people in it were relatives, but at this moment she was glad for it. After changing her paint-laden shorts, she crept down the hall for her toothbrush. Checking the tiny square bathroom window, she saw the aunts now heading to the storehouse. Aunt Beth was limping on her bad knee. That would slow them down.

Looking toward the stick barn, Lainey saw Evelyn's truck. Perfect. She could skip Waverly all together because Evelyn was like an alarm clock. She always left the house by five-forty on Friday evenings for a night on the town in Suffolk. At five-thirty she'd stop whatever chore she'd started, take a duffle bag to the powder room, and change into dressy clothes. Out the door she'd come wearing eyeliner, blush, lipstick, sometimes even glitter. She'd been doing the same thing for twenty years.

One more glance out the window—the aunts were walking toward the pond. She could hear Grandma Tessie in the front of the house with Aunt Faith. Now was the time to act. With bag packed and hooked over her shoulders, Lainey sneaked out to the old barn to wait for the coast to clear. Minutes later she hopped into the bed of the truck.

Evelyn's heels crunched the gravel. Right on time. Lainey lay still, barely breathing, hoping Evelyn didn't notice the small lump under the blue tarp in the back of her husband's pickup. The bed was lined with damp red dirt, and the tarp smelled like mildew remover. It had a little tear in the middle. As soon as she felt the truck jolt forward, Lainey ripped the opening wider to freshen the stifling, earthy air. She alternated breathing through the hole and pulling it up to one eye to gaze at the clouds as they danced above her. Grandpa Jude had always said the more cloud cover during the day, the hotter it would be at night. Tonight should be a real scorcher.

The plastic was making her sweat, and the drops of salty water were stinging her eyes, but she couldn't take a chance on Evelyn seeing her. Moving as little as possible, she settled her head on the backpack and tried to relax as Evelyn aimed at every bump. Lainey bit her lip to hold in a scream when the truck plowed through a pothole the size of Texas.

When she felt the truck jerk, shut down, and the door slam shut, Lainey peeked out. "Whatta you know?" she whispered. Evelyn, the staunch Southern Baptist, had parked her truck in the lot of Jillie's Bar on Carolina Road. A quiet giggle escaped. Itty bitty, proper Evelyn in a bar.

The parking lot was full, so she had to move before someone noticed. She tossed her bag over the side of the pickup, then ducked back into the bed when it made a thud on the asphalt.

"Stupid!" she whispered. She lifted her head again. Still clear. Lainey spied left—all she saw were apartment buildings. Right—store fronts. Her long legs slid easily over the tailgate, taking greater care not to land hard when she reached the ground. Shoulders held back, she took off toward town.

Walking with head high, she tried to fit into the quiet city backdrop. Her stomach started to growl, but the sign behind the counter at Darby's Donut Shoppe claimed they wouldn't accept any bills larger than twenty dollars. Guess she wasn't eating donuts tonight, not unless she got some change. Her stomach thundered. Lainey swallowed her fear and went up to the counter.

"Excuse me. Where's the bus station?"

The teenager behind the counter tapped the pause button on his phone and slipped a bud out of an ear with a silver stud jammed through it. The cord dangled, swinging against his belly, as he adjusted a brown visor speckled with powdered sugar.

"Huh?" he said.

"Is the bus station close by?" Maybe this wasn't such a good idea. To run away on a Friday night. Or at all. Could this guy tell she had seven hundred dollars in her backpack?

"Two blocks that way." He pointed the opposite direction from Jillie's. "Ya gonna buy something or not?"

She shook her head, so the guy put the bud back in. She turned from the counter but hesitated just outside the door. She'd felt secure enough with Evelyn only two doors away. Now she'd have to venture farther from safety, even if it was only six thirty at night.

Screw safety, she thought. Danger was better than Jeremiah. She took a deep breath and walked toward the next step of her plan.

Glancing through its glass door, the bus station looked clean enough. Not huge or busy, like in the movies. Out the wall-sized window, passengers waiting for their journey could see the whole fleet of buses lined up, side-by-side, like they were getting picked for teams in P. E. class. She braced herself and pushed through the door.

The man behind the ticket counter was much more helpful than the donut shoppe guy. His eyelids crinkled and his brown eyes glittered when he smiled. He had an inch-thick afro with splashes of white sprinkled throughout. The name Bud was stitched in yellow thread right over the pocket of his blue, button-down shirt. With a pink highlighter, he helped her map out the two-day trip to Des Moines. Transaction complete, Lainey turned to the waiting area to scope out the best spot by the vending machines. She used the change from the ticket to buy some crackers.

Half hour later, Bud walked over to her carrying a water bottle. "You might need something to drink waiting here all night." He lifted the backpack from the plastic bucket seat next to her and made himself comfortable. His shirt smelled like vanilla, oak, and sweat. His belly pooched when he leaned forward, resting his elbows on his knees. "So, miss, why are you traveling all alone?"

Lainey was prepared for such questions. It was all she'd thought about in the back of the truck. The key to a good lie was to surround it with snippets of truth. She looked him straight in the eye and spoke as fast as an auctioneer. "I guess this doesn't look good, sir, but I got to get to Iowa. My Grandpa's all I had in the world and now he can't take care of me. He was rushed to the hospital, and they kept him there. I was afraid to stay by myself at the house. So, I called my aunt in Iowa, and she told me to get on the first bus I found."

His nose twitched. He frowned. "So, she knows you're coming?"

"Yes, sir. I said goodbye to Grandpa before I left. He's the one who gave me the money for the ticket. Evelyn, our neighbor, dropped me off. My aunt, see—she has three little kids and couldn't leave them to get out here to pick me up. She's got no husband."

Lainey glanced past his shoulder at the rusty water fountain, then forced herself to look him in the eye one more time. "Don't worry. I'm not scared." Biggest lie of all.

Bud didn't look convinced, but his phone rang. "I've got to get back to work, miss." He started toward the counter, carrying her backpack.

"That's my bag, sir."

He glanced down at his hands. "Oops. Don't want to lose this, now, do you?" He apologized and set it back on the chair beside her. "Just let me know if you need anything."

Chapter 4

ELEVEN THIRTY FRIDAY NIGHT, blue and red lights flashed onto the white siding of the Weston's farmhouse. Two police cars were flanking Tessie while Faith and Beth stood a short distance away, right hands over their mouths, left arms crossing their stomachs. They still hadn't found Lainey, and Tessie was getting more fearful by the minute.

An unfamiliar car drove down the long driveway and a stranger hopped out. "Tessie!" he called.

The wrinkles around her eyes deepened as she realized who was speaking. She squinted to make sure then hurried toward the visitor. "Jeremiah!" Her arms circled his waist. "What are you doing here?"

"I figured it's time I try to make things right. Right?" He covered her shoulders with his arms.

Tessie felt eight years of distance float away. They were family. Her son-in-law was home.

They held onto each other until Tessie glanced at the passenger seat of his Jeep. "Who's that?" She pointed toward the vehicle.

"Right. Um, Ma?" Jeremiah waved the woman out of the car who then bounded up to them with youthful energy.

"I'd like to introduce you to Brooke Nelson. My fiancée. Brooke, Tessie is my—Genevieve's mother. Those are two of her sisters: Faith and Beth."

Tessie offered one slight thrust of her chin at the girl then turned back to study Jeremiah. "You look older."

He smiled. "No offense, but so do you. What's with the police?"

"Don't be alarmed, Jeremiah, but they're looking for Lainey."

"What do you mean, 'looking for Lainey'? Where's Alaina?"

"This afternoon the girls and I were talking about the possibility of her living with you. That's why I've been calling these past few weeks. With Jude being so sick—"

"What's wrong with Jude? Where is Alaina, Tessie?" he said.

She grimaced. "Lainey overheard us talking and must have heard me say she'd have to go live with you. She ran away." Tessie nodded toward Beth who still stood watching. "Beth went upstairs to see if she'd taken anything with her. Her backpack is gone, and she left her key necklace on her pillow. So we called the police."

"Where do you think she would go?"

Tessie heard sniffles behind them. Brooke was wiping the wet from off her cheeks as her orange-sized gold hoop earrings kept getting in the way. While her empathy was admirable, Tessie couldn't help but notice how quick the tears came. A real sign of youth. Jeremiah was almost forty years old. What was he thinking with this one?

"What do the police say?" Jeremiah broke into Tessie's thoughts.

"She's not been gone long enough to start an investigation, and it's obvious she left on her own accord. We have to focus on finding Lainey ourselves for now."

Madeline came rushing out of the house holding a cordless phone. "Ma, it's about Lainey!"

Tessie grabbed the phone, listened, then nodded. "Yes, I'm her grandmother. Thank you. We'll be there in half an hour." She hit the off button then stared at the ground.

"Who was that?" Faith said.

"Lainey's in Suffolk. Her bus to Iowa leaves at six in the morning," Tessie said. "Faith, you and Madeline stay behind to set Jeremiah's friend up in the guest room." Faith nodded and they started up the front porch. Brooke followed behind, glancing over her shoulder toward Jeremiah.

"Beth and Jeremiah, you're coming with me. We'll take Jeremiah's car."

⁊⧫

LAINEY DECIDED SLEEPING on plastic bucket seats was a lot harder than it looked in the movies. The curves of the seat landed at all the wrong places on her body. At least it was quiet; the vending machine kept itself to a hum. She was alone except for Bud, who closed his eyes now and then. The floors smelled like pine mixed with ammonia. No one came in the front door. Maybe they weren't stupid enough to wait all night for a morning bus.

Her stomach growled again, so she tiptoed to the desk with another hundred-dollar bill. She cleared her throat.

Bud started, his eyes opening wide.

"I need to use the vending machines, but I used up the last of my change already."

Bud repeated his screening process by holding up the bill to the light and using a special marker to check its authenticity. He nodded and licked his thumb to separate the smaller bills: four twenty-dollar bills, three fives, three ones and eight quarters. Lainey counted it twice before buying a pack of chocolate cupcakes and orange soda.

Using her backpack for a pillow, she tried to sleep under a neon sign flashing OPEN-OPEN-OPEN. Right before her eyes drifted shut, Bud laid a thin, cotton blanket over her.

Ten minutes later she felt someone shaking her shoulder and slapped at the hand. "Bud, stop."

"Young lady, my name is not Bud. You'd better start explaining why my eleven-year-old granddaughter is sleeping in a bus station and not in her own bed."

Lainey's eyes snapped open. Grandma Tessie was scowling five inches from her face, disciplinarian hat on. Lainey scootched her stuff up and yanked on her tennis shoes. Bud's blanket slid to the tile floor. "How'd you find me?" she cried. "Did Evelyn see me?"

"What's Evelyn got to do—is that how you got here?" Grandma Tessie jabbed a long finger toward Bud. "This nice man here took notice of your address on the ID tag. Didn't take much for him to get me after that."

Lainey glared at Bud who watched with wide eyes and raised eyebrows.

Grandma Tessie grabbed his right hand and shook it with vigor. "Thank you, sir. I'm recommending you for Employee of the Month or whatever award they give here."

"You're more than welcome, ma'am." Bud perched himself behind the counter, avoiding eye contact with Lainey.

Grandma Tessie grabbed Lainey's face with bony fingers, rings pressing into her cheekbones. "Now what in heaven's name did you think you were doing?"

Lainey's eyes darted right and left, looking for an escape route. All she found was a man standing with Aunt Beth. She recognized him from her Christmas photo, but this version had eyes. She'd also seen him in wedding pictures on the living room wall. He looked thicker. "What's he doing here?"

Grandma Tessie's chin rose in slow motion and pointed at the man. "Your father is here to help us decide what's best for you."

She took a seat and patted the spot next to her for Lainey to sit. The dark circles under Grandma's eyes were blacker than usual. Her normal makeup had mostly worn away. Only a few splotches of black were smudged under her lashes.

"We have to talk." Grandma Tessie folded Bud's blanket into a tight rectangle.

Aunt Beth shoved Jeremiah out the door and pointed him toward the car with one mauve acrylic. "Wait out there!" she commanded. He obeyed without a word. Then she came to sit, hemming Lainey in on the other side.

"Don't make me go with him," Lainey whispered. She looked at Aunt Beth for reassurance, who only shook her head.

Grandma Tessie enclosed Lainey's small hands into her own. "Honey, the thought of you leaving hurts me just as much as it scares you, but I know in my heart it's the right thing."

Aunt Beth started to cry, making choking noises in her throat. Bud bent his face lower, pretending to work. Every thirty seconds, his stapler clicked.

Now he minds his business, Lainey thought, dipping her chin to her chest. The tears dropped onto her lap.

❧

ON THE WAY BACK to the farm, Tessie watched Jeremiah take his eyes off the road to peek at Lainey in the rear view mirror every few seconds. She was lying with her head on Beth's lap.

Half hour in, Lainey bolted, making them all jump. "I can run away from Baltimore just as easy. Just so you know."

Tessie turned toward the back seat. "No matter how many times you run, we will find you, missy. I can guarantee you will get tired before we do. And no matter what you think of your father right now, you will treat him with respect."

"But I don't want to live with him."

Tessie sighed. If only Genevieve were here to guide them both, she'd feel much better about sending Lainey to live with Jeremiah. Genevieve had always been the stronger of the couple. When

Jeremiah refused to go to his parents' funerals, Genevieve talked him into making the right choice. When he flunked his first exam in Business Law, she baked him a cake then helped him study for the retake. When he lost his merit scholarship, she helped him find a second job. Even helped him trust in God. Until she died.

"Lainey, I'm losing my patience with your immaturity and stubbornness," Tessie said. Her voice quivered on the last word. "I have to think about Grandpa right now. I can't be worrying about you, too."

Jeremiah patted Tessie's hand as she gazed out the window into the dark night.

At two in the morning, they walked into the kitchen, and there stood Brooke leaning over the sink, eating yogurt right from a big container. Her face was painted with full makeup, and she had JUICY blazoned in sequins across the butt of her sweatpants. Her style wasn't quite at home here, but Tessie noticed something about her that made her want to smile. She had kind eyes.

Brooke dropped the yogurt container into the sink.

"You didn't have to wait up for us," Jeremiah said.

"Of course I did."

Lainey stopped in the doorway and stared. "Who's that?"

Tessie held in a chuckle. Like grandmother, like granddaughter.

"Alaina," Jeremiah began. "This is Brooke."

Tessie could feel her ears sweating. Lainey was a time bomb meeting her father and his fiancée all at once.

"She's going to be your stepmother," Jeremiah continued.

Tessie flinched at his choice of words.

Brooke's earrings clanked against her chin as she nodded. She walked around the table to Jeremiah's side and slipped her left arm through the crook in his arm.

He was staring at Lainey with feigned confidence, Tessie could tell.

"Alaina, since we're going to start over, we should start...as a family," Jeremiah said.

Brooke held out a hand. Each nail had a glittery floral design painted on the bright pink polish. "It's so nice to meet you, Alaina."

Lainey stared at the hand like Brooke had just offered her a sack of rotting fish, then turned and plopped her backpack down on the kitchen table. The sunny yellow bag was covered with dirt from the truck bed and bus station. She dug out a few pieces of clothes only to reach a white envelope folded in half. From this, she yanked a thin wad of green bills, counted out the leftover four hundred dollars one by one. Next, she stomped toward Jeremiah with the money fanned like a winning poker hand. "It's what's left of all your thoughtful birthday gifts. I won't be needing your money anymore."

She turned toward Brooke and narrowed her eyes. "My name is *Lainey*." With that, she stuffed the clothes back in the bag, said goodnight to Beth, kissed Tessie, and stomped up the stairs.

Jeremiah raised his eyebrows. "That went well. I guess I'll walk Brooke to her room, Ma."

"That's a good idea. I'll set up a cot for you in the downstairs office," Tessie said.

Brooke glanced over with a look of confusion at Jeremiah who then looked over at Tessie with a knowing glance.

"No matter age or circumstance, no unmarried couple is going to sleep together under the Weston roof," Jeremiah said to his fiancée.

"Are you serious? Who thinks that way anymore?"

"I do," Tessie said in a quiet voice.

With a swift nod of the head, Jeremiah ushered Brooke out of the kitchen.

§

THE NEXT MORNING, Tessie was working in the kitchen when Jeremiah came in with his hair sticking straight up. Evelyn had the day off.

"Have you seen Brooke? She wasn't in her room." He snagged a sweet roll dripping with white icing as she handed him a mug for coffee.

"Wait till you get a load of today's shorts with the writing on the backside." Tessie wiggled her hips back and forth like an arthritic hula dancer. "I'm pretty sure it was supposed to say FLORIDA. All I could make out was FLO and IDA."

Jeremiah put a napkin over his mouth. "She's my fiancée, Ma."

"You sure you know what you're getting into, Jeremiah?"

"Just last night you said you needed to focus your attention on Jude, so I have to—"

"I mean marrying this girl."

He looked Tessie straight in the eye then waited a full twenty seconds. "I have no idea what I'm getting into. Last week I was still trying to find ways to avoid commitment and alcohol."

Tessie raised her eyebrows and cocked her chin.

"Marriage probably doesn't sound wise to you, but I can't do this on my own. Anyhow, you don't know Brooke well enough to judge."

She shrugged and wiped the counter with a wet paper towel. "My guess is, neither do you."

"I know everything I need to. And she can help take care of Lainey."

"What about Genevieve?"

"Seriously, Tessie?" He threw the napkin on the table. "She's dead. And now I'll have to face her mirror-image every day the rest of my life. But this one hates me. Is that what you want me to say?"

"I only want to know you're making a wise choice. Difficult enough adjusting to having a young girl around." She caught his eye. "I'm referring to Lainey, of course—"

"Cut the age jokes, Ma."

She put up both hands. "From what I can tell, you don't quite have your life together; we'll get to that alcohol comment later because you know I'm not gonna let that one go. But if I believed you actually loved this girl…"

"Let's get this straight. I will never love anyone like I loved Genevieve. But if I recall, we had this same conversation back when I wanted to marry her."

"I never questioned your love for my daughter, just your timing. Your parents hadn't even been gone a month when you proposed."

"I guess that means I have a reflex that spits out marriage proposals when something goes wrong." He slid his plate away from his body and rested his elbows on the table. "I asked Brooke after I got done explaining about Alaina and Genevieve. We've been dating long enough."

"You barely know her."

"My instinct wasn't off with Genevieve, so I have to trust myself here, too."

Tessie rubbed the back of her neck with one skinny, wrinkled hand. "But—"

"But nothing. I made a promise. A rash one? Okay, yes. And you know what? I sort of feel relieved, maybe even alive. I haven't felt that way in a long time, Ma."

She blinked then slid the pan from the flames onto an unlit burner. Tessie maneuvered around the stove with arms open for a hug, a spatula raised in her right hand. One good squeeze. Pulling back, she stabbed his chest with the eggy turner. "How old is this girl, really?"

He rubbed an ear lobe and averted his eyes. "Twenty-five."

"Sweet Moses." Tessie smacked a palm on her forehead. "Go get everyone for breakfast. And wipe that egg off your shirt."

As he scratched at the yellow-orange yolk she'd left on him, Tessie could feel Jeremiah's eyes watching her. "What is it, son?"

"How do you keep everything so together?"

Tessie had been caring for people more years than he'd been alive, but she didn't feel so together. She looked up from placing napkins by each plate, her face pale and gaunt. "Just call everyone to breakfast. We'll talk about plans for Lainey afterward."

Jeremiah obeyed.

Later that evening Tessie was waiting for Jeremiah on the front porch. She'd given him some of Jude's clothes to try on for services the next day with the family in the same church where they'd all said wedding vows—the same church where they'd said goodbye to Genevieve. Tessie needed him to remember. Lainey needed him to remember.

After that, a long visit to Jude would be in order. The hallucinations would not subside for Jude without meds, so the nurses had arranged for one-on-one observation. Between those regulations and his diabetes, not to mention the danger of not knowing when he would lash out, Tessie was being forced to put him into a home. Her original plan of keeping him at the farm was no longer viable.

She hadn't yet told the family. Tessie wanted to get Lainey and Jeremiah back on track before she let them all know.

The summer sun was setting, but it was still very hot. When Jeremiah came onto the porch, she could see a bead of sweat trickling down his temple. He looked so childlike. All the tucking and cinching of the belt didn't camouflage that he was swimming like a goldfish in excess material.

"Church will bring back memories, huh?" Tessie fussed with his collar.

"Don't know why I'm letting you make me go. I haven't been part of this family for a long time. And I certainly haven't been to church." He scraped a toe of Jude's snake skin cowboy boot on the wood planks, staring at a red ant scurrying to escape the shriveling heat.

"Once a Weston, always a Weston. Plus, God's been waiting for you." Tessie jabbed an elbow into Jeremiah's side. "So, where's the fiancée?"

"Hiding in her room. Walking around the farm with Alaina earlier didn't go well." Jeremiah crushed the ant with the pointy toe. "Brooke and I will head home tomorrow, but Lainey still needs time. She can pack and say goodbye to her friends. I'll drive back down Labor Day weekend. That'll give her almost a month to get used to the idea of living with me ... with us. That also gives me a month to talk Phil into reinstating me as a broker."

"Reinstating? I don't understand." Tessie fought the urge to pull the plug on this whole arrangement.

"There's nothing to worry about, Ma. Early on, I may have lost a few clients. So, Phil, being the friend he's always been, let me stick around as a paper pusher until I got things together. I can get you quite the sale on sticky notes if you ever need them."

His attempt at a joke didn't impress Tessie. She raised her eyebrows.

"My rent is pretty cheap; I buy very little food, so even on a small salary I've been able to save up a good nest egg to get us going. And Lainey's college fund is still intact. Now, if I can make some real cash as a broker, this can work out. The commission is good when the market is hot."

"Don't you have to be licensed to be a broker?"

"A formality. I've no violations pending, so it's just a matter of passing the exam again. I did it once so..."

Tessie wanted to believe things were under control like he said. She could have used Jude's wisdom on all this. "Think Brooke's ready for this?" Tessie asked.

"Nope. But I guarantee, she's more than eager to try," Jeremiah said, taking his plate and juice out of the kitchen.

Tessie felt relief to have another month with Lainey. Without Jude at the house, things would be awfully quiet once she was gone. Her baby's baby was leaving, and she wasn't sure what she was sending her into.

⁊⁊

BROOKE PONDERED where she may have gone wrong on the walk exploring the tobacco fields with Lainey. The girl had said nothing. No matter what question was asked, Lainey stared straight ahead with her chin set.

When they called Brooke for dinner, she claimed she wasn't feeling well enough to eat and wanted to rest. But, now, she was hungrier than she'd been in a long time. She smelled something baking downstairs but was afraid to face the great Tessie Weston, especially after Jeremiah lectured her on wearing inappropriate clothing in front of such conservative people.

Her stomach growled, and she had no choice but to listen to its begging—scary woman or not. One last glimpse of her image in the full-length mirror then she had to get something to eat. She had no idea where Jeremiah was.

Brooke tiptoed down the stairs so as not to make any noise then slipped onto a stool and waited to be noticed.

Thirty seconds later, Tessie flinched when she turned around to face the counter. "Don't sneak up on an old woman like that!" Tessie grabbed at her heart and took deep breaths until her air ducts worked again.

"I'm so sorry, Mrs. Weston. Dammit. I can't do anything right in this house." Brooke felt a tear escape then balled her fist when she realized she'd sworn right in front of this pious lady. She kept her eyes on her lap.

"Brooke, look up."

She was too scared.

"I don't bite."

Brooke didn't believe Tessie, but she was too afraid not to comply. She raised her head and focused on the woman's pointy nose.

"I am the one that is sorry, Brooke. Here you are a guest in my house, and I haven't made you feel very welcome. You even skipped dinner to avoid us. I've been remiss in training Lainey not to be rude. I'll have to ask the good Lord forgiveness on that one. Could I get you some decaf coffee, a small plate from dinner or how about some cookies? I just put a new batch in."

Brooke nodded and felt more tears following the first escapee.

"Good. Grab me a mug from that cabinet left of the sink." Tessie flung an arm toward the general area then continued cutting potatoes for Sunday dinner. "I sent Jeremiah with the sisters to find the travel trunks we stored in one of the barns. Might as well use the youthful manpower while I have it. Now Brooke, it's providential that you and I have this time to get to know one another since you'll be family soon. Jeremiah was telling me you work in a law office. That must be fun."

Brooke shrugged, nodded, then stirred sugar into her coffee.

"And that you two are recently engaged."

Brooke nodded again.

"I may accuse you of having *Lainyitis* if you don't say something, dear. Why don't you tell me about how you and Jeremiah met?"

Brooke smiled. "It was in the park where he takes his coffee break every day."

Tessie nodded.

Brooke waited for another question. She was too nervous to go into detail or tell a story, knowing full well she'd say something wrong.

"You were the one who answered the phone when I first called Jeremiah."

Brooke felt the need to confess. "I'm so sorry I never gave him the message. I thought you were an old girlfriend or something. If I had known the severity of all this, I would never have kept things from Jeremiah."

"So, have you two set a date?" Tessie laid one hand over the other on the kitchen counter.

"No. Jeremiah wanted to work things out down here before moving forward with any plans." Brooke reviewed her last statement. She was fairly certain she hadn't said anything she shouldn't.

"Wise. You know what else would be wise? Not moving in with Jeremiah until after the wedding. I know I'm an old-fashioned Bible thumper and all, but I would hate for him and Lainey not to get a chance to bond together before adding another person to the mix. They have some healing to work through."

Brooke nodded, but she wasn't sure she agreed. If they bonded without her, where would she fit in once the wedding happened?

"It would be hard for Lainey if she thought another woman was trying to take her mother's place." Tessie went back to preparing the potatoes. "And with you being the same distance in age to Lainey as you are to Jeremiah, well the less confusion, the better."

Brooke's eyes bulged wide. "I could never take Genevieve's place, Mrs. Weston. And I would never try to. I just want to be with Jeremiah and hope that Lainey and I can be friends. Like best friends or something. I promise I'll do my best to be a good mom and wife."

"You mean step mom."

"Of course, step mom." Brooke lowered her head to avert her eyes from this scary woman.

"One last question for you, Brooke. Do you think Jeremiah drinks too much?"

Brooke bit her lower lip. Step dad number two had been the king of alcoholics, mean and nasty and abusive. Jeremiah was none of those. "Mrs. Weston, Jeremiah has a handle on his drinking. I promise."

Tessie patted Brooke's hand from across the counter then turned toward the refrigerator.

Brooke breathed in deeply then took her plate out of the kitchen to hide in her room once again.

Chapter 5

LAINEY SLAMMED the receiver down so hard, the battery cover popped off and hit the wall. Grandma Tessie insisted on keeping the land line because cell phone service and electricity weren't always reliable out on the farm.

"Easy now," Grandma Tessie called from the back porch. "What's with all the anger?"

Only one week left before Jeremiah was scheduled to come for Lainey, and his fiancée was annoying the snot out of her. Lainey snapped the plastic piece back on, then laid a flushed cheek flat on the kitchen counter. Her arms dangled toward the lower rungs of the stool.

"Was that Brooke?" Grandma Tessie came in through the screen door and started rinsing the yellow squash she'd picked early this morning.

"Jeremiah." Lainey's word garbled as her mouth mashed on the cold counter.

"You'll have to start calling him Dad, Father. Something more respectful."

Lainey lifted her face and propped her head on one hand. She felt the bump of her elbow move slightly on the slick granite, sending tingles up and down. "When the man earns my respect, maybe I'll call him Dad. Until then…" Bump, tingle. Bump, tingle.

"What do you know about earning respect, miss high and mighty?" Grandma Tessie gestured at the phone with a dripping gooseneck squash. "What was all that about?"

"He thinks I should reconsider being a bridesmaid." Lainey rolled her eyes. "Brooke cried when I said no."

"Honey, the girl is trying."

"I know. All I want is to stay on the farm with you, Grandma. He thinks he can bribe me with my own en suite bathroom—whatever. I don't need my own bathroom if it means living with him and his new wife. And he plans on getting a dog."

"Might I remind you; you have always wanted a dog."

Lainey's cheek sank back to the counter. "Why can't I just stay here with you? There's no reason to live with them now that we don't have to worry about taking care of Grandpa."

Lainey sat up and clamped both hands over her mouth, her face flamed red. It'd only been two weeks since a bed had opened up for Jude in the home. Grandma Tessie visited him every day. The aides warned her she wouldn't be able to keep up that pace. The administrator had even suggested not visiting at all for a whole week to give him time to settle in. Grandma Tessie had kindly thanked them all for the advice and continued to arrive daily.

Lainey hated the strange smells at the home. First, they went through the sliding electric doors where they were hit with a strong cat pee stench. As soon as they got into the lobby, the acid stink turned to metal, like she'd just poked her head into a ten-gallon pot. When she complained, Grandma Tessie lectured, "There's only so much they can do with this many people who've lost control of bodily functions."

Then came the waft of cooking smells as they walked past the kitchen. Some reminded her of boiled sausage, others like leftover sauerkraut after Grandma cooked a Sunday pork loin.

Last weekend his roommate died, so Grandpa Jude had his own room for now. He mostly slept all day. The nurses were pushing him to get out of bed so he could start physical therapy. He smiled sometimes but still refused to speak with anyone wearing scrubs. The only time he'd say more than a few words was when Grandma came through his bedroom door. His demands were all the same—"Where have you been, Tessie? Go talk to a doctor and get me out of here."

Now Lainey sat at the kitchen counter holding her mouth shut with both hands, waiting for a reaction.

Grandma Tessie set the squash aside and leaned on the counter. "I have enough to deal with visiting your grandfather. Stop trying to change my mind."

Grandma Tessie reached over and gently pulled Lainey's hands from her mouth. "Besides, I've had my time with you. You're so smart, just like your mother was. It's your daddy's turn to get to know you. He deserves that much, for all he's been through."

"Please. Grandpa's only been away a few weeks, and you're doing fine. He's had years to get over Mama dying, and he's still a freaking mess from what I can tell."

Grandma Tessie braced her hands flat on the counter and locked her elbows. "To tell you the truth, I'm not doing fine. I put on a happy face for you, but inside my heart is broken like a crystal vase dropped on a cement floor. Just grow up a bit and give us all a break."

Grandma Tessie grabbed the last of the squash and put it in the vegetable crisper, then pointed to the sink. "Take care of the dishes. I've got work to do in the flower garden." She grabbed her garden gloves from under the sink and left out the back door. The screen slammed twice against the frame behind her.

Lainey hated to make Grandma Tessie mad. All she really wanted was to stay on the farm. Or to have her own mother with her, but that was a wish that could never come true. Jeremiah wasn't going away. Neither was his sparkly pink fiancée, but Lainey was certain *she* was. And Grandpa Jude wasn't ever coming back. Nothing was the way it should be.

Lainey closed the dishwasher on the final dirty dish, pushed the start cycle button, and went to find her grandmother.

Grandma Tessie was kneeling in the dark rich soil of the flowerbed that circled an ancient oak tree. The straw hat with yellow daisies matched her yellow gardening uniform. "Head to toe sunshine," she always said.

"Grandma?"

Tessie shifted her weight to one arm as she ran the back of her other hand across her face. She said nothing.

"Can I help?" Lainey asked.

Grandma Tessie pointed to the brick pavers that circled the flower bed. "Sit down and rip all the ones that look like this. I got distracted with Grandpa for one second and these weeds went hog wild on me." She held up a white flower with soft petals. It hung limp, fragile as silk, next to the harsh gray of her bulky gardening gloves. "Rip 'em right out of the ground."

"They're so pretty."

"That's deceiving. It's called garlic mustard. Not native to our soil, but somehow makes itself at home and then spreads—"

"Kind of like Brooke."

Grandma Tessie frowned but kept her eyes on her work.

"I'll be her bridesmaid."

"That's a step in the right direction, a good step," Grandma Tessie said, before turning her attention back to the garlic mustard. "This stuff actually has a poison in it that's bad for butterflies." She yanked another, roots and all, and tossed it into the wheelbarrow. "I don't even put 'em in the compost pile because they'll sprout anywhere."

For thirty minutes, they uprooted the beautiful, villainous garlic mustard in silence. A mother robin sang to her babies. A mower hummed through the orchard.

"Is Evelyn coming back to work soon?" Lainey asked.

"Yes, ma'am." More garlic mustard flew.

"Do you miss having all the aunts around?"

Grandma Tessie sighed and plopped her backside onto the pavers. She tried to wipe sweat from her forehead but only mixed it with dirt, instead. "Look at me, making a mud facial." She used one shirtsleeve to clean her face and laughed at her clumsiness. "My secret to looking so youthful."

She propped her body up on one locked arm, knees bent to the side. "I do miss having people around, but this is no time to dwell on it. I have to concentrate on making Grandpa comfortable in his new environment."

"Are you sad?" Lainey bit her thumb nail, the sun shining through her blonde curls.

"Sad he's not here with me. Sad Genevieve isn't with us. Sad I failed Jeremiah. Sad my daughters don't live close enough to visit every day. And I'm sad my smart mouth little angel has to leave me soon."

She removed her gloves and fiddled with the huge diamond solitaire, turning it in circles around her finger. "Look how loose my rings get when I work with my hands. Most people swell up. Grandpa always did say I was an odd duck." On her left pinky was a little gold ring with two clasped hands. The fingers were holding a heart with a crown set on top.

Pulling off the ring, she held it up to the sunlight. "Grandpa gave me this the summer before we got engaged. We were at a wedding, dancing under the moonlight. We hadn't been going steady for long, so he called it a promise." Grandma Tessie handed it to Lainey. "It's a claddagh. The Irish symbol of love, friendship, and loyalty."

She reached out to tap Lainey's chin. "We have all three, me and you."

Lainey tilted her head. "Are we Irish?"

"Not even a little bit. Grandpa just liked the thought—told me I was holding his heart in my hands. And not to break it. Or run off with it." She laughed at the memory. "My oh my how I love that man."

Lainey inspected the gold emblem.

"The Irish have a tradition that how you wear the claddagh sends a message. On your right hand—heart facing out, no one has yours yet. Turned inward toward you—you're thinking about loving someone. On your left, it tells the world you've found true, eternal love."

Grandma Tessie pushed Lainey's hand away as she tried to give it back. "No, no. I want you to have it." She slid it onto the middle finger of Lainey's right hand, heart facing the world. "Right now, you're trying to figure out what it even means to love. You've heard about it at church. Seen it here with me and Grandpa. Deep down, I even think you remember loving your mother. But you're still uncertain about how to love your father. Or if he loves you."

Lainey pulled her knees to her chest with her left arm and held out her right hand like she was admiring a fresh manicure.

"This'll remind you that I love you, and we'll be friends forever. It'll also encourage you to learn how to love your daddy and maybe even Brooke someday."

Lainey rested her chin on her knees. "Thank you, Grandma," she whispered.

"You're welcome, my love." Grandma Tessie tilted her head toward the mound of dirt. "Now let's burn these weedy suckers before they sprout right here in my wheelbarrow."

❧

A WEEK LATER, Lainey met Jeremiah in the driveway and pointed over her shoulder with her thumb. "Grandma and I already said goodbye. The rest of my stuff's right inside the door."

He popped the trunk of the rented SUV, then hurried to gather her bags. "For a small girl, you have three very large suitcases."

Lainey faked a quick grin.

"I'd like to check in with Tessie. Maybe use the bathroom. Could go for a sandwich, too."

Lainey nodded, then went to settle herself into the front seat. She sat there, seatbelt buckled, until he returned thirty minutes later.

Jeremiah pointed back to the porch as he started pulling away. "I think Tessie's waving goodbye."

Lainey stayed silent. She could feel tears running down her face, but she refused to wipe them off.

For the first hour Jeremiah ventured to describe her new school and living in Baltimore, the progress on the house, how she'd get to see Grandma Tessie at the wedding in a month. Lainey wouldn't bite on any topic. Silence became their commonality.

Hours later, when they pulled into the garage in the back alley, Brooke was standing on the back porch, waving like a five-year-old on a Ferris wheel. Lainey rolled her eyes and reached for the door handle.

"Don't get out yet, Alaina. I understand you need time to adjust." His voice gained confidence. "But Brooke's going to be my wife. And your step mom—"

"She's living here?" Lainey sucked in her cheeks and set her jaw.

"Not till after the wedding. Gives you and me some time to get to know each other again."

"Again? I don't remember you at all. Just like you don't remember my mother at all."

"You don't know what you are talking about, little girl." Jeremiah took a deep breath in and out. "Why don't we agree to get to know each other then?" He reached over to touch her left hand, but she snatched it away and bent to pick up the bag by her feet.

"All right, then. Here's the deal. I expect you to give Brooke the same respect you showed Grandma Tessie all these years. No exceptions. Understood?"

Her lower jaw still set forward, Lainey nodded and got out. The stone walkway down the embankment was uneven and hard to maneuver. She stumbled and dropped her pillow. Snatching it up before Jeremiah could help, she walked straight past Brooke to the back door then paused and turned back. "Hi, Brooke. Nice to see you again," she said in a clipped manner.

"You too, honey!" Brooke gushed. "Your room's up the stairs to the right." She pointed to the lamp in Lainey's arms. "Oh, isn't that beautiful. It'll match perfectly. Run up and check things out. Let me know if you need anything."

Lainey stared at her for several seconds, then nodded and carried her Tiffany lamp up the stairs. The cord dragged behind, its plug clunking on every wooden step.

Lainey was disappointed with how pretty the house turned out to be. It was in the north section of Baltimore, called Mount Washington. She never saw the mountain, but the pale stucco facade had green shutters with moon crescent cutouts surrounding three dormer windows. Outside, all the streets curved in gentle arcs. The corner lot was bordered by waist-high shrubs that followed the lazy bend of the road. A wrought-iron gate merged with the edge of the greenery.

She loved her bedroom, though she hated to admit it. Its shiny wood floors would be perfect to slide on in just her socks. Brooke had bought a throw rug with wide stripes of purple, teal, and soft white, so soft it felt like she was walking on a polar bear's fur. And the silly pink fiancée was right—the lamp matched perfectly. She set it on the nightstand and took one more glance around. The comforter was the same soft white as the rug, with purple polka dots and beads dangling from each corner of the hem. At least seven pillows were piled at the head of the queen-size bed whose canopy also matched the purple and teal rug. Even the sheets matched. One of her windows was a dormer, with a compact window seat where she could read by sunlight, or maybe even by the moon on a clear night.

A little anxious to sleep in a strange place, Lainey decided to get all her clothes put away first. She pulled out a pile of shorts from the suitcase and noticed something tucked between them, wrapped in newspaper. Grandma Tessie had hidden a horse painting—the smallest one from her loft—reframed in antique silver. On the back was the old Christmas photo with a newer snapshot of Grandpa Jude taped underneath. There was a hand-written note.

Dearest Lainey,

You are unpacking right now and hating every minute of it, I'm sure. You're also probably hating how much you love that new house. Jeremiah sent me pictures when they closed on it. It's beautiful, isn't it? What a find on such short notice. I think he's got friends with connections. Just remember, he's trying, honey.

Did Brooke do a good job with your room? I miss you already. I know you don't agree with our decision, but I am CERTAIN your mother would want you to be with your father. She loved him with all her heart. His reasons for being away so long may have been selfish, but they stemmed from a deep well of love and grief. Remember our ring: love, friendship, loyalty. Your father has all these for you, too. He just got lost for a little while. You'll learn to love him and even gain a friendship (and maybe with

Brooke, too). But your true test of making this new life work will be <u>loyalty</u>. When you can be loyal to both love and friendship, you will have made it through this dark time.

I love you, sweets. Please behave and watch that sharp tongue. Jesus himself only got angry twice in thirty-three years. I'm sure you've already used your quota. And <u>don't bite your nails</u>! Grandpa sends his love, as do I, Grandma Tessie

Lainey withdrew a jagged fingernail from her mouth, wondering if she'd packed a nail clipper. As she refolded the letter, Jeremiah came to the door.

"How's it going, Alaina? Brooke wondered if you were hungry."

She followed his glances around the room. One suitcase lying empty under the window; a second balanced on the bed, half full. The third and largest was still zipped and propped up against the dresser.

"You know, I could help with all this tomorrow. I'm a bit tired from all the driving. I'm gonna grab a drink and watch some TV. Want to join me?"

He had a deep voice, but it was soft like he was reading a bedtime story.

"No thanks." She sneaked into the open closet to find courage, wiping her nose and eyes on the sleeve of a polo shirt. "Can I ask you something?" she said, from behind the door.

"Sure."

She watched him through the thin crack between door and frame. He was smiling, leaning against the dresser. "Do you have a nail and hammer I could use? Grandma Tessie sent a picture I want to hang."

"Sure. I'll go get them."

She stepped out from behind the door. "Um, could I ask something else?"

He stopped and waited.

"Would you please call me Lainey? No one calls me Alaina anymore."

Jeremiah crossed his arms. "That's something I'll have to get used to saying. Your mother never let me use nicknames. She didn't really like it when I called her Gen, although her sisters did it all the time. She used to say—"

"That's another thing." Lainey closed her eyes. "I don't want to talk about my mother. Ever." She opened them again and faced him head on, spinning the claddagh ring. "It's hard to believe she actually loved you like everyone says."

Jeremiah tapped on the freshly painted trim of the door frame. "Lainey it is then. I'll go get that hammer and nail."

She could hear him descending the creaky stairs. Crap it all. Grandma Tessie would've death-stared her on that one. Jeremiah didn't even blink.

Lainey finished placing the letter back in the envelope and stuffed it under her mattress, right next to her Genevieve notebooks.

❧

LAINEY WOKE TO A SUNNY MORNING and a light breeze cutting across her room. *This place is so damn nice*, she thought. Then she looked around, certain Grandma Tessie could sense from the farm she'd just cussed in her head. Only Lainey was stuck in Baltimore and her stomach ached from missing everyone. Grandma would be finishing her morning coffee; Evelyn cooking or cleaning something; Grandpa would be making phone calls from the old folk's home demanding to know when Grandma was coming to visit.

While unpacking last night, she had noticed a few plaid skirts and matching polo shirts already hanging in the closet. A navy-blue cardigan. Uniforms. With skirts, ugh. She dreaded being the new kid tomorrow at what Jeremiah called a charter school. The kids would be snobby, she was sure. Jeremiah had won some kind of school lottery to get her into "the best free school in Baltimore." They were very lucky, apparently. She didn't feel so lucky. She felt cursed to be held hostage in a city where she had no friends. Cursed to live with a man who only pretended he loved her. Cursed to have to be nice to some crazy lady who wanted to replace her mother.

With fresh Baltimore tears, Lainey smooshed her face in the new, down feather pillow. The sheets smelled like plastic packaging. Brooke didn't know enough to wash new stuff before using it. Grandma Tessie always said, "Never use things straight out of the package. You don't want factory crawling all over you."

She already missed the good smells of Virginia. The rose bushes, Grandma's cotton-breeze fabric softener, the clean linen-scented spray she used to freshen furniture. The sweet flowering tobacco leaves. Lainey craved the smell of burnt ashes from when they prepared the seedlings.

Most farms grew corn or had cows that made the farms stink like manure. Grandpa said he liked the simplicity of the tobacco farm. It didn't require any new-fangled contraptions or technology. And even the crop rotation was easy enough with soybeans. The farm could stay simple, just like he planned on doing. The outside smells were sometimes fresh and earthy—sometimes sweet like sugar. Pink, sticky flowers in July covered whole fields like a fancy carpet. They stuck straight up above the leaves in the regal fashion of a flowering Hosta plant.

Grandpa's attack happened right before all the tobacco companies normally would send representatives to purchase the harvested leaves. That's when the smell was sweetest, right after the cropping. He used to tell stories of how they'd take the cured tobacco leaves into city warehouses for auction, "back in the day." The sell-outs, as Grandpa would call them, were now cultivating new crops and not just for rotation. Others were switching to livestock rather than tobacco. Lainey wondered what Grandma Tessie would do with the farm now that they didn't need to keep things the same. Was there really something evil behind such a beautiful plant?

Lainey got out of bed to shut the window so she couldn't smell the flowering hydrangea below her window. The neighborhood looked like the too-perfect paintings found in small-town bookstores. Grandma Tessie had told her all about the row house her parents had owned when she was a baby. Classic Baltimore style—flat roof, red brick. It sounded tiny with no lawn to run around on. Now, Jeremiah had found this tranquil place in the midst of chaos. Weird to think she'd been born right here in this city but felt like a complete stranger.

Jeremiah had promised to take her dog-shopping today since he was off from work. She chose light gray shorts with a pink tank top and glanced in the mirror. She practiced frowning to hide her excitement about getting a dog. Even though she didn't want to take anything from her father, what else was she going to do here? No friends, no real family. She'd take the dog and name it Jude Too.

As she set her jaw for a death stare if needed, a knock sounded on the bedroom door. The old wood sounded hollow. "Breakfast, Alaina—I mean Lainey."

She slipped on hot pink flip flops and swung the door open so fast her hair lifted from the woosh of air.

"Almost ready to get us a dog?" Jeremiah stood there with wet hair flopping on his forehead, a stupid grin plastered on his face. He pointed at her chest. "Your shirt says, 'Princess.' That was Brooke's nickname growing up. You know, she even has a tattoo—"

"I'm too old to wear stuff like this anyway." Lainey spun on one heel back into the closet, shut the door, and changed into a blue t-shirt with gray and white stripes that matched her shorts. She came into the room, hands on her hips. "I want a Cockapoo." She slipped by Jeremiah, pressing against the door frame to avoid touching him, and headed toward the kitchen.

He followed behind. "A what?"

She kept the conversation going over one shoulder as he ran down the stairs, trying to keep up. "A mix between cocker spaniel and poodle. If we get it young enough, we can tell them not to chop off its tail."

Rather than eat the eggs and bacon he'd already made, Lainey grabbed the box of Honey Nut Cheerios off the top of the fridge, then opened five cupboards, searching for a cereal bowl.

Jeremiah silently placed the untouched plate by the sink and offered her a spoon, handle first. When the toast popped, he grabbed both pieces and tossed them onto the cold eggs. "Sounds like a plan. As soon as Brooke gets here, we'll head on out to buy a Cockatoo. I mean poo. Cockapoo."

Lainey stuck her head into the fridge as she reached for the milk, biting the inside of her lower lip to keep from laughing.

From out of a wash basket on the kitchen table, Jeremiah pulled out a ratty college sweatshirt with bleach stains splattered over a big K. What should've read DUKE looked more like DUI E. "Pet stores should be open on Labor Day, right?" he asked. When he slid the sweatshirt over his head, his hair went every which way but straight.

She shrugged and chomped cereal with her mouth wide open. This would have driven Grandma Tessie insane. Jeremiah didn't seem to notice.

"I'll go make some calls." Once he was out of sight, Lainey reached over the sink to grab a piece of bacon.

Brooke spent the whole rest of the day with them. First, they bought the dog, which took Lainey all of five minutes to find the right one. Later, Jeremiah cooked burgers and hot dogs on the grill for dinner. After cleaning up, Brooke insisted on a forty-five-minute drive to a dairy farm for what she called, "the best ice cream in Maryland," even though they had to stop ten times to let the puppy out to pee.

Okay, the ice cream was good, but Lainey refused to say so, mustering a curt thank you and finishing her double scoop in silence. She petted JT's speckled soft fur with her free hand.

Because the wedding was so close, Brooke refused to eat any desserts. "I have a dress to fit in. I'll just sit here with this cute puppy while you order." Not having her mouth occupied gave her free rein to start 'sharing' during the ride home.

After three more potty stops for JT, Jeremiah dropped Brooke off at her apartment. She wiped hot fudge from his mouth with a napkin while he walked her to the door. Lainey looked away as they kissed goodbye, which took forever.

As he jogged back to the car, the shimmering pink fiancée yelled for the whole neighborhood to hear, "Only two weeks, babe! Two weeks and we'll be husband and wife."

Lainey felt mint chocolate chip creeping back up her throat.

Now she really regretted that weak moment she'd agreed to be maid of honor. The only flipping bridesmaid, to be exact. Tomorrow after school Lainey had to go for a fitting. Brooke had already picked out a turquoise taffeta with tangerine silk belt that matched the tangerine spaghetti straps. She looked like a poufy mermaid.

So far, there was only one good thing to come out of this impending wedding. Grandma Tessie had agreed to come to Baltimore while the newlyweds honeymooned. Aunt Faith would fly in from Boston to take over visiting Grandpa Jude. Lainey would have her grandmother to herself for five whole days, while Jeremiah and the pink future stepmother partied in Florida.

Lainey picked up JT, the second good thing to come out of this disaster and let him lick her face. She and Jeremiah didn't say one word the rest of the ride home. Silence had become their new best friend.

Chapter 6

LAINEY CONVINCED JEREMIAH she didn't need a babysitter at the bus stop on the first day of seventh grade. He actually bought it and left her there to wait alone. The public transit bus ride was short, which was good because the back seat smelled like burnt rubber and rotting seaweed.

Most of the teachers at the school seemed nice. She had to get a P. E. uniform and was required to cover all her textbooks in brown paper grocery bags by the next day as fancy book covers were against the rules. When she told him this, Jeremiah laughed. "Charter schools, the great equalizers." Whatever that meant.

Lainey made a friend in homeroom. Deena had straight, thick black hair, was two inches shorter than Lainey, and slightly plump and curvy. She'd moved to Baltimore two years ago because her mother had remarried, causing enough anger brewing in her to create some havoc. Just the right amount of rebel to get Jeremiah to worry he was screwing up and send Lainey back to the farm.

They'd only known each other a few hours, but Deena didn't waste any time sharing all her stories with Lainey. In one day, Lainey learned more about the world outside of the farm than she ever did from sneaking peeks at cable TV. Once, when Deena's parents had gone out, she'd invited some ninth-grade boys over to shoot pool, then watch TV in her bedroom. The boys had been playing hockey with brooms in the street and invited Deena to play, too. "Joey had to go home early, but Benny stayed until late, so we snuck out to that pizza place on Charles Street. They sell slices for a dollar after midnight." Another time she drank a whole package of her dad's beer while visiting him, then puked all over his girlfriend's shoes.

Yes, keeping this wild girl around just might be the trick.

The whole ride home on the bus, Lainey tapped her foot in excitement. She couldn't wait to see how JT had made out all day. What she didn't want was to see Brooke, who'd taken off from work to start house-training him. The woman's perfume alone was enough to stunt her growth, she thought, let alone JT's. Plus, Brooke felt way too "at home" already, which was evident as soon as Lainey walked in the front door.

Brooke was standing in front of the sink squirting disinfectant on the basin. "So how was your first day?"

"Where's JT?"

"I got him settled down in his new doggie bed. Go look at the bottom of the stairs."

Brooke had sectioned off a 'room' for JT. Lainey stared at her puppy locked behind wooden slats painted banana yellow. The crafty pink fiancée could make anything tacky. Lainey released her puppy from his prison and raced him around the backyard until dinner time. With JT to care for, she could pretend to be happy. The only other thing that offered any consolation at being stuck in Baltimore occurred once a day. At least for the two more weeks before the wedding. Jeremiah still made Brooke go home every night.

Lainey waited in the window seat of her bedroom until the back door clicked shut and the bolt jammed behind her future step mom around ten o'clock, then she shut her light off. Jeremiah wouldn't try to say goodnight if he thought she was asleep.

❧

THE COUPLE SAID their vows in a historic Presbyterian church built in the 1850s. The ceiling was chock-full of gold-tinted scrolly trimmings. The sanctuary was so enormous, it looked like five people showed up for the ceremony since only a few friends and co-workers were invited. The reception was held at a waterfront restaurant under blue and white lights.

Tessie asked Lainey to start the dollar dances which would require she dance with her father until someone cut in by paying to dance with him. When Jeremiah reached for Lainey's hand, she turned and grabbed Brooke by the elbow and started to dance with her instead. Brooke giggled the whole thirty seconds until Jeremiah's boss cut in, giving Lainey the chance to bee-line to the bathroom.

Jeremiah and Brooke left the party just before midnight. Their plane to Miami was scheduled for eight the next morning.

"The house all to myself," Lainey said with a smile when Tessie brought her back to Jeremiah's house. "No kissing couples or hugging step moms or annoying questions. Peace at last."

Tessie took off her black patent sling-backs and left them by the welcome mat. "What a beautiful reception. Wasn't being on the water just divine?"

"Sure." Lainey ditched her dyed kitten heels and sequined belt as soon as she shut the front door. Humidity had turned her ringlet curls to frizzlets hours ago.

"You shouldn't have refused to dance with your father. You almost caused a scene." Tessie propped her feet up on the ottoman in the family room.

Lainey shrugged as she cozied up on the couch. "Did you see the doorknobs on the stalls in the bathroom? They looked like real gold."

Tessie ignored her deflection with silence.

Lainey squirmed in her seat. "Well, I think it's inappropriate for a girl to dance with a man she doesn't really know. I heard Grandpa say so plenty of times to Evelyn before she got married."

"Not so sure I've missed that sharp tongue of yours." Tessie dug into her up-do to remove the bobby pins holding a tiny, coral-colored hat in place. "I assume tonight is a good indication that you've been giving them both a hard time."

"No, ma'am."

Tessie's eyebrows rose and her chin sank to her collar bone in disbelief.

"Okay. Maybe a little. But it's so horrible..." Lainey growled the last words from deep in her throat, "...when she's here."

"Brooke can't be that bad. She really enjoyed dancing with you, even if it was for only a second."

Lainey huffed, then started ticking off faults on her fingers. "First, she has the most annoying laugh." She mimicked, shrugging her shoulders and bobbing her head, "Teeheehee, teeheehee."

She held up a second finger. "Second, her crappy, fruity perfume sticks in my nose for hours, even after she leaves. I follow her around spraying Febreze, and she thinks I'm teasing."

"I see." Tessie set the hat on the couch beside her and stroked the scratchy veil between her fingers. "How about your father? Is he annoying, too?"

"He's trying too hard to make me happy. Like I'm just going to ignore the fact that he was starting a whole new family with no thought of me. I swear at any moment he's gonna realize how deep a creek he's gotten himself into and he's going to bolt. He's soooo not ready for a family." Lainey reached into a tote Tessie had brought back from the wedding and pulled out a large chunk of white cake wrapped in plastic on a paper plate. "Want some?"

"No, thank you, Lainey. I had mine with everyone else while you were hiding in the fancy bathroom with gold nobs."

"I told you, I had to really go. It's not my fault they cut the cake without me."

Tessie nodded in slow motion.

"I didn't do it on purpose. Honest." Lainey took a large fork full and shoved it into her mouth. "Do you mind that I named my dog after Grandpa?" she asked.

"He'll be thrilled to have such a legacy." As if on cue, JT jumped up on Tessie's lap. He circled five times before curling up to sleep. She smiled and scratched his ears. "Don't be such a pig, sweets. Take smaller bites."

Lainey slurped half a glass of milk.

Tessie sighed. She was at a loss on how to make Lainey see how wrong she was. Sure, she could punish her granddaughter for being a smart mouth and force her to be polite, but unless Lainey's heart changed, what did compliance matter? Or was she right about Jeremiah?

ॐ

FOR THE NEXT WEEK while the couple honeymooned, Tessie and Lainey explored Baltimore, but only after homework was completed. They found a starving artist expo down by the waterfront, bought another horse painting, and took a boat ride on the Bay.

Their last night before the newlyweds returned, they made a batch of brownies. "Things are better when you're here, Grandma. You should stay."

Tessie raised her eyebrows. "Are you wearing your ring?"

Lainey held out her right hand for inspection.

"Then I'm always with you, sweets." Tessie grabbed Lainey's finger to inspect the position of the ring. "So, you're still looking for love?"

Lainey gave a slight shrug. "I guess."

"You know, honey. I think I got it wrong."

Lainey jerked her hand back. "You mean I can come home with you?"

"Settle yourself." Tessie patted her hand. "I mean, I got the order of things wrong. I asked you to try to love your father. What I should've asked is that you try to be his friend. Like you were when you were little. You two were thick as thieves."

Lainey slumped and reached for another brownie. She slid lower in the dining room chair and nibbled on the gooey chocolate middle.

"It's hard to love someone you've essentially just met." Tessie reached over to tap her shoulder three times, which meant *sit up straight*. "I see that now. But you can work at being friendly. Try to find things to like about your father. And Brooke, too. After that, the love may come."

"How am I supposed to like people so gross, pink, and lame? And love them, too? Grandma Tessie, you clearly have no idea what you're asking."

"Yes, I'm just an old woman who has no idea about anything." Tessie shrugged.

The newlyweds came home late the next morning. As Lainey lifted the suitcase into the trunk of the silver Pontiac, Tessie said she had one more snippet of information to discuss with her granddaughter. "I need to step back for a while."

Lainey jutted her chin forward. "What does that mean?"

"Honey, if I keep hogging your attention, I'll be stepping on your parents' toes."

Lainey opened her mouth, but Tessie glared. "Don't try to argue," she said.

Lainey snapped her mouth shut.

"Like it or not, Brooke's your stepmother now. If I keep showing up, you'll never adjust."

Lainey slammed the trunk, making the car bounce and creak. "What about my birthday? Or Christmas?"

"The sooner your life gets easier here, the sooner I can be back in it." Tessie leaned down and patted her pouty face. "So, get to it, missy."

Lainey gritted her teeth. "I'll … try."

"Trying isn't good enough. Lainey, I'm afraid of what it's going to take to make you grow up. This is your family, and you have a responsibility to them." She tapped the claddagh ring. "When you can honestly turn that around to face you, showing the world you're thinking about loving your father, then call me for a visit. Until then. I'll pray for you every day."

Tessie slipped into the driver's seat. She pulled off her shoes for the four-hour drive, then tossed them onto the passenger seat. "Step back, honey. This old woman's a bit crazy in reverse."

BROOKE QUIT HER JOB two weeks after the honeymoon, saying that Jeremiah was doing well with his promotion and needed her to run the household. Brooke insisted on laying out clothes for Lainey every night. In response, Lainey would promptly throw them into the hamper when she woke up. She felt a little guilty, but she had to keep control somehow. And Brooke never seemed to catch on to the multiplying laundry. She packed Lainey's and Jeremiah's lunch every day. "Cafeteria food isn't good enough for my family!" she said.

Lainey would leave for school with the drawers slightly askew or her shoes strewn across the closet floor. She'd come home to rolled socks stuffed in a row like packaged sausages. T-shirts layered dark to light. Underwear with no creases because Brooke ironed them. To drive her step mom batty, Lainey took to squirting toothpaste on the mirror or shaking baby powder over the dresser and nightstand. She had to do something to make her father and step mom want to send her back to the farm. If she had to be a brat to make that happen, then she would do it with flair.

Jeremiah, on the other hand, appeared to love all the attention from his wife. Brooke tied his tie for him in the morning while he listened to the news. At night, she'd sit in his lap to watch TV. He even let her feed him from her own fork across the dinner table. The one time he pushed her hand away, she cried, so he groveled until she forgave him. Lainey complained to Deena every day.

"Your dad's happy cause he's getting some all the time now," Deena told her.

Lainey just laughed, pretending to be comfortable with what Deena meant.

Her next dread was her twelfth birthday—the first one in Baltimore. Back on the farm, Grandma Tessie always threw a party the night before her birthday, no matter what day of the week it fell on, then she and Grandpa Jude had her all to themselves on the actual birthday. Each year over pancakes they'd re-tell the story of how they'd made it to Baltimore in record time after Genevieve called to say her water broke a week early.

"Almost six pounds with long, lean fingers; a piano player, maybe," Grandpa said every year. Lainey had taken lessons for two weeks from an eighty-year-old organ player, but she refused to practice because it took her away from the farm. Grandpa Jude had been on her side like usual, telling Grandma how much he needed Lainey's expertise.

All her aunts would send birthday cards which Grandma Tessie then hid in her backpack to read throughout the day. After dinner they'd give her a special present and, of course, Jeremiah's card. As soon as she was alone, she'd throw his money into the box, and the stupid card in the trashcan. Who cared what he had to say?

Lainey wished that were true, but in reality she had read every message. Just a quick glance, but the result was always the same. In anger, that's when she would chuck his words in the trash.

Brooke first mentioned Lainey's birthday on Halloween morning. For the next two weeks Lainey heard nothing but birthday talk, almost as bad as the endless wedding plans she'd suffered through.

The woman insisted on a luau-themed party. None of the aunts could take time off to visit so close to Thanksgiving, and Grandma Tessie agreed with Jeremiah it was still too soon for her to come back to Baltimore. To fill the guest list Brooke had invited her own family, then she forced Lainey to invite a friend. The only person she really talked to was Deena, so she told Brooke to add her to the list.

Lainey considered ways Deena could cause trouble and planned to let her friend choose. First on the list was bringing beer for them to get drunk on before the party ever started. Lainey had never tasted the stuff and the smell made her gag, so she really hoped Deena didn't choose that one. Her other suggestions all seemed too lame, so Lainey added "rebel's choice" as the last option.

Brooke bought everyone a grass skirt and plastic, floral leis. Then, she made flip-flop shaped invitations, which looked kind of cool, though Lainey would never admit it aloud. They were yellow foam cutouts with green pipe cleaners for the straps. She painted a human-size picture of hula dancers on plywood, with the faces cut out so guests could stand behind them to take pictures. The party had the feel of a school carnival—all well and good if it had been June. But a luau with eight people the week before Thanksgiving, inside a stuffy kitchen because it was forty degrees outside? Everyone got sweaty and cranky, and the picture-taking station kept falling against the hutch in the dining room.

Hovering with Lainey in the corner, Deena pointed at Brooke's brother Bill. "That guy smells like salty bologna." Deena was holding JT close to her face, making baby noises to him. Animals were the only thing on earth that made Deena act friendly. And JT loved attention.

"And wearing that plastic crap around his neck just angers the meat stench," Lainey agreed. She looked at the tall, bald man leaning over the aluminum foil pan as he picked out the best pieces of smoked pork. "He's a rotting bologna sandwich in a Hawaiian shirt."

"Ha!" Deena laughed outright.

Right then Brooke pulled out the karaoke microphone. "It's time for our special activity! Everyone into the family room."

She walked up to the girls and pulled Lainey to the front row for hula lessons. Bill's wife was in charge of teaching the traditional dance she'd watched on some kids' television show. "Hips sway to the left four steps, back to the right four steps more," she chanted into the microphone. The arm motions represented the words of the song: fishing, basket, rain, and sun.

Brooke stood behind Deena moving her elbows up and down. "Isn't this a hoot?"

While Lainey felt relief that Deena hadn't brought any beer, Lainey stared with disappointment that Deena was not going to cause any trouble. And now Brooke had accepted Deena with no questions asked. Her fear was growing; she'd have to acknowledge this woman as a replacement for her mother. She couldn't ever let that happen. Her mind raced with plans on how to get back to the farm.

As soon as the song ended and she escaped Brooke's grip, Deena dragged Lainey behind the half-empty gift table. "Your mom's a trip." She shoved Lainey's shoulder. "But I could be at a real party right now." She ripped the velcroed grass skirt from her waist. "With boys. And booze."

"Step mom, thank you very much. And you could have brought us beer like I suggested."

"Dude, it's lame to drink just the two of us. Plus, you've got plenty in the back of the fridge. I checked. If you really want to cause a problem, then just call your step mom a bitch to her face and be done."

Lainey closed her eyes. Grandma Tessie definitely wouldn't approve of her new friend. She didn't have the guts to be like Deena.

As they dumped the grass skirts into a large plastic tub, Brooke resumed her instructions over the microphone. "Let's get everyone to the dining room. I've made space for a limbo contest. No excuses! Come on, Jeremiah. You're up first."

As the small crowd began to chant Jeremiah's name, Deena leaned over to whisper in Lainey's ear. "I'm outta here. No way I'm watching a bunch of old people bend over." She raced out the back door, leaving Lainey to endure the rest of her party alone.

ONE EARLY DECEMBER morning, Brooke made a big breakfast for Lainey. By seven Lainey was dressed in the new jeans Brooke had bought, paired with her brick-red hoodie. As a reward for exemplary student behavior, the charter school removed dress code regulations between Thanksgiving and Christmas. Lainey had informed her that Deena, of course, still had to wear a uniform because she'd cut class to ride motorcycles with two boys from the high school. Deena hadn't even gotten out of the school parking lot before the principal noticed and dragged her back to his office. Next day she wore black tights with giant holes cut out of them in protest. Administration sent her straight home with yet another warning.

Brooke was a little worried about that friendship.

Lainey buttered toast while Brooke washed Jeremiah's breakfast dishes by hand. She felt she could get things cleaner than any machine. She was excited that Lainey had chosen the new clothes without any fight, so she wanted to offer positive reinforcement. With wet fingers, Brooke grabbed Lainey's waist, then turned her in a complete circle. "Those jeans look fantastic! I think you might be getting some curves."

"Stop!" Lainey held the knife above her head and brushed Brooke off with her free hand.

"Getting taller, too. Another six months, you'll have me beat. Maybe you shouldn't wear that sweatshirt to school. Dress up. Make the boys take notice."

"Geez. I'm only twelve. And everybody wears this."

Brooke grabbed the end of Lainey's ponytail, inspecting it for split ends. "Then how about you let me straighten your hair?"

Lainey whipped her chin to the side so hard Brooke heard her neck crack. The ponytail flew out of Brooke's hand, smacking Lainey in the nose. "No straightening. No makeup. I'm going to school just like this, Brooke."

Brooke's shoulders drooped. "I wish you'd call me mom or something."

Lainey moved her breakfast to the table.

"I was thinking maybe we could take our first family trip over Easter break," Brooke said. Yes, she could start planning a trip. That would help build rapport with each other outside of their normal routine.

Lainey rolled her eyes at JT, who sat at her feet waiting for scraps. In just four months, he'd grown as tall as a footstool. His rib cage bulged like he'd swallowed a bowling ball. His soft fur was a mix of four dark colors: brown, tan, black, and gray. Lainey tossed him a piece of crust. "It's not even Christmas yet."

Brooke wagged a finger like a metronome. "Don't feed him people food!"

Lainey dropped another piece of crust straight into his open mouth.

Dang this girl was defiant. Brooke laid the dish cloth over the faucet and pulled out two pieces of flax bread for Lainey's sandwich. She wanted to be patient, so she took a deep breath. "Maybe your father could take the whole week off. Ever been to Disney world? Or maybe we could find a beach house on the Chesapeake. Try water skiing if it's warm enough."

Lainey bit into the toast where butter globbed the thickest. "Screw Florida. Screw the Chesapeake; I'll take a bus to Virginia since you aren't going to let me see Grandma Tessie over Christmas." She sipped orange juice.

"Don't talk like that." Brooke finished filling the lunch bag and tucked in a bright yellow napkin. Being patient made her chest feel tight, like she'd burst if she didn't tell her bratty stepdaughter what she really thought of her. Brooke held the lunch bag out in front of her until Lainey took it. "You can't go to Virginia. Tessie agreed to give us time to—"

"Grandma Tessie said only until I was adjusted to my new setting. Well, I'm as adjusted as I'll ever be." Lainey upended the nylon lunch bag and shook the contents onto the counter. The sun-colored napkin floated to the floor. "I'm so adjusted, I'm willing to tell you the truth. I hate organic peanut butter cause it's impossible to swallow. Apricot preserves are the nastiest thing I have ever tasted." She set the sandwich and a baggy of celery side by side next to an apple.

Brooke scooped up the fruit and held it a half inch from Lainey's nose. "And what's wrong with this, young lady?"

"As a matter of fact, I'm not in the mood for an apple today. Not in the mood for any of your lunches 'made with love.' I'm not in the mood to make you happy cause you'll cry like a baby if I don't. And I'm not ever in the mood to be called 'young lady'—young lady."

Grabbing a yogurt from the fridge and a spoon off the drying rack, Lainey threw her backpack onto one shoulder and ran out the front door.

Brooke swung the door open. "You call that adjusting?" she yelled down the street.

She let the door close softly as Lainey ran to the bus stop two blocks away. Brooke tried to hold back the tears, not wanting her stepdaughter to be right about her.

Chapter 7

THREE-THIRTY THAT AFTERNOON, Lainey raced up the stairs to her room to change clothes. By four forty-five she was being steered back downstairs by Jeremiah to the dining room table. She stood behind the high back chair while he complained he hadn't been able to get any paperwork done because he had to field calls from Brooke every hour trying to stop her tears.

"Sit down," Jeremiah said.

Lainey plopped down then propped one foot up on the cushioned seat, pulling at the frayed seams of her oldest jeans. They'd grown an inch too short in the last three months, but they were better than wearing the clothes Brooke had bought her. She focused her gaze on the slow continuous spin of the ceiling fan meant to keep the warm air closer to the ground.

"Where's Brooke?" she asked.

"Young lady, we need to have a chat about the outburst this morning."

"What is it with you people and 'young lady?' I have a name." By accident she glanced Jeremiah's way. His chin was set like he was biting the inside of his cheek.

"Yes, you do." Jeremiah planted himself on the chair facing his daughter. "One I'm not allowed to use even though I picked it twelve years ago. Alaina Rose Traynor. Daughter of Jeremiah and Genevieve Traynor."

"Don't mention her." Lainey crossed her arms and leaned back on the high-backed, maple chair.

"Or what? You'll be a rude smart ass? You've used that trick already today."

To avoid any more eye contact, Lainey looked at the mustard-yellow painted wall, lined by a white chair rail then turned her gaze toward the deep red curtains which draped into a pool of fabric from the floor-to-ceiling windows. Brooke had wanted the dining room to be luxurious. Lainey had told her it looked like Ronald McDonald's house instead.

JT crawled under Lainey's chair, his normal post for when crumbs fell.

Jeremiah took a deep breath. "Let's try this again. Please look at me." He reached over to touch Lainey's chin and tilted her face toward him. "I'm sorry I yelled."

She slid his hand from her face with one finger. "I'm not afraid to look at you. I just don't want to."

"Young la—" He tightened his jaw and clenched both hands. "Lainey, it's been four months, and I've given you space. Things were getting better for all of us."

She snorted. "No, they weren't. You're just too busy with the pink wife to see how much I hate it here. How much I hate *her*."

"Weren't you raised by a Christian? Isn't hate kind of a big no-no in that world? And to think Tessie raised your mother as well. You are nothing like her. She would have been much kinder to Brooke. Especially since Brooke's been nothing but nice to you. She called me crying at eight this morning. Is that what you want? To make her cry?"

"Like you care if I cry."

He slammed a hand onto the tabletop right next to her ear. "How would I know when all you do is hide in your room? Now, sit up. I'm not letting you get away with treating your mother like this."

Lainey jumped out of her chair. One spindle scraped the drywall, gouging a long line in the paint.

"I meant stepmother."

"You can't replace my mother with that witch. And you're wrong. If Genevieve were alive, she would never have met Brooke." Lainey stepped over the fallen chair and ran through the kitchen. JT bopped along behind, wagging his fluffy tail.

☙

BROOKE CAME HOME an hour later to find the dining room chair lying on the floor. She wrote a note on her daily calendar to touch up the scratched paint on the wall, then went to find some help for dinner. With the pads of her fingers, she tapped lightly on Lainey's door and peeked in. The young girl was listening to her headphones and reading old journals. Brooke could see her eyes were swollen from crying.

The first week she'd moved in, Brooke had found those notebooks under the mattress while changing sheets. She'd read a few entries, all stories about Lainey's mother growing up. Perfect Genevieve from the perfect Weston family. In comparison, her own family looked like a nightmare. At the time, she'd felt a twinge of guilt for prying and slipped the notebook back into its hiding place before anyone found her snooping.

Now Brooke sort of wished she'd read all the entries, since last week she had started peeping through a white container Jeremiah had shoved behind an old fridge in the basement. Inside were his own memory journals of Genevieve. These were more bullet lists of every memory he'd ever had of her. Her favorite clothes, his favorite clothes on her, favorite board games, a whole page of Genevieve's made-up words like 'slurpilicious'. Even though the writing held little sentimentality, the time he'd taken to make the lists said everything.

When she got to the entry entitled <u>Firsts</u>—first date, first kiss, first movie, first time they said, 'I love you'—she felt nauseated. His memories of Genevieve were intimate. She had to stop reading when he described the day he found out Genevieve was pregnant with Alaina. Brooke worried that the only connection she really had with her own husband was physical. If she pushed him where Lainey was concerned, she'd chase him away for good. Her mother had taught her that.

Brooke was anxious to find out what had happened with Jeremiah and Lainey, so she tried knocking on her stepdaughter's door again and opened it three more inches. "Lainey, I need help with dinner."

The girl didn't bother to look up.

Brooke clicked the door quietly. Since Lainey was flat-out ignoring her, she went searching for Jeremiah. He was sprawled on the couch, watching a Ravens' game on DVR and balancing a half-empty glass on his stomach.

"Please don't spill on my new couch, Jeremiah." She counted to ten. "How'd the conversation with Lainey go?"

"Not well." His eyes stayed focused on the wide screen.

"What happened to the dining room wall?"

He grunted and turned up the volume.

Fine, she thought. She could be patient with the father as well as the daughter. She had to make dinner anyway.

After preparing red baby potatoes and chicken for the oven, she took the slimy packaging out to the industrial garbage bin in the mud room. As she shoved the Styrofoam tray deeper into the trashcan, she noticed a spot of blue material. She went back to the open doorway and called to Jeremiah. "Could you come here, please?"

She had to ask twice.

When he appeared, she held up a pair of pants with a broom handle.

His eyebrows came together as he squinted. "What's that?"

"The new jeans I bought Lainey. She wore them to school today."

He ripped them from her hands. "She can't throw perfectly good clothes away just because you—"

"Wait." She held up a finger. "Look." She rummaged deeper with the broom. Under a chipped Frisbee and cracked eggshells, Brooke lifted a pair of white cotton panties with a rose-petal print. One section had a dark brown stain centered with a red spot the size of a half dollar coin.

"Is that …?" He scratched the belly of his sweatshirt and looked away. "Oh."

"I clean her room every day, so she must have brought the ruined clothes out here to hide them."

His left eyebrow raised an inch higher. "You clean her room every day?"

"Not the point right now." Brooke threw the panties back in the can and buried them deeper. "No wonder she was so snippy this morning."

Jeremiah fidgeted from foot to foot. "I am not the one to talk to her about this."

"Agreed. Becoming a woman is such a big deal. Talking to you might embarrass her."

"You're the best." He left her holding the broom.

"You're welcome," Brooke whispered. She scraped coffee grounds off the back pocket of the jeans then went upstairs to tour the bedrooms in search of other dirty clothes. When she reached Lainey's, she opened the door, without knocking this time, and dropped a basket on the floor with a thud. "I'm washing your jeans from today. Toss in anything else that needs cleaning."

Lainey stared like a trapped badger. Then she bolted off her bed to the hamper and threw a shirt into the basket. Brooke snatched up the load, shut the door, and left the young girl to stew.

Brooke stopped short on the landing. Such a life-changing event and the poor girl didn't have Genevieve or Tessie to help her anymore. Brooke set the basket down and marched back up the stairs to the bathroom. First off, the girl needed supplies.

"Lainey?" This time Brooke knocked lightly before opening the bedroom door again. She tip-toed across the room and set a package of panty liners on the bed. "You wanna talk?"

"No." Her stepdaughter snatched up the package and stuffed it under the bed skirt.

"Need anything? I mean—do you understand what's happening?" Brooke patted her own stomach.

Lainey's neck blotched red. "Grandma Tessie told me all about it before I left Virginia. And Deena gave me stuff to use at school. Just leave me alone. You're the last person I'd ever ask for help."

Brooke bit the inside of her lip and backed out of the room. She closed the door, then squeezed the bridge of her nose. Lainey didn't need or want her.

While she treated the stains in the laundry room, tears and negative thoughts nagged. At the rehearsal dinner the night before her wedding, step dad number three had taken her aside, breath hot and moist as he whispered, "He's just marrying you to take care of that girl, you know." Then he ran a thumb from her temple to her chin and smiled.

She shuddered, remembering his fat clammy touch. Brooke had told him to shove it as she wiped damp residue from her ear lobe. He didn't know them well enough to make any judgments, the old perv.

He wasn't the only one to say something. Her old boss at the law firm had kindly informed her at the coffeemaker that she was too young to be a mother to a teenager. And boy, had Tessie been bothered with the thought of her precious Jeremiah marrying someone so young.

The sisters-in-law were just as bad. Faith had written on their wedding card, *Sure hope this works out for you both!*

She was starting to believe she'd made a big mistake.

Lainey had eaten her alive this morning, and Brooke hadn't been able to defend herself. *The girl was right*, she thought. I'm not her mother. I have no jurisdiction—not unless Jeremiah gives it.

Jeremiah … something felt different. He'd barely acknowledged her presence, speaking in grunts like she was the dog. A fight was bubbling in her gut by the time she slammed the washer door. "I'll just force him to talk to me," she said to herself, "he would never have treated Genevieve this way."

Brooke marched to the family room and stood in front of the TV screen for a whole minute waiting for Jeremiah to say something; she wasn't going away without a fight.

"We can deal with it later, Brooke." He glanced as high as her waist, avoiding eye contact. "I just don't have the energy."

She arched her back and lifted her shoulders. "A few weeks ago, you would've turned the TV off as soon as I came in the door."

"What's wrong?"

"You aren't acting normal, Jeremiah. What happened when you tried to talk to Lainey earlier?"

Ice clinked the sides of the glass as his stomach lifted up then down with each breath. "I told you, it didn't go well. That's it. Sorry she made you cry, but I said I would deal with it later. Look, I had a really long day at—"

"Jeremiah, why'd you marry me?"

"What?"

"I know you're not comfortable saying affectionate things, but do you love me even the slightest?"

He lifted his head to down the last of his drink. "Don't be silly."

"It's simple enough to answer. Do. You. Love. Me. Because those journals you have hidden in the basement would suggest that Genevieve was your only love. How can I compete with that?"

His moment of silence hurt her ears and heart.

Without sitting up, he muted the sound with the remote and patted the couch cushion next to him.

She shook her head. "No. I'm staying right here until you answer."

"Brooke, you know I care about you," he said in monotone.

"Obviously not enough to tell me you love me. You didn't seem to have any problems loving Genevieve."

Jeremiah took another deep breath. "Ever since we got married, it's been nice to have you around all the time."

"It shouldn't be this hard to tell your wife you love her."

He sat up and propped his feet on the coffee table. "You have a good heart ... you're obviously a beautiful woman."

Brooke crossed the room and knelt in front of him, placing a hand on his knee. "Then why don't you love me?"

The clock ticked loudly; the washing machine purred in the distance. He looked straight into her eyes. He brushed her hand off his leg and slipped the thin gold wedding band off his finger. "I can't do this right now."

Jeremiah tossed the ring next to the remote control. Before the gold circle stopped spinning, his Jeep was pulling out of the back alley.

℈

AT MIDNIGHT, LAINEY TIPTOED down the hallway toward the back stairs, hoping to get a snack without waking up her oh-so-helpful step mom. On a normal day, if she even glanced toward the kitchen, Brooke was all over her. "What do you want, what are you hungry for, can I make you something?"

As Lainey opened the fridge, she noticed the glare of the TV illuminating the family room with a dull gray light, the sound muted. Crumpled tissues were strewn all over like tiny white lily pads. Every thirty seconds a muffled sniff escaped the depths of the couch.

Halfway back up the stairs with milk and oatmeal raisin cookies, Lainey heard the back door thump shut, the deadbolt click. Ten seconds later came a tinny jingle as Jeremiah tossed keys on the counter. He took broad steps toward the sniffling, his left tennis shoe squeaking like a hamster's wheel in need of oil.

Lainey positioned herself on the top stair for a good view of the action. When this fell apart, she could easily convince Grandma Tessie to let her come home.

Jeremiah flipped on the overhead light. Brooke's hair draped the armrest like a brown doily. She hugged a throw pillow to her chest. He walked around the couch, scooped up soiled tissues from the floor, and turned off the TV. Brooke didn't move an inch, only squeezed her eyes tight.

He dropped the tissues into a trashcan. "Brooke. Open your eyes."

"No."

"Don't act like a child."

Her eyes darted open. "What did you call me?"

"Oh good, you're awake. Now sit up." He reached down to swing her legs into a sitting position.

As her stepmother grabbed another tissue, Lainey bit into a cookie, thankful they were too soft to make crunching noises.

Brooke sniffled. "Our first fight, and you run away."

"I'm not good with confrontation. I get this claustrophobic pressure squeezing my head like a baseball helmet, and I have to get out."

Lainey had felt that helmet before when Grandma Tessie had told her the news. *I can't let you stay with us.* The first thing Lainey had done was run.

"Are you drunk?"

He shook his head. "No, but I wanted to be."

Brooke pulled his wedding ring off her thumb and held it out in her palm. "You scared me."

"I'm sorry." He reached for the ring and clenched it in a fist. "It's not like we were arguing over normal things like whether the toilet paper roll should hang over or under."

"O—over." Brooke hiccuped.

Lainey nearly choked on her milk. Pink step mom was sassy.

He sat down on the couch and tried to put an arm around Brooke's shoulders, but she shrugged it off.

"We rushed into this," he said as he slid the ring back on his left hand.

"Where did you go?"

"The ocean. Yelled at the seagulls. When you brought up my journals about Genevieve, I panicked." He pressed his head back into the cushion. "So, instead of getting a drink like I wanted, I called Tessie."

Lainey put down the glass of milk and pushed the plate of cookies toward JT, who enthusiastically dug in. This was better than any movie.

"Are you kidding me?" Brooke stood up and paced. "That woman promised to give us a chance."

Jeremiah grabbed her elbow as she passed behind the couch. "That woman is the closest thing to a parent I have left. It was that or the bottle."

Brooke jerked the arm from his grip.

"She offered some perspective." He patted the cushion beside him. "You might be interested in hearing it."

Brooke circled the couch once before joining him. She leaned her back on the armrest and crossed her legs. "Fine, enlighten me."

"We have to work harder at getting on the same page. We're in different stages of our lives. That's what she said to me."

Lainey watched Brooke purse her lips and squint her eyes so tight, wishing the pink wife would literally burst.

"Keep going," Brooke said.

"You're still young. You want romance and warm fuzzy—"

"Every woman wants romance, Jeremiah—"

"Please." He held up one palm. "Let me finish."

"Fine." She folded her hands in her lap like a good girl praying in Sunday school.

"I've already done all that romantic, fuzzy-feeling stuff," he said. "I was happier than any man had a right to be."

Brooke's chin lowered to her chest.

Defeat? Lainey started making a mental note of the clothing she needed to pack first.

Jeremiah sat on the coffee table to face her. "Brooke. Look at me. I didn't choose to let go of that love. It didn't walk out on me. It was stolen from me without any warning, and I can't pretend to feel any different."

"Don't you think I know all this? Genevieve was perfect. Genevieve was beautiful. She's the only woman you'll ever love." She punched the cushion with the back of her fist. "You needed Tessie to tell you these things? All you had to do was read your own words hidden in the basement. It's quite clear there."

Lainey grabbed the spindles of the railing and held her breath.

"Let me talk, please?" He lifted his eyebrows.

Brooke reached for another tissue with her left hand, giving him the floor with a wave of the right.

"Thank you. Yes, I will always love Genevieve. And yes, she was all those things to me, but I refuse to apologize for it."

Brooke stroked the fringe on the throw blanket as if it were a kitten.

"Here's what I do know," he said more gently. "You are the one who's helping me get ready to move on. Your good heart makes me believe in love again. I adore how much you want to take care of Lainey and me, whether we appreciate it or not. Tessie helped me realize that feeling all those things … it's a good place to start."

Brooke raised her chin and looked straight into his eyes.

"What I'm trying to say is I'm *falling* in love with you. All those things I'm feeling…they mean I really like you. You make me laugh when you argue with other drivers on the road. I smile when I read those silly notes you leave in my lunch every day."

Worry lines creased her brow. "Silly?"

"I trust you with my heart and with my daughter. If Lainey turns out half as kind and loving as you, we'll have done a good job with her."

Brooke grabbed his outstretched hand and pulled him back onto the couch. "We've got our job cut out for us on the kindness front. Where'd she get that tongue?"

"We'll blame Tessie. She had her for eight years."

Brooke snuggled into Jeremiah's embrace. "So, you're falling in love with me, huh?"

"On the beach tonight, I started worrying about how frightened you must be. That's when I realized with certainty how much I need you. Right away, I wanted to come back to make sure you were okay. If that isn't the start of a strong love, I don't know what is." He kissed her forehead. "I'm sorry about the ring. That was unfair."

Neither of them heard the footsteps heading toward Lainey's room, the door shutting, or JT lapping up spilled milk from the hardwood floor.

Chapter 8

IT WAS MARCH NOW, four months since the big blow up. For the first eight weeks, they walked on eggshells around each other, but Lainey refused to apologize to her dad or Brooke. Then, Brooke announced her pregnancy and the adults' focus swayed in a different direction, giving her more freedom to plot out ways to get herself back to Virginia.

For her latest scheme, Lainey carried Deena's overnight bag up to her bedroom. With a fake pouting lip, Lainey had told Jeremiah how much she missed having a best friend, and he folded. Grandpa Jude would have said like a cheap tent.

The girls figured it would be better not to tell Jeremiah that neither of Deena's parents had wanted her around that weekend. That morning Deena called her father a real jack-hole over the phone then went and pierced her nose with a sewing needle and ice. It was still blood-stained.

"Brooke's been throwing up for a month," Lainey told Deena. She wanted her friend to be prepared for any hormonal craziness that might happen, like the time her step mom cried for an hour because Lainey threw a half-eaten banana in the trash. "If she loses more weight, they might have to put her in the hospital," Lainey finished. "She can't do anything normal."

The family's daily routine went out of whack once news of a little Traynor-to-be was broadcast. Lainey started making her own lunches and still had to help make dinner. She had to help take care of the pregnant pink step mom whether she liked it or not.

"Mandatory participation is what Brooke calls it. Says it'll make us a stronger family unit. Ugh. Plus, she says she's trying to prepare me for marriage." Lainey threw Deena's clothes into a heap on her bed. "I'm only twelve!" Lainey didn't want to be an adult yet. She wanted to go back to the farm with Grandma Tessie like it used to be.

Deena set down a blue tote with white and yellow flowers scrolling every inch of the bag, even the straps. It was large enough to hold two bowling balls. "Wanna see what I brought?"

Lainey wrinkled her nose. "That bag looks like something my grandma would buy."

Deena grinned. "That's the point. Adults don't get curious if you cover things with flowers."

Lainey laughed, but her stomach fluttered. Rather than butterflies, it felt more like moths trying to munch their way out. She was glad to have a friend, but Lainey never knew what to expect with Deena around. "Okay. What's the big secret?"

Deena pulled out a pack of cigarettes, a lighter, and a red box of strike-on matches.

"That honking big bag for cigarettes?" She was relieved it wasn't anything worse. At lunch yesterday, Deena had threatened to bring pot a "friend" had left in her locker. "You know we can't smoke these, right?" Lainey said.

"Why not? We'll just open a window." Deena ripped off the packaging with her sharpened tooth. Right before her mom remarried, Deena had gone through a vampire stage and filed the left cuspid to look like a spear. She used it to open everything.

Next, she pulled a match out of the box.

Lainey followed behind Deena, picking up all the crumpled cellophane tossed to the area rug and shaking her head. "Uh-uh. Opening the window never works to get rid of the smell."

Deena struck a match and watched the flame travel down the wood until it got close to her fingertip. The wood melted like ice in the sun, then turned a chalky black. Lainey's room filled with the soft, acrid stench of egg mixed with campfire ash.

"Deena, I'm serious. We can't light a cigarette in the house. Plus, Grandma Tessie would kill me if she found out I ever smoked one."

"Sounds a bit hypocritical to me, living on the tobacco farm and all. Plus, Grandma Tessie's not here. What's the big deal?" Deena lit another match and watched it burn. When it reached the tip of her nail, she squealed and flung it away. It landed on the oak floor, still smoking.

"Watch it, Deena!" Lainey's moths were eating her stomach alive. She was regretting all the plans to use Deena's rebellious nature to get back home.

"Lighten up, would ya? No pun intended." Deena guffawed then shoved Lainey aside. "I've got an idea. Ever see an aerosol can shoot flames?" Deena lit two matches simultaneously this time and watched the two orange flames race toward her fingers.

Nerves rumbled deep in Lainey's stomach. The moths were restless now. She shook her head.

"Excellent! Go get some hairspray."

With the should I/shouldn't I wrestling in her brain, Lainey sneaked down to Brooke's bathroom and took a large can of Suave aerosol from the cabinet. She was tempted to go back and tell Deena she couldn't find any. Playing with fire was stupid, but she also wanted to stick to her original plan—get in trouble so they would send her away. Plus, the moths made her feel alive.

Just as she was leaving the master bedroom, Jeremiah stopped her short in the hallway. "Need something?"

"Uh, no. We were just doing each other's hair and wanted something to make it stick." She held up the Super Hold and shook it.

"Do I smell matches?"

"Um, yeah we lit a candle." Lainey wanted to get away from Jeremiah more than anything.

"Okay. Brooke and I are watching a movie if you two want to join us."

"No, thanks." She shook her head and ran back to her room.

"Doing our hair. What a freaking liar!" Deena grabbed the can and ran into the bathroom. "Bring the lighter. Matches don't work so good for this."

Time stood still, like a pivotal scene in a movie. She could see Deena's lips moving, but her heart was beating louder. It was Lainey's moment to leave Grandma Tessie's goody-two-shoe warnings and Jeremiah's lame attempts at being her father all behind. Lainey reached into the dangerous, floral bag for the lighter then followed her friend to the bathroom.

Deena waved Lainey over to her. "I'll spray and hold the lighter up and poof— you'll see a big flash."

Lainey swallowed the twig-like scratch welling up in her throat. "Wouldn't it be safer to do this outside?"

"Don't be so lame. We're surrounded by water." She spread her arms, pointing to the sink and bathtub. "If something happens, we'll just chuck the can in the sink."

Lainey bit the inside of her lip as Deena pressed the nozzle. A fine mist floated from under her finger. Deena flicked the lighter. A foot-long tongue of blue-red flame blazed toward the sink. Both girls shrieked then shushed each other.

"I feel like a dragon," Lainey whispered. The moths were soaring. She could honestly say, it was fun trying to piss off the parental units. The girls soon got into a perfect rhythm of spray, lighter, flash; spray lighter, flash; spray, lighter, flash.

On the tenth round, the lighter failed to spark. Lainey glanced toward Deena. "What the—" With her finger still on the nozzle, the Zippo ignited. A burning sensation jolted her hand back. Aerosol fumes shot fire toward the clear shower curtain. Fueled by melting plastic, flames hit the ceiling in two seconds.

Screams and the smoke detector sounded simultaneously.

Footsteps pounded down the hall and Jeremiah raced in. The girls hovered by the toilet watching the ceiling paint bubble into black. He lunged through the flames to turn the shower on. "Get out of here!" he shouted. Jeremiah grabbed a plunger and shoved the melting curtain rod down into the tub. The pelting shower head doused the flames, but the ceiling was charred.

He spun toward them, thrusting the plunger like a giant accusing finger. "What the hell were you doing?"

Deena ran past him, out of the bathroom. Her chunky shoes thundered down the stairs.

Jeremiah studied the burnt plastic debris floating in the tub and winced. "Loyal friend you got there. So much for lighting a candle, huh? Are you hurt?"

"No." She held her breath to force back tears then pointed at the blobs of clear blisters forming on his hand.

"Son of a—" He ripped the battery out of the shrieking alarm and chucked it into the tub with the rest of the junk. "Didn't hurt until you pointed it out." He sank onto the toilet lid and held the burnt hand above his head. "Let's get a plan of attack to keep Brooke from worrying."

"Worrying about what?" Brooke stood in the bathroom doorway, taking in the blackened ceiling, the pile of plastic char in the bathtub, the can of hairspray lying abandoned in the sink.

Jeremiah slid his hand behind his back, and Brooke strained to peek around his shoulder. "What are you hiding? What's that smell? What's wrong with Deena?"

"She's fine. Just needed to go home." He steered her from the room with his good hand and coaxed her to lie down. "No need to stress the baby. I'll take care of all this."

He got her settled in for a short nap after she gave him three lists of items to buy to fix the damage, then told Lainey to get in the car. "I need a doctor. You need a new shower curtain. And a good whupping."

The emergency room made them wait two hours because Jeremiah, gritting his teeth, modestly claimed his pain was at level four. In the waiting room, three TVs broadcast CNN, the bottom line scrolling faster than Lainey could read. A lady behind a thick wooden door screamed shrilly every thirty seconds, "I'm not sick! I'm not sick! Let me outta here, I'm not sick!"

The doctor allowed Lainey to join them in the examining room. Lainey's shoes kept sticking to the tile floor like they'd washed it with bubble gum. The exam room was only a cubicle made of metal rods and a blue curtain with bleach stains. A poster on how to save a choking victim hung on the back wall of the exam room. Someone had drawn cartoonish body parts on the 'model' with a black marker.

When the doctor finished examining Jeremiah's hand, he called it a second-degree burn. "This is so deep, it could turn to third degree if not treated correctly," he admonished him. "First grill of the season?"

Jeremiah smiled. "Something like that. Can burns get worse like that?"

The doctor nodded. "You're looking at three to four weeks to heal. The nurse will set you up with sample meds till you can get to the pharmacy."

Hours later as he drove them home with one hand on the wheel and the other propped over it, Lainey could feel Jeremiah glancing over at her. She was sucking on the end of her ponytail like she had done when she was little. It felt like the moths had died right there in her stomach.

"Look at me," he said.

Lainey turned her head toward him.

"Next time we go to the emergency room, pain level is a ten. Got it? This thing hurts like hell."

She spit hair off her tongue and whispered, "I'm really sorry, Jeremiah." She was holding a bag from Target close to her chest like a Teddy bear. A new shower curtain rod ran between the front and back seats. A can of white ceiling paint sat at her feet.

"How stupid do you have to be to shoot flames inside the house?"

"It was under control; we'd done it ten times already."

"Even if you don't care about me or yourself, Brooke is pregnant. What if the house had caught fire? You do know Genevieve died while she was pregnant, don't you?"

The silence lasted an eternity.

Lainey felt the tears welling into extra-large droplets on her bottom lashes. She let out all the air in her lungs. The thought of a brother or sister was too much for her. "I'm real, real sorry about your hand," she choked out.

"And I am sorry I mentioned your mother. That was cruel. I never told anyone about that." Jeremiah scratched at his nose with his bandage. "I'm a bit out of commission, so you're in charge of repainting the ceiling this weekend. I consider that light punishment for such a bonehead move."

"Yes, sir. Jeremiah?"

"What?"

"Are you going to tell Grandma Tessie about this?" She couldn't stop the tears from streaming down her face. She was torn. Her plan had worked. If he called Grandma, Lainey might be able to go home, but something felt wrong about that now.

"We'll have to see." Then he reached for his phone. "I'll give you one call to make sure Deena made it home, but understand this," he held the cell just out of reach. "That girl will not be invited back for a long, long time."

That was a relief. She wasn't quite feeling up to the rebel lifestyle anymore.

&

LAINEY LAY DAYDREAMING on her bed one rainy Saturday morning. School had been out for two weeks, and she longed to be back on the farm. In Baltimore, summer moved at a sloth's pace. It was only the end of June, but it felt like each week was a whole year. Jeremiah had gotten far behind in work with his burnt hand, so vacation was out. She'd secretly hoped they'd change their minds about letting her visit the farm, but Brooke was as round as a watermelon and just kept taking more naps. They weren't going anywhere, anytime soon.

Lainey closed her eyes to picture Grandpa Jude walking the rows of tobacco in his Wrangler jeans and straw cowboy hat. Did he miss his home something fierce? The summer months were the second busiest, other than harvest, and she loved following behind him. Now they were both missing it. She got a lump in her throat thinking how he might not even remember the farm. Or her.

She could imagine the three-foot plants rustling in the breeze with tall flowers splashing one long chain of pink. Sometimes she allowed herself to picture Genevieve, and the baby she'd been carrying, there with her on the farm smelling the tobacco plants. Lainey couldn't stay in that daydream long. It was too sad.

The Weston farm was still successful because, according to Grandpa, everyone else had sold out. Would Grandma Tessie sell out, too, now that Grandpa wasn't there?

She imagined herself climbing the ladder to her loft to look at her the horse paintings. Grandma Tessie had promised she wouldn't get rid of them. Lainey sighed. The longer she was away from the farm, the less likely it was she'd get back there, so what did it really matter? Her rebel plans had been deflated the day of the fire. Now, Grandma Tessie only spent five minutes a week on the phone with her—just long enough to ask how JT was getting along in his obedience training. Lainey had taught him to roll over and sit; next they were working on shake and play dead.

One good thing—when Jeremiah found out how much she liked horses, he'd made her a deal. If she did the housework for Brooke in the morning all summer, he'd get her two memberships: one for the public pool in the afternoons, the other for a horse farm where she could take equestrian lessons on Saturday mornings. Today's riding lesson on her usual horse Tulip had been canceled due to the rain. Being an equestrian was much different than just riding old Sam bareback around the farm. Now she had to sit on a saddle and wear paddock boots. If she improved enough to enter competition, she'd have to wear the tall leather boots. The riding pants had a weird name she couldn't pronounce—jodhpur—they made her feel a foot taller.

Helping Brooke was a small price to pay to have some actual fun. Plus, she still felt a little guilty about putting them all in danger with the bathroom fire. Lainey hadn't seen Deena since the last day of school, but they hadn't been getting along since the incident, anyway. Deena had started hanging with Joey and ate lunch in the cafeteria with him the whole rest of the year. When Lainey tried to stop her from stuffing eggs in a locker to rot over the summer, her "friend" had thrown one at her head and ran. Lainey had ducked just in time.

Saturday riding lessons were the only time she was alone because Brooke insisted on going to the pool with her every day. "Baltimore's not like Waverly, Lainey. You can't just run around by yourself. And if I have to rest, might as well be by a pool," she'd said, following it with a smile.

Sometimes Brooke would step down into the shallow end to float, her hair spreading like brown seaweed, her whale-like hump protruding from the water. She still wore a sequined red bikini. Personally, Lainey preferred a one-piece suit that hugged tight, right up to her collarbone. Who wanted to worry about private parts popping up out of the water? Not that Lainey had anything too impressive to worry about yet.

The cleaning started the day after school let out. Brooke wasn't comfortable having someone else do her housework, so she followed Lainey checking for missed dust bunnies and window streaks.

"I used to help Grandma Tessie all the time," Lainey huffed. "I know how to clean."

Brooke hugged her from behind. It was like being squashed by a bony kangaroo with a full pouch. "I know, honey, but I feel sort of useless, so I'll keep you company."

"Great," Lainey said in monotone.

Each morning over cereal and whatever else wasn't making Brooke queasy at the time, they would plan the day's course of action. Lainey could get three main chores done from eight thirty to eleven thirty while Brooke followed along. They'd eat lunch, then be at the pool by one. On rainy days, she'd take her to the movies or set up a T.V. marathon in the family room. If Lainey hadn't been so determined to get back to the farm, it could've been a nice summer.

During the cleaning sessions, Brooke took to chattering about her own childhood. At first Lainey tried not to listen, keeping her face smooth as the kitchen tile she was mopping. She heard about Brooke's first kiss and how she didn't learn to ride a bike until she was eight. Lainey counted to one thousand in her head to tune out the story of the 'Princess' tattoo from spring break, Brooke's senior year in high school. Something about best friends, a double dare, and needing to feel special.

Brooke's father had left when she was only two. Her brother Bill was fifteen years older, so he'd left the house soon after. As Lainey emptied the dishwasher, Brooke once asked, "Ever notice how my brother Bill smells like lunch meat?"

Lainey couldn't help but giggle. She wished Deena had been there to hear that.

"The smell grew when he stopped eating carbohydrates. He lost weight for sure, but boy did the abundance of meat permeate his whole body."

July passed, and the more Lainey learned about Brooke, the less she was able to ignore her, which was also annoying. Then she'd think of Genevieve and resolve to be loyal to her mother's memory, even if Jeremiah wasn't capable of doing the same.

This morning in early August, as Lainey cleaned the master bathroom, Brooke sat on the toilet seat lid and started talking like usual. "I had to live in foster care for four years."

Unnerved by the information, Lainey sprayed three times as much Scrubbing Bubbles on the tub as was needed. She turned toward Brooke. "You might not want to be in here with these chemicals. I got carried away."

"Oh!" Brooke grabbed her belly and went to lie down on the king-sized bed, talking louder. "Bill had already enlisted in the Army by the time I was four. My dad had been gone for two years. Mom lost the apartment and had nowhere to turn."

Lainey wiped down the melting foam with a wet sponge, then sprayed the tub again for good measure. She heard the rustle of sheets against the comforter.

"Mom had been seeing some man she met at the grocery store. So, one day while she was at work, the boyfriend emptied her bank account. He'd got the numbers from her checkbook and signed my dad's name. She hadn't changed their info at the bank, yet."

Sponge in hand, Lainey came out of the bathroom and sat on the tan speckled carpet by the door.

Brooke pounded the pillow under her head. "She didn't even find out until a week later when her rent check bounced. We got evicted. So, she packed up all the canned food, and we lived in the car for a month. I still can't eat canned peas or smell Spam. You'd think I would've been too young to remember that."

"I have one memory from when I was four." Lainey brought back the image of her clinging to Jeremiah's khaki pants leg. That was the first time she let herself remember it as it truly happened.

Brooke patted a spot next to her on the bed. "Come sit over here so I can see you."

Lainey held up the wet sponge with her pruney hand. "Can't." Ammonia fumes burned her nose.

Brooke leaned her head on one hand, propped by an elbow. "Then we ran out of food. Mom still hadn't found a job, so she took me to a girl's home downtown. I remember her saying, 'Sit here while I go get us some juice.' The bottom step was crumbling. I watched an ant carrying the tiniest bit of apple. I remember worrying someone would step on him before he got the food to his family. One of the workers took me inside to watch cartoons. But they couldn't keep me there without knowing where I had come from, so they put me into the foster system when Mom didn't come back."

"Wasn't there anybody else to watch you?" Lainey leaned her back on the door frame.

"Just Bill, but he couldn't have left the base even if he had known. Mom was an only child; our grandparents had died already. She never even met my dad's family." Brooke sighed. "Anyway, it took her four years to get a job and come find me."

She laid her head back on the tan, black and red plaid pillowcase. "Need to rest my eyes a minute."

Lainey stared at Brooke's protruding belly button rising and falling in slow motion under the thin yellow t-shirt. She wondered what it felt like to have a baby living inside. Genevieve had been pregnant twice. Grandma Tessie four times. Lainey stuck out her own belly but couldn't get a decent lump. She grabbed a throw pillow from the side chair and shoved it under her shirt. Back in the bathroom to check the mirror, she rubbed the pillow in small circles like she'd seen Brooke do.

A flicker of light bounced off her claddagh ring. She raised her hand, and the pillow dropped to the floor. *Friends first, then love,* Grandma Tessie had instructed. She thought of Brooke left on the steps all alone, worrying about an ant. Four years old. Motherless. They had something in common after all—parents desperate enough to leave them behind.

At least she'd had Grandma Tessie and Grandpa Jude. Brooke had been alone.

❧

TESSIE HELD THE CORDLESS phone half an inch from her ear, peeling paint from the porch railing with a fingernail. The farm was quietest during early evening, but with summer days so long, the sun still burned her face.

Jeremiah's voice echoed in her ear. "I find myself getting frustrated with Brooke. She needs so much attention. With all the pressure at work, I don't have time for it."

Tessie pulled off a six-inch chip of lead paint and watched it slip right through a crack in the boards. She'd have to tell Amos to hire a young kid for repainting. "Jeremiah, if she needs a little attention then why not give it? It doesn't hurt to give someone you love what they think they need, especially the woman carrying your child. You do love her, right?"

She hoped he couldn't detect the lethargy in her voice. Tessie hadn't been feeling like herself. Usually, these conversations with family or friends brought joy, but that was no longer true. Now, she just felt alone.

"Of course, I do! I just can't stop comparing everything to when Genevieve was pregnant. I find myself wanting to go into hiding all over again. Whiskey sounds a whole lot better sometimes. What if I can't protect Brooke?"

Tessie counted to ten, watching a butterfly flap its delicate green wings. "Brooke isn't Genevieve." A wave of emotion forced tears to her eyes, but she held the steady tone in her voice. "Can't give in to fear, son. Only a month till that little one gets here, then everything will feel right again." She closed her eyes, feeling hypocrisy wash over her—a sinner's baptism.

"I guess you're right, Ma. Are you coming Labor Day weekend? We want you around when the baby's born."

She took a deep breath. "That's a mother's job. I wouldn't want to intrude."

"Brooke doesn't really care for her mother's help, so we need you. Faith already offered to come take over your visits for Jude. We'll put you in the baby's room. He won't be using it right away."

"Oh." Tessie's heart skipped for the first time in months. "It's a boy?"

"Don't tell anyone." Jeremiah's whisper tickled her ear through the phone line. "We're thinking of calling him Caden Wendell."

"Caden Wendell Traynor. Sounds almost presidential," she said. "You haven't told Lainey?"

"Brooke wants it to be a surprise. It's her first time experiencing all these things."

"Might be better to include Lainey in all the preparation."

"So, how you holding up, Tessie? Anything different with Jude?"

She didn't want to talk about her husband. Maybe she could just hang up. She sighed as her mind grasped for a response that didn't sting. "Jude's heart issues are under control for the time being. He's ornery about getting out, about coming back home. Can't remember where that is much anymore. Now he's obsessing about strange details like did the porch wrap all the way around the house. Or how much land sits to the left of the garage. Then inevitably he ends with some comment about my putting him in that God-forsaken place so I can get rid of the farm just like all the other sellouts.

"He can't remember the grandkids' names anymore, and he's just getting meaner." Tessie sighed again. Talking about her situation drained her heart. "Overall, we're making it through the daily grind with the Lord's mercy and grace."

"Can't believe it'll be nine years since the accident," Jeremiah said. "I've always put my head in the sand or in the bottle every August and plowed toward September till I could breathe again."

"You aren't drinking, Jeremiah?" Tessie felt a twinge of regret for sending Lainey back to her father.

"One here and there. I haven't told Brooke yet, but I think I want to spend the anniversary day alone. I just need to wrap my mind around all these changes."

Tessie leaned an elbow on the arm of the rocker, placed the ear piece on her forehead, and spoke directly into the mouthpiece as it dangled. "Not a good idea, son. You've got to trust her with your feelings, good and bad. Go talk to your wife. And to your daughter. Stay away from the booze."

"I hear you, Ma. I'll figure something out." The dial tone buzzed in her ear.

Tessie rested the phone on her girdled belly. "But you don't really listen," she said to the still air. She closed her eyes and leaned back. Evelyn was gone for the day; Amos was working on accounts in the office. Dusk enveloped the farm in a hug like it wanted to say goodnight.

Rather than dwelling on the fact that God had taken away every person she'd ever loved, Tessie imagined Jude rocking next to her, his steel-toed boots clicking on the wood boards. The red bandanna he loved to filch from her top drawer hung out of his back pocket. He casually slung his blue cotton, plaid shirt onto the railing. She could faintly smell the sweaty musk from the damp, white undershirt tucked tightly into his jeans. The faded bronze belt buckle with antlers centered under a slight pooch, and blonde curls threaded with gray escaped from under his John Deere cap. Which he re-adjusted every three minutes. Tessie sat with eyes closed, watching him there till the moon filled the sky, her cheeks wet with tears.

Chapter 9

LAINEY WOKE TO BROOKE standing by her nightstand slamming buttons on her alarm clock. Brooke wouldn't let her use her new cell phone as an alarm because she didn't trust the battery to stay charged. Lainey tried to explain she could keep it plugged in all night, but Brooke wouldn't listen.

"What are you doing?" Lainey mumbled from under the covers.

"Go back to sleep." Her whisper sounded like a radiator's hiss. "We're making today a family holiday." Brooke dropped the alarm clock on the nightstand.

"Let me do that." With a scratchy grunt, Lainey shut off her alarm, flipped the pillow over her head, and hunkered right back into dreamland. She half heard the door click as Brooke tiptoed out.

A little after nine, Lainey shuffled into the kitchen. "Why did you wake me up, just to tell me to go back to sleep?"

Brooke scowled and pointed to Jeremiah sitting at the kitchen table with orange juice in front of him. "I was up at five to see your father off on his 'personal holiday.'"

Jeremiah looked like he'd been run over by a dump truck.

"As you can see, he's getting a slow start." Brooke poured a juice for Lainey then started beating a second batch of pancakes with unnecessary force.

Lainey took plates out of the dishwasher. "Why are we taking off on a Monday? What about the chores?"

"Seems it's going to be another family tradition." Brooke stopped mixing to flip three golden brown silver dollar pancakes onto an already tall stack of five. "From now on, the fifteenth of every August, your father will drive to the ocean all by himself, while his wife and daughter have as much fun as they want somewhere else. Oh, and he'll also drink himself into a stupor. Great plan, huh?"

"Why can't you understand I just need some time to myself?" Jeremiah's voice was only above a whisper.

Brooke dropped the bowl onto the counter. "Oh! I understand! I understand so well I'll even get out of your way."

Lainey scratched out crusty eye gunk and propped her elbows on the counter, blowing softly at the strands of loose hair that tickled her face. "Well, I still don't understand."

"Historically speaking, August has not been kind to your father, and he needs a day to gather his thoughts. He wants to do it alone."

Lainey realized Brooke was referring to her mother's car accident. Grandma Tessie hadn't ever dwelt on it, at least not in front of her. Sometimes Grandpa would mention a 'heavy atmosphere' at the end of summer. He'd always blamed it on locusts, though. She remembered sitting on the front porch when she was nine. They had just finished breakfast and were enjoying the fresh morning air. The day hadn't yet gotten too hot. Not saying a word, Grandpa patted Grandma Tessie's hand as she dabbed her eyes with a handkerchief.

Lainey noticed a screeching sound coming from the trees which kept getting louder and louder. "Grandpa, what's making that noise? Sounds like the bugs are screaming at each other."

"The locusts came for a visit, Pumpkinhead. As they make themselves comfortable in our neck of the woods, they rub their hind legs together like two sticks trying to start a fire. Always heaviest around this time, but every seventeen years they really swarm on in and take over."

That reminded her of something she'd heard in Sunday school. "Like in the Bible. Are we surrounded by a plague?"

He reached over to tap her head and chuckled. "No. We're surrounded by August, Lainey girl."

That was the summer they'd first told her the details of her mother's death. Up to that point they'd only said things like, "God wanted Genevieve with Him." Or, "She's protecting you from her mansion in Heaven." Once Lainey realized rain had caused her mother's death, storms haunted her. A flash of lightning could make her jump a foot off the couch. The rumble of thunder squeezed her stomach like a nutcracker.

Brooke slammed a platter of pancakes onto the counter in front of Lainey. "Eat these. And while you're at it, why not ask your dad what's in his orange juice this morning."

"Damn it, Brooke, it's more juice than vodka. A simple screwdriver."

"You mean nine screwdrivers, don't you? One for each year of pain?"

Jeremiah got up from the table and stuffed his car keys in the front pocket of his jeans.

Brooke looked up from the frying pan. "Where do you think you're going? You can't drive in your condition."

"I don't believe I asked your permission."

Brooke dropped a spatula and rushed over to Jeremiah. She reached into his front pocket. Before her hand could get a grip on the keys, Jeremiah shoved her back with a grunt.

Avoiding eye contact, Lainey used her fork to spell words in the syrup that had pooled next to the pancakes. Lainey noticed movement by the stove in her peripheral vision. She glanced sideways from her plate just as Jeremiah looked over her shoulder.

"Don't write her name," Jeremiah barked.

Lainey froze, the hairs on her arms sticking straight up. She realized she had started to spell her mother's name into the syrup.

"You're not Genevieve," Jeremiah whispered in Lainey's ear. He pointed toward Brooke. "You're not Genevieve either." Jeremiah grabbed Lainey's fork and threw it across the kitchen into the sink then stormed out the back door.

Lainey tried not to cry. Brooke stood motionless. His vehicle pulling out of the driveway was the only sound they could hear.

"Are you okay, Brooke?" Lainey asked when she was able to stuff the tears down into her throat.

Brooke turned slowly then wiped the tears off her face. She whipped open her robe revealing the red bikini and baby bulge. "If he's hell-bent on killing himself, then we're out of here. I know of a beach where dogs are allowed. It's only an hour away."

"We're what?" Lainey stared at the bulging stomach, pale skin stretched white. "Are you sure that's a good idea? Jeremiah's pretty bad off. And you're having a baby. Like, in less than a month."

"Jeremiah is no longer a factor here. Don't worry about me. I'll sit under an umbrella."

Brooke re-robed and set the last of the batter on the top shelf in the fridge, a sheet of plastic wrap on top. "Go get your suit on while I finish cleaning up. That cute polka dot two-piece I bought for you last week. And bring down a flat sheet from the linen closet. I'll pack us a fun lunch."

Lainey left to get ready, leaving the sound of slamming cabinet doors and running water behind her. She slumped on the edge of her bed wearing a one-piece racing Speedo with just a t-shirt and flip-flops. Lucky me, she thought as she tossed the polka dot bikini under the bed, with the tags still on. Today I'll commemorate the death of my real mother by spending time with my step mom avoiding any conversation about my drunken father.

❧

LAINEY TRIED TO MANEUVER the rush of emotions she was feeling as they drove south on Interstate 83 through downtown Baltimore. Jeremiah was right in what he had said. Lainey wasn't her mother. And Brooke wasn't her mother either, or even step mom. She was Fakemom. Lainey gave a small smile. Deena would've laughed at that.

Grandma Tessie on the other hand would not have.

The drive was slow-going because Brooke refused to use the outer loop around the city even though everyone told her it was faster. She also checked for messages on her phone every three minutes. Lainey assumed she was waiting for Jeremiah to reach out.

JT sat between Lainey's knees with his tongue hanging out. Warm drool dripped on her thigh. The windows were open, blowing their hair in all directions. Her ponytail whipped her face and stuck to the goo of her raspberry lip gloss.

Once JT snuggled down for a nap, Lainey opened her Genevieve-journal to re-read some stories. She thought maybe she could make herself feel better by remembering her mother.

"What you got there?"

Lainey focused her gaze on the words in front of her. "Just some stories Grandma Tessie told me."

"Anything I'd like to hear?"

"Nope." Lainey snapped the notebook shut and shoved it into her backpack. "I get sick reading in the car anyway." She shifted her hips in the bucket seat so her spine faced Fakemom. Trees rushed by in a blur. She closed her eyes.

When Brooke hit her fifth pothole, Lainey tried to imagine Genevieve at the wheel instead. Blue eyes like robin's eggs, wearing a simple, mom-type bathing suit. Maybe one with a flared skirt. She too had grown up on the tobacco farm, and just like her, Jeremiah had taken her to Baltimore, away from the family. Grandma Tessie hadn't ever said if Genevieve had been happy to leave.

As her mind wandered, she spun her claddagh ring round and round. What had Grandma Tessie told her? If it's facing toward me, I'm contemplating love? By no means was she ready to turn the ring around. She certainly didn't love her dad or Fakemom any more than before, although she didn't despise being in the same room with Brooke now. She had JT, and riding Tulip at the stables almost made her want to stay. Almost. But every time her heart softened, Jeremiah would say or do something stupid like this morning. Lainey's anger boiled once more.

She turned to Brooke. "Are you mad Jeremiah went off without us?"

"Yes, ... and scared." She laid her left hand on her belly and rubbed in a circle. "Scared that he'll get in a wreck or something worse. But, I also have a hard time blaming him."

"Are you serious? I can blame him, easily. He was horrible this morning. I can't believe he shoved you like that." The dog simpered in his sleep, grinning as Lainey scratched his soft ears.

"He loved your mother more than life itself." The hand rubbed faster. "More than—than me."

"More than me, too."

The car jerked as Brooke clutched the wheel harder and pumped the brakes. She canceled cruise control every time a car in front of her drifted slightly. Lainey braced her hands on the dash to steady herself and the dog.

"No, Lainey," Brooke said. "That's what you don't understand. You came from them. Loving her means loving you. Jeremiah can't separate the two." She pressed the resume button on the wheel, restoring the speed to seventy-two. Another Brooke rule: Don't drive so fast that cops notice, but not so slow even nuns will pass you.

Lainey turned to face her. "He separated the two for eight years! He left me with Grandma Tessie and didn't look back. Then he planned a whole life with you with no thought of me. He didn't even think of me until he was forced to."

Brooke reached over and rubbed Lainey's forearm. "That's not the way it was. He decided to come get you before he knew anything was wrong with Jude."

JT bolted upright and scratched her again.

"Dumb dog. Why can't you just sit still?" Lainey tossed him on a blanket in the back seat.

"Lainey, your father left you with family when your mother died. People who loved you, wanted you. Not everyone's that lucky."

Brooke reached under her sunglasses with a pinky to wipe her eye. Even when she cried, she followed her freaking rules—only wipe with your pinky; it's the weakest finger so you won't damage blood vessels under the skin. And by no means rub. Because, according to another Brooke rule, "Boys don't look at girls with dark circles or lines under their eyes."

Lainey really didn't feel like talking about Jeremiah anymore. "You weren't lucky at all growing up were you?"

"No, I wasn't. And it makes me fume to watch you both throw away … when I would have given anything to …" Her lower lip quivered.

"To what?"

"To have a father who loved me as much as Jeremiah loves you."

"He has a funny way of showing it. How can you forgive him?"

"Who says I have? Just because he's a jackass doesn't mean I don't love him. I've lived through a lot worse, Lainey."

Lainey was confused at Brooke's calmness. "Did you ever try to find your dad?"

"Wasn't worth it." Brooke slid her sunglasses up like a headband to push back her hair. "He came back once, though. That's why my mom got me from the foster home. A shame because I really liked my new family. Their kids were grown and out of the house. This humongous, white mansion outside the city with a pool and tennis courts. They gave me my own room with pink furniture. They set up a college fund. Mr. Thompson was a VP at some pharmaceutical place. I can still smell Mama Thompson's butterscotch cookies. They called me their Little Princess." Brooke's voice faded to a whisper. "It was the safest I ever felt in my life."

Lainey fidgeted with a loose curl tapping at her sunglasses. "Is that why you got the tattoo?"

"To remember what it was like to feel special, I guess. Plus, I was kind of drunk." She gasped, then jabbed a finger at Lainey. "Don't tell anyone I admitted that to you. And don't go taking any pages out of my book!"

No worries there.

"Anyway, my father came back into town and made mom look for me," Brooke added. "The whole goal of foster care is to bring families back together, so the Thompsons had no choice but to let me go."

Fakemom's family was beginning to fascinate Lainey, almost as much as Deena's. Life with Grandma Tessie on the farm had been downright boring. "What do you mean he made her look?"

"When he came back, mom was waitressing at his favorite diner, so he asked about me. She had to admit she hadn't seen me in four years."

Lainey scrunched her forehead. A mother not wanting her own daughter around was impossible. Fathers, yes. Mothers, never.

"Bill told me dad was so angry, he smacked her jaw right there in the diner. Didn't take long to find me. I mean, she knew exactly where she'd left me. So, they tracked me down and set up a place for us."

Brooke steered the car with one knee and made air quotes. "Our 'home' lasted two months. Haven't seen him since. Mom went out and got me Step dad Number One."

She took the next exit off the highway toward Metapeake. They parked seventy-five feet from the water after Brooke paid the three dollars for park entrance, then she asked for directions to the dog-friendly section.

The thin grains of sand softly tickled Lainey's toes. No buildings were in sight, only beach walkers and a few families who also had dogs. Lifeguards, who'd just set up their station at the public swimming area where dogs were not allowed, were rubbing thick globs of white sunscreen on noses and shoulders.

Brooke took a deep breath of ocean air and pointed toward a more secluded area, away from the swimmers' beach area. "Let's get our little private beach camp set up over there by the jetty."

Lainey set to digging a hole for the umbrella. The orange and yellow stripes leaned to one side with loose material that flapped in the breeze. Brooke laid out the bed sheet, using magazines and flip-flops to hold down the floppy corners. "Sheets keep you cooler than a blanket and are much easier to brush sand off of than a towel," she said. After their day camp was assembled, sunscreen applied, and JT tethered to a chair, Brooke sat facing the slow, rolling bay waters. Lainey stood staring at a sailboat as it bobbed in slow motion on the horizon.

"That chair won't hold the dog unless someone is sitting in it," Brooke instructed.

Lainey rolled her eyes but sat down.

Brooke tapped Lainey's shoulder. "Sorry you had to do most of the work."

"That's okay."

JT was caught in a cat and mouse game with a sand crab, until the leash yanked him back.

"See? If you hadn't been sitting, we would have been chasing him down the beach." Brooke tied her hair up in a messy bun.

"You have a lot of rules, just like Grandma Tessie!" Lainey rolled her eyes one more time. Grandma Tessie would have said there was no need to work out her eyeballs so much.

Brooke asked for a drink from the cooler. "I'm getting heartburn again."

When Lainey secured the lid back on, Fakemom cleared her throat. "I want to ask you one more thing, okay? Then we'll just enjoy the rest of the day not thinking about your father."

Lainey lowered into her neon-green chair and handed Brooke a water bottle. "I won't answer if it's about my mother."

"Fair enough." They shook hands as if signing a business deal. Then Brooke grabbed both arms of her beach chair and scooted it toward Lainey. "What I want to know is—why you don't have any friends other than that girl who started the fire."

Lainey set her jaw and stared at the horizon, away from Brooke's intense gaze. "We both started the fire, and I don't know." She'd been expecting nosiness about Virginia, the farm, school, something easy. Lainey shrugged. "Why get close to people? Either they'll leave or I will."

"But why her? You could have made any friend, but you chose a very troubled girl."

"Deena was nice to me on the first day of school. That's all. No big mystery." She wasn't lying. Deena had been very kind to Lainey, even protective, when a boy started picking on her.

Brooke tilted her beach chair back. "Deena reminds me a little of myself back in the day. Living with my mom, rebelling up a storm. That should be one of our goals when school starts. To make some friends." Her eyes sparkled. "I'll try to meet some of the parents once Baby C arrives. You can find more girlfriends to hang out with. What do you say?"

Lainey shrugged and jumped out of her chair. "I'm gonna see how cold the water is." She grabbed the cooler to replace her weight in the chair then ran into the thin foamy ripples up to her ankles. It felt chilly in patches, like sweet tea after the ice melts. She pushed forward through the calm water. It was so cold; her legs went numb. When it almost reached her chin, she heard Brooke yell, "Don't go out too far!"

She dunked her head then floated in a V shape with only her toes and head sticking out. Her butt almost touched the bottom before her ears started filling with salt water.

With her back to the shore, she could float and daydream about the sailboats in the distance. One had *MY CHARLOTTA* painted on the bow. Lainey chuckled at the memory of her goose egg she had named Charlotte, back on the farm. A yipping bark jostled her back to reality. She paddled her body around setting her eyes on JT. Brooke had removed his leash and was tossing a ball to him. Lainey lowered her toes to the mushy ocean floor, stood, and pushed back toward the shoreline.

Halfway back, she called out, "JT, come!" She kept pushing her legs through the heavy water.

As the cockapoo raced toward the water's edge, Brooke cradled her belly bulge, bending over as if she was looking for JT's ball. She plunged to her knees.

"Hey!" Lainey shouted. She untangled a string of seaweed from one ankle and ran toward the chairs, gritty sand stinging the backs of her legs. "What're you looking for?"

Brooke's face was white and puffy. She waved Lainey down, sucked in air and held her breath. Releasing the breath like a leaky tire, she gritted her teeth. "Feels like a knife."

Every bone in Lainey's body shook. Her head and forearms itched. A hot breeze flushed her cheeks. "I don't know what to do," she whispered. It felt just like when Grandpa Jude fell on the farm.

"Help me to the—" Brooke squealed one high pitched wail, then buried her face in her hands. "Car," she mumbled, breathing long strokes in through her nose and out her mouth.

Lainey dropped down to her knees and grabbed Brooke's hand. She had to bite her lip every time Fakemom crushed the small bones in her hand. With the free hand, she dialed Jeremiah's number from Brooke's phone. The call went straight to voice mail.

Lainey heard someone speaking behind her. "How can I help, sugar?" A lady holding a chihuahua tapped her on the shoulder. Her lime green suit took on the glare of the high sun and a large-brimmed straw hat hid her eyes. "You want me to get a lifeguard?" she asked.

Lainey tossed the phone to the sheet and pulled Brooke to her feet with care. "That's okay." She pasted on a confident smile. "I just called my dad to hurry up. He's on his way to meet us." She wasn't sure what made her say that.

The lady patted her cheek. "Well okay, sugar, but you just whistle if you need anything. I'll be right over there."

Lainey nodded then walked Brooke to the car, propping her by the elbow. "Are you sure we shouldn't call an ambulance?"

Brooke plopped down into the passenger seat, sweating and holding her belly. "I'm fine now. Just too much sun. Get the air conditioning on."

Lainey dangled the key chain that claimed *Brooke loves Jeremiah* in front of her eyes like the hypnotist she'd seen on TV once. Brooke had bought the tiny turtle-shaped wood carving on their honeymoon. She turned the ignition and asked Brooke how they were going to get home if she was sick.

"You just let me rest here in the air conditioning while you get all the stuff. I'll be ready to drive by the time you're done." Brooke closed her eyes and breathed slow, deep breaths through her nose.

Back on the sand, the straw hat lady was glancing Lainey's way. She took JT and as much as she could carry back to the car then yelled, "My dad's here!"

The lady waved, less concerned than before.

Trying to give Brooke enough time to rest, Lainey tied the leash around the door handle, thankful that side of the car was in shade. "Don't bark, JT. I'll be right back." She reached down to pet his head. He licked her hand and jumped on her leg.

During the long walk back, she said several short prayers. "Please don't let anyone steal JT. Please don't let Brooke die. Please." It took three trips to get all the stuff back. She called Jeremiah again after every lap, ticked off that she was having to be the adult for both of them.

Once everything was in the trunk, she sat on the front bumper to rest. The backs of her legs were frying on the Chevy Impala's hot metal, but it almost felt good. Jeremiah had purchased the car when Brooke first got pregnant. Her old car had been a junker, and he wanted her safe out on the roads. He said another loan payment was worth it.

So where was he now? Lainey turned to check on Brooke through the windshield. She had reclined the seat as far back as possible; her mouth was open as she tried to breathe through the pain.

Lainey didn't know what to do next. Grandma Tessie would tell her she needed to pray for an answer. "If anyone lacks wisdom, let him ask of God," she'd say. Well, okay.

Or ... or ... she could try to get them home herself!

Lainey had driven Grandpa Jude's truck plenty of times and the riding mower every week, once she had been able to reach the pedals. Brooke had filled the gas tank when they'd reached town. No cars were parked directly in front of them, so she could pull right out and get away with it as long as no one noticed how young she was. As long as the gas held out. As long as it didn't start to rain. She shuddered and checked the sky—not one cloud.

"I can do this." She untied JT and settled him in back. "Don't distract me now, boy."

Lainey punched their Baltimore address into the old GPS, hoping it still worked. She then scooted the seat closer to the pedals.

"What are you doing, Lainey?" Brooke asked without moving a muscle. "I'll be ready to drive soon." Her only sound was the breathing in her nose and out of her mouth.

Lainey ignored her. She needed a small boost to see over the wheel, so she folded two beach towels and the sheet to prop her butt higher. Then she adjusted the mirrors like Grandpa Jude had taught her in the truck. Brooke had to do this every time Jeremiah drove her car.

The dash clock blinked two o'clock. She started the engine and listened for directions from the old school technology. A lady's soft voice said, "Turn left in one hundred feet." As she pulled forward and glanced at the side mirror, the right side of the car rose like she was driving over a speed bump, but the tire never came back down. She pressed the gas to go forward, then tried reverse. The car wouldn't budge.

Brooke's eyes flew open. "What was that?" Brooke tried to sit up but couldn't get the electric seat to move.

"How could I have hit something?" Lainey asked as she flung open the car door. "We didn't go anywhere!" Dropping to hands and knees, she looked under the car. "Brooke, we're stuck on a blob of cement," she yelled.

Brooke finally got the seat raised and wiggled out. "What were you thinking, driving the car?" Brooke grabbed her phone from Lainey.

Lainey squeezed her eyes tight trying not to cry when Brooke hung up the phone after calling a tow truck. With a deep breath, she reached under the driver's seat where Brooke had hidden her wallet then handed it to her. "I tried to call Jeremiah; he just won't answer."

"I'll text him. Then he'll answer." Brooke dialed the phone and waddled toward a picnic table.

Brooke was right. Lainey watched the animated gestures from her free hand as Brooke spoke with Jeremiah. The pregnant lady sat on the bench and put her forehead on the table, still holding the phone to her ear. Lainey could only hear a word here and there, but from the looks of it, the phone call was not going well. Minutes later, Brooke returned.

"Let's wait in the car. Even if there's damage, the air still works."

Lainey obeyed with speed. She'd never heard Fakemom sound so confident and in control.

"A truck probably dumped a blob of concrete right on the ground and didn't even know he did it. Did you know cement and concrete aren't the same thing?"

"No, no I did not." Brooke's attempt at conversation baffled Lainey.

"Cement is actually an ingredient of concrete. I did a research paper on it in middle school."

"Okay." Lainey didn't know how to respond to the useless information Fakemom was so keen on giving her. For five minutes they sat in silence.

"What do you say we go on another trip?" Brooke turned toward Lainey with her eyebrows raised.

"Um, what if the car won't drive?"

"We'll have the tow truck take us to the bus station if we need to. All I know is we are not going home, and I have plenty of credit cards."

Lainey was downright scared of Brooke at the moment. "You sure you should travel anymore? What about the baby?"

"Resting helped. I was just a little overheated. Now it feels like I have some anger stirring my belly. Literally and metaphorically."

"What did Jeremiah say on the phone?"

"Your father is still completely wasted with no plans of sobering up. So, we're on our own, and I don't know for how long."

"Where are we going?"

Brooke couldn't answer for the fresh tears.

Thirty minutes later as the tow truck driver latched their car to his chains, Lainey couldn't wait any longer. "Brooke?"

"Hmmmm?"

"Grandma Tessie only lives a few hours from here."

Brooke glanced over with a grin that didn't match her sad, tearful eyes. She nodded in slow motion.

Once the car was loosened, it ran perfectly fine. Brooke paid the tow truck driver with her credit card number and pointed to the Impala.

"Hop back in the car, Lainey. We're going to the farm."

Chapter 10

LATE THAT NIGHT, as light rain misted the tobacco leaves on the Weston farm, Tessie heard a knock on the kitchen door. A dog yipped and scratched at the screen. Tessie flipped the back-porch light switch up. There was Lainey, hair damp and hands waving through the windowpane. "What in the world, child." She unlocked the door. "What have you done?"

Lainey grabbed Tessie's waist and squeezed. "Did Evelyn make any mint tea today?" She dropped her backpack onto the breakfast bar. JT pawed at Tessie's leg, tongue out, already begging for a treat.

"Down, boy." Tessie shoved him lightly with one foot. "Does your father know where you are? How'd you get here?"

The suntanned girl filled a glass with ice from the front of the fridge.

"Answer me!" Tessie grabbed her granddaughter's elbow. Cubes bounced off the linoleum.

Lainey pulled her head back and pointed at the back door. "Brooke drove me."

Tessie turned to the doorway and noticed the very pregnant woman, hovering in the entrance.

"Hey there, Tessie," she said. "Thought you might want some visitors."

Tessie shut the screen softly behind Brooke then rested her back against the weather-proof door.

"Girls, what are you doing here? Where's Jeremiah?"

Lainey heaved herself onto her usual stool at the breakfast counter and explained the disastrous day she'd had with Brooke who had settled herself at the kitchen table, one hand tangled in her hair, the other resting on her belly.

"Okay. Enough with the whats, I want the whys."

"You might get mad." Lainey took a sip from her glass.

"I reserve judgment until I've heard the whole story." Tessie joined Brooke at the table. "Who is going to make me angry?"

Brooke cleared her throat. "Last time I spoke to Jeremiah, he was still drunk off his ass at some bar in the Inner Harbor, and I refuse to go home. Forgive my language."

"Brooke almost passed out on the beach today," Lainey said. "It freaked me out."

Tessie jerked her head back toward Brooke. "Are you okay?"

When the fragile girl nodded, Tessie clapped her hands together once, firmly. "Then first things first. You are safe, praise the Lord. Next, Lainey go shower. Find some old clothes to put on while I heat up some mac-n-cheese. Brooke and I are going to find an urgent care open tonight to check out baby and mama. No arguments." Tessie glared at Brooke, daring her to say something.

Lainey raised her eyebrows.

"Get a move on." Tessie pointed toward the staircase.

Twenty minutes later, Lainey came back down wearing sweatpants from her old dresser.

Tessie slumped back in the recliner, dangling an arm over the rest, staring at her granddaughter from across the room. She looked older. Taller. Her hair was long and dripping wet, the only time it stayed straight. "Look how you've grown in less than a year." Lainey had scrunched up the pants legs around her knees. The tank top looked two sizes too small.

"This underwear is cutting into my thighs." She squirmed and pulled at the leg bands.

"Well, come eat some dinner."

Seeing the heaping plate of mac-n-cheese on the kitchen table, Lainey grabbed a big spoonful. "Where's Fakemom?"

"Brooke is in my bathroom. We're going to leave soon. You can stay or come, whatever you want."

"I should make sure JT gets settled and doesn't make a mess of the house." Lainey took another bite of macaroni then went to the fridge to find some leftovers for JT. She opened a tuna casserole and laid it by the screen door. "Grandma?"

"Hmmm?"

"Is Jeremiah going to leave us here?"

Tessie sighed and picked up the kitchen phone. "Let's not overreact, not until we reach him." She dialed Jeremiah's number for the fifth time which yielded no result.

Tessie turned and grabbed Lainey's head to kiss her forehead. "It's so good to have you home."

"Is it okay I brought Brooke? I didn't know what else to do. You wouldn't believe what he said to us this morning," Lainey said while finishing her dinner.

Tessie patted Lainey on the back. "Of course, it's okay you brought Brooke. She's family. We'll let Jeremiah sleep this day off, make sure Brooke and baby are healthy, then figure the rest out later. My guess is we'll be taking the long drive back to Baltimore tomorrow."

❧

LAINEY WAS ASLEEP when Tessie and Brooke returned late that night, tired but healthy. She'd made a bed for JT to sleep by the door, but the dog was roaming the house. Tessie went to her own room but couldn't go to sleep. Instead, she kept calling Jeremiah's phone, then the house. At one a.m., he answered.

"Ma, I can't find Brooke or Lainey."

"Why not?" Tessie almost felt guilty for being deceptive.

"No one was here when I got home. Brooke was pretty pissed when I talked with her this afternoon."

"You're drunk, Jeremiah. You're still drunk."

"A few drinks is all."

"Why can't you find your wife and daughter?"

"I told you, Ma. I don't know where they went. Brooke won't answer her phone."

"Jeremiah, Brooke and Lainey are here."

"What? Lainey left a message about going home. I assumed ..." Jeremiah cleared his throat.

"You can figure out what to do on the drive down here to get her. After you sober up, of course."

"What if Brooke doesn't want me to come?"

Lord Almighty, here we go again. Her mouth tightened. "They are welcome for as long as needed, but Jeremiah," she paused and set her jaw, "make sure it doesn't take eight years to come get them." Tessie hung up before he could reply then went down to the kitchen to clean the dinner dishes, scrubbing the casserole dish with fury.

Finally, she gave up. As she filled it to soak overnight, Lainey shuffled back into the kitchen, gnawing on the end of her ponytail.

Tessie shook her head. This habit wasn't much better than nail biting. "Why are you up?"

"I keep dreaming about Brooke falling over on the beach. Then there's a coffin with her big belly sticking out. They can't get the lid closed, so Jeremiah—with a bottle of beer in one hand and a tobacco plant in the other—asks me to jump on it."

Tessie shook her head. "I wouldn't be able to sleep either with that haunting me. Sit down. I got hold of your father, and he's fine. No coffins, no more booze he says. He's sobering up so he can come get you all tomorrow."

Lainey unclenched her jaw, but her eyelids drooped. "Grandma?"

"Yes, dear?"

"Do you think Brooke will want him to come?"

"Jeremiah asked the same thing."

"It was bad, Grandma. He keeps screwing up."

Tessie nodded. "What matters right now is Brooke and baby are healthy. That you are safe, and we get to spend part of the day together before Jeremiah arrives."

Lainey stared hard at her then turned and left the kitchen.

AT TEN, Evelyn started making noise in the kitchen. By the time Tessie got downstairs, Evelyn had started mopping the floor. She glanced up then propped both hands on the mop handle. "Mrs. Weston, why didn't you warn me you were getting a dog?" She pointed to a yellow puddle by the door. One under the breakfast table. One by the fridge. "I'm thinking this pooch has got himself a nervous condition, going like that everywhere."

"I was up late trying to locate Jeremiah, and Lainey had already fallen asleep. We just plain forgot to let the poor thing out." Tessie grabbed the mop handle. "Let me finish that for you."

Evelyn's grip tightened and raised an eyebrow. "We?"

"Gracious, Evelyn. Lainey and Brooke came down from Baltimore last night. Dragged along that silly dog she's named after Jude. He answers to JT."

After the dog's messes were taken care of, Tessie pried Evelyn's hands from the handle and leaned the mop against the wall. "I'll finish all this in a bit. We both need some caffeine." At the table, she filled two large mugs and offered Evelyn the French vanilla creamer. "Afraid we've had a bit of a setback. Jeremiah jumped headfirst off the wagon yesterday."

Evelyn clucked her tongue on the roof of her mouth.

Lainey entered the kitchen dressed in the same scrunched sweatpants and another too-short tank. With a wave of the hand, she presented herself like Vanna White bestowing the grand prize on Wheel of Fortune. "So, if Jeremiah decides to bail today, maybe we could get some clothes that fit?"

"Oooh, come here, my little cantaloupe. How I've missed you!" Evelyn grabbed Lainey tight to her chest and twisted, making Lainey's arms flop like a landed fish. Lainey wheezed as Evelyn squeezed all the air out of her. "You got so tall, looking like you're old enough to graduate high school. A whole head taller than me, now."

"Shopping is a great idea." Tessie rinsed out the coffee mugs as Lainey filled a bowl with raisin bran. "Eat some breakfast, brush your hair and teeth, go walk the dog, then we'll be off to town. There's an extra toothbrush in the hall closet. And we'll see if Brooke is up to coming along. Won't that be fun?"

Lainey watched milk soak into the flakes, twirling a finger in long, slow motion circles. "Woo hoo!"

THAT EVENING, Tessie dropped the sixth and last shopping bag onto Lainey's old bed. Two bags held clothes enough for a week or so in Virginia and some basics for the new school year coming up. After refusing to take any of Jeremiah's calls, Brooke had decided to stay back at the farm, asking only that they buy her a few items to get by.

Tessie pulled navy blue knee socks out of the Belk's bag. "I guess I like the idea of uniforms, but it sure does take some of the joy out of shopping."

Lainey crouched on the floor to empty the drawers for her new things. "There won't be much to donate to the church like we did last year."

Tessie started ripping tags off, preparing for prewash. "Pastor Tim never did locate fifty homeless people like he promised."

She couldn't stop the constant flutter in her stomach as she watched Lainey. Tessie had never dreamed of having her back again at all, never mind for such a small thing as cleaning out drawers. That's when you treasure time the most, she thought. Watching kids grow up and move on in the shape of shrunken, outgrown clothes. "We should check the attic or spare room for an old suitcase. You need it to transport all this stuff back to Baltimore."

Lainey twisted her mouth, as if she'd bitten into a rotten peach. "Please, please don't make me go back."

"Don't start this," Tessie said.

"I belong with you where I can just be a kid. Can you really say you trust him after this? Did Brooke tell you he—?"

"I said don't. As soon as Brooke and Jeremiah have a heart-to-heart, you will be going back to Baltimore. This was just a setback." Tessie wished she could believe herself in this moment.

"Fine." Lainey jerked the bottom drawer open. "I saw a suitcase in the barn loft once. Aunt Madeline said Mama took it to college. Can I use that one?"

"Sure thing, sweets, but we'll get it later. We've got a few days at least."

Tessie picked up a pair of jeans they'd bought from the juniors department. She was pleased her granddaughter hadn't inherited her own flat posterior. She draped the pants over Lainey's head. "Now that you're all beautiful and filled out, do you like any boys?"

"Boys are stupid. And they don't think I'm beautiful." She ran a hand through her curly ponytail. Halfway through, her fingers stuck in a knot.

Tessie jabbed a finger into Lainey's arm. "Don't you get in any hurry because they will very soon." She sat on the side chair, a nightshirt wadded in her lap. "What do you say we visit Grandpa while you're here?"

Today's shopping adventure had been the first break she'd taken from visiting Jude in a month. The nurses and aides scolded her every morning for not taking more time for herself, but the feeling of guilt and being solely responsible for locking a loved one away was too much for her. Tessie wasn't the kind to spend fifty years devoted to a man, just to let him sit all alone twenty-four hours a day because he got sick. She'd promised herself that when Jude forgot who she was completely, then she'd take more breaks. Until that day, this was her job. Her duty. Seven days a week. No breaks. No holidays. Not unless Lainey girl came to town.

Tessie watched her granddaughter shut the last drawer and look at the clothes heaped around her feet in a perfect loop. A princess in the middle of a moat. JT was snoring on a pile of socks.

Lainey pointed to the multi-colored layers on the bed. "Can I wash all the new stuff in one load?"

Tessie sniffed. "Sure can. If you want your white sweatshirt to turn blotchy pink. You have a red T-shirt there just begging to bleed."

"Got it." Lainey stepped out of the circle of clothes to make dark and light piles with the stiff, new ones.

"You get the laundry started then throw the old stuff in bags. I'll go see what Evelyn's cooked up today and check on Brooke. I may have smelled chocolate cake."

Tessie walked downstairs, one hand dragging over the bumps and divots on the banister. Somehow having Lainey back made her feel lonelier. And guiltier. Her husband was still alive, but she was living here on her own as if he were already dead.

THEIR WEEK CONTINUED in the same manner. Wake up to breakfast, make sure Brooke felt rested, then a few chores. Next a visit to the skilled-nursing home. Jude was pleasant, even jovial, the first few visits. Lainey mentioned how much better he looked than last time she'd been there. He looked healthier since going through physical therapy, even walking faster than he had before the attack, a year ago. The aides all told Lainey how much they loved her grandfather. "Mr. Weston's quite a charmer!"

Thursday afternoon on the way to the home, Lainey shifted in her seat like she was uncomfortable. "May I ask a question?" she said quietly.

Moving to Baltimore had softened her approach a bit, Tessie noted.

"Sometimes it feels so normal with Grandpa. Why can't we just take him home?"

"He's not always this lucid, honey." Tessie stared straight ahead. It had been a good week for Jude.

"What's lucid mean?"

"Clear-headed. Sometimes he thinks he's being held captive by the Navy." She started flailing her arms for effect. "Yells, 'Release the prisoner' or 'I'll sink this ship myself'.

"Then there's the medicine. The doctor has to keep changing dosages to regulate his heart and diabetes, plus the dementia. I couldn't do all that at home." Tessie parked in the spot directly outside his room. A weeping willow tree stood ten feet from the window. Rain dripped off the bird feeder hanging eye level from its lowest branch. She could see him lying on his bed, staring at the ceiling, scratching his nose. Tessie had come to notice how bad weather made the patients here ornery. When she saw the weather report today, she'd tried to talk Lainey into staying home. It was bound to be a bad visit.

"Didn't we have fun yesterday making up games?" Lainey asked. The three of them had sat at a square table in the common gathering room, Jude and Lainey batting the tissue box back and forth in a round of air hockey. Then she folded one into a thick, triangular football and flicked it toward his face. He giggled and shot it right back. They entertained each other for half an hour this way.

"You're both nuts," Tessie had muttered.

Jude went through stages with the Lewy Body Dementia. The doctors claimed it was normal for the proteins to attack one part of his brain, sometimes another. That meant his symptoms changed, too. Sometimes she'd arrive and he couldn't walk or swallow his food. A month later he wouldn't be able to stop drooling but could speed walk down the hallway. That's when he'd get in trouble with the nurses for not using the walker. Plus, when he wandered, he often couldn't find the way back to his room. The staff posted large name tags by his door, which sometimes helped. Tessie was always on edge; no one could predict where the little protein buggers would attack next.

When they reached Jude's room that afternoon, he wasn't there. The desk nurse directed them to the physical therapy wing. As Tessie and Lainey turned down yet another pale blue hallway, bingo players were leaving the recreation room. Wheelchair after wheelchair rolled past in a line, most escorted by recreation staff in neon-orange polo shirts. Tessie spotted Jude at the end of the hall tottering toward them. It was a walker day. His therapist, a twenty-something girl with a severely tight ponytail, was holding onto the back of his sweatpants.

When he came up to the line of wheelchairs, he started yelling, "Get these god-awful freaks outta my way." He lifted the walker half an inch and swung at the wheel of another old man's chair.

The last wheelchair shot out of the room, the patient's outstretched arms swinging side to side like airplane wings. She cheered with the breathy voice, "Whee! Whee! I'm flying. Whee!"

"I'll whee you right where it hurts, old woman," Jude shouted after her. "Get the hell out of my way!"

As a stocky aide with bunny print scrubs rolled the flying patient to one side of the hall, Jude turned on Tessie, slamming the walker with each word. "Where. Have. You. Been?"

She laid a hand on his shoulder and leaned in to plant a little peck on his cheek. "Well, hello to you, too. Lainey and I took care of some chores at the farm. Then we came right here."

He slapped her hand away, bouncing it off the metal of the walker. "How dare you leave me with these crazy people?"

Tessie pointed at the physical therapist, peering close at her name tag. She swallowed to keep her voice steady. "Kim is here to help you. Why are you yelling?"

"You're my wife. You should take care of me."

She moved around the walker to stand beside him, set a hand on his back, and guided him toward the hallway chairs. "The doctor hasn't released you yet," she said calmly. Inside, anger and fear were stirring. She swallowed again. "I can't be in charge of all the medicine and the therapy and what-all you need right now." She tried to pat his arm.

He shrugged her off again. "Then get out!" His voice thundered down the north and south wings. "Just get yourself and that skinny little girl away from me. I'll find a way out of this place myself." He dropped down into the side chair, still mumbling.

Tessie felt a presence by her shoulder; Lainey was moving in slow motion toward Jude.

"Just leave it be, sweets," she warned. "Let them get him back to his room and comfortable—"

Lainey held up one palm. A brave calm washed over her face as she stepped forward. "Let me just say goodbye."

Lainey took three more steps toward Jude and covered his dry, cracked hand with her soft, smooth one. His nails were thick and yellowed. Hers were neatly painted purple. His gray hair was buzzed a quarter inch from his scalp, his own curls lost for convenience. Lainey's bouncy curls frizzed uncontrollably on rainy days like these. She reached over the walker and kissed his cheek. "I love you, Grandpa."

Jude blinked his blue, misted eyes and slid his free hand over her slender one. "I love you too, Genevieve."

❧

WHEN THEY REACHED the farm, Lainey dropped onto the porch swing. Her whole body shook.

Tessie stroked her hair. "Don't cry. You did good. Real good." She tucked a folded handkerchief into the girl's hand.

Lainey blew her nose on an embroidered rose petal. "I just want to throw something. First, Jeremiah makes a point to tell me I'm not Genevieve, and then Grandpa mistakes me for her. I feel like

I'm battling a ghost." Lainey handed the moist wad back to Tessie, who took it between thumb and forefinger. Tessie pushed the soiled handkerchief in her pants pocket and dug anti-bacterial lotion from her purse.

Brooke joined them on the porch with her hair twisted into a messy bun and the new maternity sweatpants hanging below her belly. "Why's Lainey crying?"

"Rough day with Jude." Tessie pulled Lainey closer and scooched over to let Brooke squeeze in with them on the swing.

"I don't think I should test the weight limit on that thing." She pointed to the porch ceiling.

Tessie patted the open seat again. "Jude made this thing so sturdy; it could hold 500 pounds. I guarantee we are not at risk."

When Brooke settled herself in, Tessie pulled Brooke's head to her own shoulder and rested her chin on the top of Brooke's head. "Jeremiah called again, didn't he?"

Brooke nodded and sniffed. "I'm overreacting, Tessie. Maybe it's the hormones."

"What's keeping you from saying 'come get us'? Have you forgiven him?"

"He broke my trust, I guess. But there's some truth to what he said. I'll never be Genevieve."

Lainey gave a hard shove at the porch floor with a toe, jerking the swing into motion. "Of course, you can't trust him. He left me here for eight years; you better get used to living on the farm."

Tessie swatted Lainey's shoulder. "You don't get an opinion here, miss.

Lainey slammed both feet flat on the floorboards, and the swing creaked to a protesting stop. "In all his phone calls to get Brooke back, has he asked about me at all?"

No one answered.

"Right. So why can't he just let me stay here where I belong and go on with his new family like he planned in the first place? I remind him of Genevieve—which he refuses to admit unless he's drunk."

Tessie took a deep breath. "First off, this is not about you. Brooke is hurting and you need to check yourself. Second, I'll never let that happen. You and your father need each other, and if it kills me dead, I'm going to make you two grow up. And maybe even love each other."

Lainey screwed up her mouth like she planned to spew venom.
Tessie raised her eyebrows.

Instead, Lainey sprinted off the porch, screaming, "I hate him!" A blurry blonde mass of curls dashed toward the barn loft.

"Well, I'm not so thrilled with him either," Tessie said in an angry whisper.

"We haven't done a good job with her," Brooke admitted.

Tessie stood up from the swing, trying to keep it from moving. "Brooke, we can only do our best. Looks like my best was creating a mouthy monster. I'm very sorry for the way she treats you."

Brooke sighed in relief. "You know, Tessie, I was so scared of you when I came to the farm. And when you came to the wedding. And when we were driving down here. But not anymore. I finally understand where you're coming from. Thank you for all you've done for me. I'm not even family."

"Of course, you're family. You're married to my stupid son-in-law." With that, Tessie went on into the house and slammed the front door only a little bit on purpose. In the foyer she dropped her purse on a long, narrow side table made of cherry wood. She glared at her haggard reflection in an oversized mirror above the table. "Stubborn fools, all of them. Lainey looks like Genevieve but acts more like that father of hers."

"Mrs. Weston, ma'am?" Evelyn was hovering in the hallway that led to the kitchen.

Tessie watched her own face and neck blotch red. She turned. "Evelyn—just talking to myself again."

"Had a phone call while you were out. Jeremiah needs you to call him back." Evelyn handed her the portable receiver.

Tessie felt the blood draining from her neck. "Lord, I don't know how to get him back on track," she said. Before she could push the ON button for a dial tone, it rang.

"Hello?"

"It's Jeremiah. Don't hang up."

"Why would I hang up? But the person you need to be talking to is your wife."

"I have an emergency and I need your help, Tessie, especially with Alaina."

Tessie clenched her teeth, feeling her face heat up once again. This time with anger. "Jeremiah Traynor. If you called to tell me you want me to finish raising your daughter for you altogether, I—"

"Tessie!"

"... will ring your neck after—"

"Ma! Stop. I actually need to come get them tonight, whether Brooke is ready to forgive me or not."

"I agree." Tessie couldn't ease the bitterness gurgling in her throat. "I'm losing all patience here, Jeremiah."

"No time for details. Get them ready to come home; you are the only one that can convince them. I'll be there as soon as I can to explain it all. I might finally have found a way to make it up to everyone."

He hung up and Tessie tossed the phone onto the counter. She breathed in and out until her heart slowed to a normal pace. "Evelyn! Go get Lainey from the barn and tell her to bring that suitcase. Looks like they are going home."

Chapter 11

JEREMIAH MADE IT TO THE FARM around eleven that night. Lainey was looking out the window when she heard the car pull up. To her surprise, Deena got out of the backseat, looking like she'd been in a fight.

By midnight both girls were in the barn loft sitting on top of sleeping bags. Grandma Tessie sent up three industrial fans and another lamp to make them comfortable. "Wouldn't you prefer air-conditioning?" she yelled up the ladder. "Heat rises."

"I want her to get the real farm experience," Lainey said. "That means sleeping with bats!"

"Excuse me?" In two seconds flat, Deena started climbing back down the ladder. "I'm outta here."

Lainey giggled and pulled her back up by her wrist. "Just teasing, loser. For someone who acts so tough, you sure are a scaredy cat." She called down the ladder, "Grandma, tell her there aren't any bats up here."

"You're on your own." Then Grandma Tessie mumbled something about crazy kids and left for the cool house.

Deena reached up with one finger, testing the puffiness of her bruised cheek. Her lip rings had been removed. Three little black holes gaped on her face like the top of an anthill.

Lainey still felt surprised and nervous to see her friend, let alone in Virginia. They hadn't spoken all summer. Now here she was with black and green marks all over her arms, most of her body swollen like she'd been stung by hundreds of bees.

Lainey couldn't hold her curiosity in anymore. "Was it your drug-dealer boyfriend or dear-old-dad that did this?"

"I haven't seen Joey all summer," Deena muttered and sat back on the camouflage sleeping bag. "He's not my boyfriend anymore."

"Your father got this mad? What the heck did you do?" Lainey reached out to touch the squishy bump under Deena's left eye, only to have her hand smacked away.

"Not him either. I lasted one week in his new double wide, and he sent me back. I was getting in the way of his new girlfriend." She punched a pillow then laid her head down and closed her eyes.

"Aren't you going to change your clothes?" Back in her bedroom, Lainey had slipped into sleep shorts with the blue-ribboned pattern Grandma Tessie had bought. The white t-shirt smelled freshly washed, like Ivory soap and mountain air.

"Too tired." Deena turned her back on Lainey in slow motion, grimacing when her hip bumped the floor.

"Fine. If you won't tell me what happened, then I'll just tell you about my own trip."

Deena's top shoulder shrugged. "Whatever."

Lainey crossed her legs and toyed with the tip of her ponytail. "When Brooke and I got down here to Grandma Tessie's, I found out Corinne had a new best friend, Grandpa is much worse off, and to top it off, Jeremiah is a complete mess. Can you believe he just—"

"Shut up about Jeremiah." Deena's voice was low but hollow.

"Not only did he ditch us for the day, he shoved—"

"Idiot." Deena lifted her head and glared over her shoulder. "You're so selfish, you can't see how lucky you are."

Lainey hugged her pillow. "You're the idiot. I mean, look at what your boyfriend did to you."

"It was my step dad, all right?"

Lainey's eyes stretched so far, they looked like cue balls. "But—why?"

Deena laid her head back down. "I'm not telling anyone what happened."

"We're friends. You can trust me, but you refuse to see that."

Deena sat up. "Okay, okay. Just shut up, please!" She lifted her nose to the ceiling and snorted back snot. "It's embarrassing, and you can't talk about it. Ever. To anyone." She reached out a curved pinky finger with chipped purple polish. "Double—no, triple pinky swear."

Lainey linked her finger in the crook of her friend's. One nail was growing back from when she'd bit it clear off, but it was still scabby. It felt kind of nice to have a friend again, bruises and all. "I pinky swear."

"Monday, I snuck out of the house and got a new piercing." She stuck her tongue out for inspection.

Lainey stared at a red cavernous hole in the middle then scrunched her nose. "Ewww."

"When I woke up on Tuesday, my mom kept hounding me about why I wouldn't speak to her. It's real hard to talk with one of those things in, you know?"

Lainey shook her head. "Uh, nope."

"Well anyway, she didn't figure it out before she left for work. So, she called Lorne—"

"Who?"

"That's my step dad's name." Deena let her tongue drag out the name. "Lorne. When he got home for lunch, he knew right away what I'd done." A tear slid down her cheek.

Lainey reached up to the desk drawer and pulled out a tissue then decided to grab the whole box. She scooted over to Deena's sleeping bag and put an arm around her shoulders.

"He wouldn't stop yelling, but I refused to show him. He grabbed my face and pried my mouth open with his fingers. He flipped out, shouting, 'Cheap slut! You know why girls get those things, huh? Someone needs to clean up your act.'"

Deena took another tissue and delicately wiped her nose. "That's when he grabbed me and ...and started...I tried to push him away, but he held my arms tight, right above the elbows." She lifted a sleeve to show finger marks making a perfect circle.

"He kept ..." She shuddered from head to feet. "He kept poking his tongue in my mouth to find the metal. I got loose and he yelled, 'Just giving what you're asking for, Bitch!' When he reached toward his zipper, I ran fast.

"Got as far as the kitchen sink, about to hurl vomit chunks all over. While I gagged, he lunged at me. I started swinging. Any body part I could reach. I think I broke his nose. That's when he pounded on me."

"Did he ...?" Lainey didn't want to finish the sentence.

"No. Beating me was enough thrill for him, I guess."

"How'd you end up with Jeremiah?" Lainey whispered.

Deena lay back down on the sleeping bag and pushed Lainey back over to hers. "Turn off the light, would you?"

She unplugged the small floor lamp. The moon covered their heads with a dim glow through the window.

"Lorne had taken off, and my mom found me bleeding all over the carpet. Said I deserved it, so I took off and ran straight to your house. Obviously, you weren't there."

"I was here. Brooke collapsed right in front of me; we had to go somewhere."

"Jeremiah's been great, you know? He let me sleep it off in your room while he took care of everything. Your dad spent all this morning at Social Services getting emergency custody till the court sorts it all out. He said I'll never have to go back to my mom again if I don't want."

"But your step dad never bothered you before. I don't get it."

Deena shrugged. "Just how my life works, I guess. Something about me makes people snap." She bent the pillow in half, propping her head higher.

Lainey pulled a double-sized cotton sheet over both of them. "It's okay now. Jeremiah will make sure you're safe," she whispered, not sure if she was hoping or lying through her teeth.

As they settled in under the light cover, Lainey spun her claddagh ring in circles, thinking about trying to love others. Why did they have to make everything so hard?

§

THE TRAYNOR FAMILY, with Deena in tow, was back in Baltimore by mid-afternoon the next day. Brooke immediately went into labor. Seventeen hours later, Caden Wendell Traynor was born, sleeping under a lamp to help with his jaundice. His condition wasn't enough to keep mother and baby from coming home the next day. Lainey noticed all of Brooke's and Jeremiah's hurt and anger had dissipated at the birth of their son.

A week later, Brooke sent Jeremiah out with the girls to pick out bunk beds. "No matter how long Deena stays with us," Brooke said, "she deserves her own bed."

In front of Lehman's Furniture Emporium, Jeremiah gave instructions. "Stand side by side and listen closely. Don't go picking some girlie looking set. No pink, no purple, no flowers. Or polka dots. These bunks have to go in Caden's room when he's old enough. And we aren't made of gold, so nothing extravagant."

Lainey grabbed Deena's hand. They both yelled, "Whatever!" then ran through the double doors.

With his help, they chose a knotty pine frame, double bed on the bottom with a single-sized loft structure for the top bunk. They could remove the canopy from Lainey's bed and fit the top bunk over it, saving the bottom section for Caden's room when he would be old enough.

While the salesman went to the counter to ring up the order, the girls begged to eat dinner out. "Please?"

"Great. In stereo." Jeremiah dug a credit card out of his wallet. "After we pick out a bedspread for Deena. But fast food because we need to get home."

He encircled Lainey's head with one arm, rubbing her skull with his knuckles. "How'd I ever get roped into this whole shopping deal?"

"Ow!" She wriggled free, jumped between him and the front counter, then bent her head back to look up at him. "Don't know. Don't care. Can I start the car?" She held out a hand and wiggled her fingers.

He sighed and dropped the keys. "Start it *only*. No driving around the parking lot looking for cement blobs."

"Not funny!" Gripping the keys in her fist, she ran toward the door. "Come on, Deena!"

"No fooling around! Last thing we need is to get the car stuck again," he called out after her.

Lainey waited as Deena took three quick steps back toward Jeremiah, bruises glowing green under the fluorescent lighting. "Thanks, Mr. T."

He nodded as the automatic doors swallowed the girls.

In McDonald's, it was Lainey and Deena's turn to give instructions as Jeremiah leaned against the cold metal of the condiment counter. "Stand by the ketchup and do not embarrass us by saying anything corny. We need twenty dollars," Lainey held her hand out and ran to the front of the line.

The boy running the register blushed as Deena leaned over the counter to touch his name tag. "Liam," she said aloud in a high, sing-song tone. "I like that name."

"Hey," Jeremiah yelled. "Number five with Coke."

Lainey nodded, then turned back to smile at Liam, too. The lanky boy grinned, braces glimmering like silver dollars in the sun. The swelling on Deena's face had gone down, but the bruises would be visible for a while. Even with the green and blue marks turning yellow, she was much softer without those distracting piercings.

They were back to Jeremiah's post in five minutes.

"What'cha thinking about, Mr. T?"

Jeremiah blinked and looked down. Deena stood by his side, handing him a paper cup with brown droplets puddled on the plastic lid.

"How expensive children are and how much things can change in a year." He slurped off the excess soda.

"I sure hope so." She pointed to a back booth. Lainey sprinted over, trailing fries in her wake.

Through dinner they talked about where to put Deena's clothes. The conclusion was it wouldn't be hard since she hadn't brought much with her in the first place. Then Lainey asked for money to buy school clothes.

"No more money. I just paid for a new bed, sheets, and comforter," Jeremiah said. "Which—by the way—are pink, purple *and* polka dot!"

Lainey snapped her fingers, then pointed one finger in the air with a brilliant idea. "You got good Labor Day sales, and school starts Tuesday, so we've gotta have something to wear."

"What's this new interest in clothes?"

"I'm growing up. It happens."

"Well, nice try, but you wear uniforms to school." Jeremiah jabbed a stubby, thick finger at Lainey. "As I recall, you've already been set up nicely by your grandmother. A suitcase full of new clothes that you can share with your friend here?"

She raised her eyebrows and smiled. "It was worth a shot."

He popped the last fry in his mouth. "We can talk about buying Deena some more things, but it's about time we got home. First, I've got to tell you girls something."

Lainey sipped her drink. "Yeah?"

"Somehow, Pam Forman got our number and wants to see Deena. Brooke texted me. She'll be at our house by sev—"

"Hell, no!" Deena slammed her paper cup onto the tray; Sprite erupted like clear, bubbling lava.

"Now, listen."

"She called me a whore, just like her creep of a husband. And—"

Jeremiah put up his hands in surrender. "You don't want to see her. Understood. But we don't have a choice here. If she makes a stink, we won't be able to keep you with us. We can't make any waves."

Deena blinked back tears and slumped farther into the booth. "I hate this."

Jeremiah leaned forward on his elbows. "We can't do anything to jeopardize your situation. Right now, you're safe—so long as you keep away from matches and hairspray, right?"

When Deena rolled her eyes and stuck out her tongue, another hole glared like a Cyclops eye.

He grimaced. "Really, no food gets stuck in that?"

She scrunched up her mouth. "Actually, it kind of does. I have to rinse it out every night."

"That's foul. Seriously though, if we fight, kick or scream, Deena might have to go home. Right now, we play her mother's sick game which starts tonight in our living room—in half an hour." He stacked the trays and tossed wadded napkins on top. "Let's go. Can't hide from the inevitable forever."

⁊ঌ

BROOKE WAS STANDING on the porch in blue fuzzy slippers, cradling Caden on her chest, when Jeremiah pulled up in front of the house with the girls. While they'd been shopping, she had changed into some old office clothes—a brown pencil skirt and striped button-down shirt. Now, the material looked baggy everywhere except for the small pooch left over from carrying Caden for so long. Her hair was tied in a knot at the nape of her neck, thin brown strands tickling her temples.

Jeremiah rolled down the passenger window. "How much time we got?"

"None." She held the baby closer and scooted down the front steps. "She's early. Brought a lawyer, too."

"What the ...?" He jammed the car into park, jerking all three of them forward.

"I know." Brooke spoke through the passenger seat window. "She wouldn't give any details. Said she'd wait for you."

"Get back inside while I park. Girls, go on in with Brooke but don't say anything. Got it?"

Lainey nodded and slid out of the backseat lugging plastic bags to the sidewalk. Deena stalled, one leg dangling out the door. Brooke stepped back waiting for Deena to get out of the car.

"You have to face her, Deena."

"What do you think she wants, Mrs. T?"

"To win. But we can't help you from the car, so come on."

Deena slid out and shut the door. At the front gate, she paused and breathed in deeply through her nose. Brooke followed closely behind her.

Jeremiah honked and motioned them forward.

Deena nodded then obeyed. Slowly. Lainey and Brooke followed her in.

Brooke glanced sideways at Pam Forman sitting on the sofa in the front room. She wore a loose floral skirt with a gray, short-sleeved suit jacket. A man sat next to her on the edge of the sofa cushion wearing an expensive-looking, wrinkle-free navy suit. The reddish-brown leather of his shoes perfectly matched the leather of his briefcase. His gelled hair looked plastic.

"Jeremiah's parking the car. He'll just be a minute," Brooke said.

Lainey stood next to her while she fussed over Caden, laying him in the bassinet under the bay window.

Mrs. Forman nodded and pursed coral-red lips. She turned to look at her daughter, who stood rigid in the foyer. "Hello, honey."

Deena bee-lined toward Lainey then whispered in her ear.

Mrs. Forman stiffened. "I said, hello."

Deena glared. "I heard you." She walked down the hall into the kitchen. The clang of glass hitting marble echoed through the house.

Brooke tapped a finger on her lower lip. "Probably just getting herself a glass of water. Long week with traveling. Started in Virginia just over a week ago, then Caden was born."

The only response was the slam of a cabinet door in the kitchen.

Brooke jolted. "Lainey, why don't you go check on Deena; see if she'll come chat with us?"

Lainey raised both eyebrows.

Brooke frowned. "Go on."

Before she could obey, Jeremiah appeared from the kitchen, ushering Deena back to the company. He scanned the room. "Lainey, take Caden to the kitchen and feed him a bottle or something."

"I've never done it before. I haven't even held him by myself yet!" Lainey glanced at Brooke.

Brooke nodded with affirmation. "You'll be okay," she said. "He's asleep right now."

Jeremiah didn't even look Lainey's way. "Go up to his room and rock him; you'll be fine. Deena, sit on the piano bench, right there."

Lainey scooped the baby up from the bassinet with great care.

"Make sure you hold his head steady," Brooke instructed as Lainey left the room.

Jeremiah turned to the visitors, offering an outstretched hand. "I'm Jeremiah Traynor. You've already met my wife."

She flipped a hand in a short wave. "Call me Brooke."

Jeremiah cleared his throat. "We were expecting you, Pam, but I see you've brought a friend. Can I get anyone a drink? Water, tea, there may be a light beer in the back of the fridge."

The woman leaned forward and placed a hand on her escort's arm. The carnation pink acrylics flashed brighter against his dark suit. "It doesn't seem wise for you to have alcohol in the house from what I've been told. Does it, Mr. Traynor?" Her voice had a gravel tone to it that made a person want to clear her throat.

Brooke wondered how much dirt they'd mustered up on them all.

Jeremiah stared straight ahead.

"This here's Frank Morris. My lawyer. He's come along to ensure we're all clear on my intentions."

"Then let's get to it." Jeremiah gave a slight nod. "What are your intentions?"

"Well, Mr. Traynor. I plan to make it very clear to the courts, the police, to anyone who'll listen, that my daughter is lying." She pointed, her pale arm—fat dangling like loose jowls—toward the piano. "My husband's not the one who beat her."

"You're the rotten liar." Deena spun on the bench to face the piano and slammed a fist onto the keys. Brooke flinched.

Mrs. Forman lowered her voice, glaring at Deena. "You invited that boyfriend over after I left for work. He did this to you, just admit it." She sidled closer to the lawyer, gazing into his eyes like a beagle begging for attention.

Frank Morris patted her hand and nodded at Jeremiah. "Mr. Traynor. Mrs. Traynor. My client is prepared to bring to light the true nature of Deena's situation. Deena's biological father has relinquished all rights to seeing the girl. As of three weeks ago, he's moved to California. Obviously, Mrs. Forman wants nothing more than to have her daughter home, her family together again. This includes Lorne Forman, the man who lovingly adopted the girl a year ago."

"Who brutally beat her." Jeremiah walked over to the piano and squeezed Deena's shoulder. "I won't let you bully her. She'll be staying here for as long as she needs us."

Brooke glanced at Jeremiah's muscled hand pressing Deena's shoulder. If Deena was anything like she had been as a teenager, she knew Deena was happy to see someone take on her mother. And win.

Dabbing her watery eyes with a hanky, Brooke cleared her throat and pointed to the door. "Mrs. Forman. Mr. Morris." Her voice rose in volume with every word. "Please show yourselves out. And FYI, we're prepared to fight," she added, folding her arms.

"I see you are in the dark, Mrs. Traynor. Your husband can't be the savior for very long. Do you want to tell them the truth, Mr. Traynor, or do you want to wait until it all comes to light? I'm good at biding my time." Frank Morris got up, offered Mrs. Forman an arm, and escorted her to the front door.

Jeremiah held his head steady. Brooke stared at him, wondering what the lady was talking about.

Mrs. Forman spun back, pointing a half-inch acrylic. "You don't fit in here, Deena." She flashed a glare at Jeremiah. The whites of her eyes and teeth were yellowed. "Better watch yourself, Mr. Traynor. She likes to come on to older men, then tell lies about them. There are some truths out there that could hurt you as well."

"Get out of my house," Jeremiah gritted through clenched teeth. He squeezed Deena's shoulder tighter. She bowed her head and ran a finger under her left eye as her mother slammed the door behind her.

"Jeremiah, what kind of threat was that? What does she want?" Brooke asked.

"They are bluffing just trying to scare us. He's probably not even a real lawyer. Deena is safe here, and we will keep it that way. Don't you worry."

Brooke nodded. She had to believe Jeremiah had things under control.

Chapter 12

TESSIE ARRIVED at Heritage Manor at two o'clock. Visiting Jude after lunch seemed to work best since mornings here were dedicated to mopping floors, patient showers, or physical therapy—a chaotic frenzy of goodwill. Evenings often turned horrible with what the nurses called sundowning. Most patients got meaner and more confused as the sun sank on the horizon. A full-moon crazy, every night of the week.

Jude had started calling Tessie a dozen times every evening, not remembering he'd just spoken to her. Sometimes he'd cry. Others, he demanded she come get him. He'd hang up if she offered excuses like she wasn't allowed to drive at night anymore or the doctor hadn't released him yet.

She tried to disconnect his phone line, but he irritated the staff too much by asking them to make calls for him. The nurses didn't like to say no because it agitated him even more. "It's our business phone, Mrs. Weston. We can't have him using it all night." So, she gave the nurses permission to lie to Jude about the phones no longer working.

As she signed in at the front desk, Tessie heard her name coming from somewhere behind her. "Mrs. Weston? Mrs. Weston, I was just about to call. Could we talk?"

She nodded at Dr. Miller's head as he peeked out his office door from behind his computer screen. The doctor was surrounded by stacks of manila folders. His pot belly rested on the pencil drawer; his loose, oversized glasses pressed down on the pockmarks under his eyes. Tessie latched onto her purse handles, knuckles pale, face hot, and sat down. Her knees touched the tan metal desk. "How's Jude doing, Doctor?"

He rifled through the stack of folders and would not look her way. "As you know, Mrs. Weston, this disease is unpredictable." He pointed vaguely into the air, keeping his eyes peeled to the paper in front of him. "Please take a seat."

I am sitting, she screamed in her head. "He's worse, isn't he? Dozed most of my last visit. Pastor Tim was with me, which usually keeps him on good behavior, but the nurse said he hadn't slept at all the night before. She caught him trying to call me at four in the morning."

The doctor folded his hands in front of the keyboard and moved one thumb back and forth in rapid motion. His gaze aimed over her left ear. "One of the signs of pending decline is a loss of appetite."

"I could visit during mealtimes if that would help." Tessie dug into her purse for a hanky.

The doctor's thumb kept moving, keeping beat with his lips. "Keep to the schedule you've set. Up till now, he's been most cooperative with a plate of spaghetti in front of him."

"Jude always did love his food. Ice cream, especially Rocky Road. Until the diabetes came on. But even then …"

Dr. Miller re-folded his hands, but this time started thumb-wrestling himself. Tessie wondered what happened when one thumb beat the other. Was the doctor a sore loser either way?

"Mr. Weston hasn't eaten much of anything the last three days. We thought it might be a passing phase because he complained about not feeling well right after he choked on a small piece of meat. Low-grade fever, too. Today he stopped eating altogether. The nurse and aides have tried everything. He just slaps their hands away.

"We're required to document any erratic or abnormal behavior. This might be the start of a more serious decline. I want you to be prepared, in any case."

She wadded the hanky in one hand and gripped the purse handles with the other. "Thank you, Doctor. Is there anything I can do?"

"Like we said when he first arrived, the only thing any of us can do is to let this disease run its course. We'll continue to make him comfortable, keep him safe. And notify you regarding dosage adjustments."

Tessie stood, purse dangling at her sides. "Thank you, Dr. Miller."

"Wait a moment, please." He motioned her back into the seat with that dang thumb. "I'm afraid there's one more difficult issue we need to discuss."

She sat again on the edge of the chair, latching back onto the purse handles with both fists.

"Mr. Weston's been testier at night. Last week's reports gave cause for new concern. We tried to give him a roommate. Two hours later we were forced to switch the poor man to another room. Mr. Weston threatened to shoot him if he ever found his shotgun—12-gauge to be exact."

Tessie flinched.

"The hallucinations have gotten worse. One night last week, he again was under attack in the Navy. This time fighting like a twenty-year-old hostage when the staff tried to soothe him. It took seven aides to secure him. He's still a very strong man."

She stared at the doctor's blotchy forehead. The red was brightest between his eyebrows, like he'd just finished plucking them.

"Mrs. Weston, if this aggressive behavior gets more dangerous or turns chronic despite the meds, we'll have to find a new place for your husband. There's a good geriatric-psychiatric ward down in Suffolk."

"Thank you, Doctor." She stood again and shook his hand before exiting. Back into the psychiatric ward. Her brain felt dizzy walking down the hall. Jude, in a crazy house. She stopped at the water fountain and leaned down to the spigot. "Lord, help me," she whispered as lukewarm water ran over her lips, and her tears mixed with chlorine and sulfur.

In room 109 there were two of most everything. Two beds, two rolling dinner trays, two dressers, two walkers, two nightstands, two decrepit side chairs. Jude sat on the sofa that separated two TV stands. The center curtain was pulled to divide the room. The window shades were up, the window cracked. Fresh air blew a gust of musty, old-man stench up Tessie's nose.

Pushing his walker to the side, she positioned a chair to face Jude. Its cushion was indented; the red and tan stripes of the backrest were faded. She laid down a hanky to cover a suspicious-looking stain. "How are we feeling today, my wonderful husband?"

Jude lifted a gaunt face. His blue eyes had lightened to soft gray, but when he saw her sitting there, they sharpened and sparkled. "Feels like I woke up from a long nap. I've missed you, Tessie Green. What took so long?"

"Now, don't go acting like I haven't been around. What about yesterday afternoon? We played Bingo, and you ate an ice cream sandwich with some of the other patients. Seems that's the only thing you've eaten in the last few days, Mister."

"I remember driving my truck to check on the fields and stopping at the barn to find a tool, then feeling tight in my chest. How's the farm? Feels like I've been gone months."

Tessie wasn't about to tell him it'd been twelve, exactly. "Amos Lowry is working out great. Your short absence really forced him to step up his game. Got things running so smoothly, you wouldn't recognize the place. We're all waiting for you to recover and get back to wreaking some havoc." It didn't even feel like lying anymore.

He reached out dry, ashy hands. "We're getting old, ain't we, love?"

Tessie laid her hands on top. "And wrinkly."

Jude and Tessie gazed at each other like they were in a staring contest.

"Doctor says you haven't been eating," she scolded.

He ran a thumb down each of her fingers. The dryness scratched at her own wrinkles. "From the looks of the tray over there, ain't missing much."

"Now, Jude. Doesn't matter how it looks or tastes. You need strength. Let me get a fresh plate." She tried to stand, but he held tight to her hands.

"Stop it, woman. Just let me look at you. I promise to eat five plates of whatever watery mush they bring, but right now let me gaze into the eyes of my one and only."

She dropped back into the seat, sniffing back tears. "I'm lonely without you."

He frowned. "Where's ole Lainey girl? She's not helping out?"

"Jeremiah came and got her. She's been living with him in Baltimore. He got remarried—a much younger girl."

Jude smiled.

"Now don't go grinning and smirking about younger women. This girl's only twenty-six. Jeremiah's thirty-seven."

"Tessie." His voice dropped half an octave. "Genevieve's been gone a long time." His eyes glazed over like a man caught in a daydream. "Is the boy happy?"

"Well." She let out a long breath. "When he's not getting blind drunk or stressing out over work."

"Let the kids be, Tessie. They'll figure it out."

She moved from the chair to sit next to him on the couch, pressing shoulder to shoulder with him. She slipped her hand into his. His eyelids started drooping, but she was afraid to leave. These lucid moments were peaceful for her soul.

She could hear his breathing settle into a light snore. "Jude. Would you like to take a nap?" She squeezed his hand one more time.

He nodded and grunted.

Tessie helped him into bed, covering him with three white cotton blankets. She stood at the edge of the mattress and tapped one of his shoes, those dang Velcro, orthopedic things he insisted on wearing day and night. "Anything else I can get you, my dear?"

"Real therapy, so I can come home," he slurred. "Want you to take care of me."

"I'll see what I can do. Promise me you'll eat next time they bring a meal. Hear?"

She leaned over to kiss his cheek then left before she cried in front of him.

❧

IN THE SCHOOL CAFETERIA in late September, Lainey removed her navy-blue cardigan to hang it over the back of the chair. Her short-sleeved, white button-down shirt lay loosely over a black tank top she wore for modesty. She had to do something to hide the colored bras Brooke kept buying her. Today's special purchase was leopard print.

With just enough time to review her notes before the first test, Lainey wanted to go over the key facts she'd highlighted last night. She opened her history book directly in front of her then methodically set each item of food in a moon-like half-circle. Brooke was back to making Homemade Lunches with Love but made a point of asking Lainey what she wanted almost every day.

As she bit her turkey sandwich, she soaked in the peace she felt with being alone. It was nice not to have too many classes with Deena this year and even nicer not having lunch with her. They were best friends and all, but the girl was hard to live with. She wouldn't make her bed, which looked even worse hanging over Lainey's neat, tidy one. She refused to clean anything in the bathroom and threw clothes all over the floor. Only if Brooke or Jeremiah were around would she scrape a plate in the sink or open a textbook, pretending to study. Lainey was afraid to tell Jeremiah and Brooke she was doing both their chores and even some of Deena's homework. If they found out, they might have to send her back to Social Services. Or worse, home.

Then there was the loud music when she was trying to study. Rather than listen with headphones like a normal teenager, Deena cranked up the big speakers on Jeremiah's old stereo. If Lainey moved to the family room, she followed within five minutes then turned on the TV, full blast. Brooke and Jeremiah were so involved with baby Caden, they didn't seem to notice.

Grandma Tessie used to lecture good and hard about the benefits of work. "Every child is a crystal ball into the work ethic of his parent," she'd say. "Show me a kid who does chores without being told, I'd hire his parents to run this farm. Then take a nice long vacation." Lainey snickered at the thought of Grandma Tessie whipping Deena into shape. But that wasn't going to happen. Grandma wasn't here.

She crunched a bite of a carrot just as Deena ran into the cafeteria. Her plaid skirt was wrinkled, as usual, shirt untucked on the right side. A knee sock puddled around one ankle.

"What are you doing here?" Lainey slid the pencil behind an ear. "You're supposed to be in class." She glanced at the clock high up on the cement wall. "Like, five minutes ago."

"Can't think straight, and school just makes it worse." Deena plopped onto the tabletop, planting her butt right next to Lainey's lunch.

"Jeremiah said you have to stay out of trouble. No waves, remember?" With one swipe of her forearm, she scooted her complete lunch farther from Deena's backside. "That means keeping up with schoolwork."

"It's just … I think I'm gonna go see my mom today."

Lainey glared through squinted eyes. "Are you totally stupid?"

"I guess I am stupid because I'm going!" She grabbed a carrot from the sandwich baggy and crunched.

"Hey! Eat your own lunch."

"Did already." She filched another carrot.

Lainey slapped at her hand. "Why do you want to see her?"

"You hit like a girl. I don't want Joey to get blamed for what happened to me, so I have to make her understand."

"You're stupid for hanging out with drug dealers."

Deena slammed a hand on the tabletop. "Stop calling me stupid! I'm not into that shit anymore. No drugs, no beer, nothing since I moved into your house. My piercings are all closed up. Even my hair dye is fading. I'm totally legit." She poked at Lainey's stomach with her toe. "Boring, just like you."

"Don't touch me with your nasty feet. And pull up your sock while you're at it." Lainey shoved Deena's foot away.

"I need her to believe me about Loser Lorne, the perv. Anyway, I want some things from my room. I want some of my stuff."

"Ask Jeremiah. He'll go get it for you. He does everything for you."

"Dammit, Lainey. You're the stupid one. I want to talk to my mom. I'll grab my junk and be back by dinner."

"He said not to talk to her."

Deena shrugged. "*He* doesn't need to know everything."

Lainey liked the thought of having an ally against Jeremiah. "Want me to go with you? What if Loser Lorne's around?"

"Nah, just go home like normal. If I'm there and gone by four, I won't have to deal with step-creeper! Bleecchhh. When I think of that slimy tongue ..."

They shuddered in unison.

Deena grabbed one last carrot and sighed. "Guess I better show up for the end of English. I think they're taking a test."

"What?" Lainey looked up from her lunch. Her delinquent friend was already halfway to the door.

WHEN DEENA WASN'T HOME by dinner time, Lainey informed Brooke that she'd stayed at school for tutoring. She really didn't like to lie, even if it was to Fakemom. She also didn't want Deena to get in trouble. They were all trying their best not to make waves. When seven p.m. rolled around, Jeremiah knocked on her bedroom door.

"Come in." Lainey had set herself up on the bedspread with a science textbook and notebook paper surrounding her.

"Brooke wants you to feed the dog." He glanced around the room, frowned. "Deena's not back yet?"

"Nope."

"She stayed at school?"

"Yup."

"School can't still be open, right?"

She grunted and focused on counting the purple polka dots on Deena's bedspread hanging from above her. She was gonna kill Deena when she got home. She'd never really had to cover for anyone before.

"Cut the one-word answers. Tell me what's going on."

She gripped the pencil so hard her hand began to sweat. "I don't know."

"Need more than that if I'm going to find her. Maybe where to look, for instance?"

She stopped counting dots at twenty-two and looked at his anxious expression. There were wrinkles across his face, and if she didn't know better, she thought she saw the start of a tear in his left eye. A switch flipped deep in her heart. "Like when you came back for me when my mother died? Oh wait. That's right. You didn't bother!"

"You're bringing that up now? I thought we were past that stage."

"Stage?" She held up one palm like a date book and tapped the tip of the pencil on her tongue. "Let's see. When would be a better time to bring up the abandonment of your only daughter? How about I schedule a fifteen-minute meeting for Friday? You're so involved with your new son and protecting Deena, I'm not sure you'll have enough time. And don't forget, I'm not Genevieve."

Jeremiah grabbed the pencil out of her hand and snapped it in half. He pursed his lips shut. "I said I was sorry for the Genevieve comment. I wasn't in my right mind. I don't know what else to do."

"Same old story," Lainey filled in the silence. "The only difference here is, you'll go searching for your precious Deena. I'm the only person you screw over."

"Alaina Rose. The longer you hold out telling me where Deena is, the more trouble your best friend is in. If the courts find out, they'll take her away."

"Fine." Lainey chucked the pillow to the floor. Her neck felt on fire, heat rising to her jaws and cheeks. "She went to see her mom."

"Why would she do that?" Jeremiah threw the pencil pieces on the floor. "I specifically told her not to!"

"You're quite easy to disobey." Her eyes darted back to the polka dots.

His nostrils flared. "I need help, not smart-ass comments."

"She thought she could convince her mom she's not lying."

"That makes no sense. She knows the woman's unstable."

Lainey shrugged. "At least she has a parent who wants her around."

Jeremiah sat on the rolling desk chair. "There doesn't seem to be anything I can do to make you forgive me or even understand. So, I'm done apologizing."

"Don't bother. Your precious Deena will be home any minute."
Lainey kept her gaze on the bedspread. Her dot count was up to
thirty-four.

"What time did she go there?"

Lainey shrugged slightly.

"You've gone from grunting to nothing."

She scooted to the edge of the bed, leaning elbows on her thighs.
"Why do you want to help Deena so much?"

"Redemption, maybe. I promised Genevieve we could adopt
one day. I just want to make good on at least one promise to your
mother."

"Jeremiah ... does it bother you when I call you that?"

"Yes."

"Good." She crossed her legs like a pretzel.

"Watch the attitude, Lainey. I can only fight so many battles at
a time."

"Since you're so concerned about doing the right thing for
Deena, I have another question."

"Shoot."

"Was leaving me with Grandma Tessie the right thing to do,
too?"

His lips tightened. "No."

She smirked and tilted her head left. "Now who's got the one-
word answers?"

"It was the most selfish choice I've ever made in my life." He
spun the chair backwards and straddled it, resting his chin on the
leather back. "As was the drinking. When God took Genevieve away,
I lost my mind. I honestly didn't plan to leave you when I went down
there. It was too hard making decisions about her burial right there
in the hospital. A whole day passed, and I couldn't remember if I had
even fed you.

"And I was furious when Jude and Tessie insisted the funeral
be in Virginia, but it was easier to just let them have their way. They
immediately shipped her body to the church. All I could picture as I
drove those two hundred miles—with you asleep in the back—was
her casket with a big POSTAGE DUE stamp right in the corner.
Once she was in the ground, I couldn't take any more, so I made a
bad choice. Every huge decision of my life—good or bad—has been
a rash one.

"It took ten minutes and five shots to convince myself you'd be
better off without me. I just wanted some time to sort things out.

Some time turned into years." He hid his eyes behind his hands. "Someday I hope you can forgive me."

"Grandma Tessie talked about Genevieve all the time. We never do."

"Might I remind you that on your first day back in Baltimore, you told me not to talk about her. And every time I tried, you stopped me. Man, I love her so much—"

Lainey shook her head. "Loved."

"No. I still do. So much that whenever anything good happens—to you or me, Brooke or Caden—I have this overwhelming urge to tell her all about it. And I do. I talk to your mother all the time."

"Really?" She'd tried that a few times, too.

Jeremiah laughed out loud. "She doesn't talk back."

"Does that make Brooke angry?"

"Hurt more than angry, but she understands more now. We really are trying our best here, Lainey."

She lay back on the bed. "Calling you Dad feels weird. I tried it once, looking in the mirror. I actually had to make a face..." she scrunched her lips and squinted her eyes. "To get it out."

"Well." He shook his head. "Just be creative, then. Like you were with Fakemom."

She shot straight up, eyes wide.

"Yeah. We're not deaf. Maybe I can be Fakedad until you're ready to shorten it." He stood up and wheeled the chair back under the desk. "We'll be okay, I promise. Go get a jacket. We'll pick up Deena at her mother's, so she doesn't have to take a bus back." He left the room quietly.

Lainey felt numb from her scalp to her toes, but tears still dripped past her ears, turning a pink polka dot on her own blanket a muddy brown. A few moments later, she wiped her eyes and slid the claddagh ring off her finger. She walked toward her dresser and set it next to a framed picture of Genevieve. "Help us out, Mama. I want to forgive him. I want to trust him. I just don't know how to let it all go."

She stuffed her arms into a blue corduroy coat Deena had left on the closet door handle. "Wait for me, Fakedad," she called down the steps.

&a.

NO ONE ANSWERED the door at the Forman's row house. Lainey studied the cracked asbestos shingles on the house across the street while Jeremiah knocked for the third time. The Forman's screen door was more rust than white paint; a large corner of its netting flapped in the breeze. The surrounding blocks offered illumination like a high school football game on Friday night, but the Forman's street was pitch black, its only light shattered. Ambulance sirens chirped a few streets over.

Jeremiah leaned against the wrought iron railing, next to Lainey. "Good thing Caden's a boy. Maybe I won't lose him like I seem to lose you girls."

She laughed politely as headlights approached and parallel-parked right up on the sidewalk, five cars behind Jeremiah's Jeep. Pam and Lorne Forman got out and walked up the pavement with a confident ease.

"Why, Mr. Traynor! Good to see you again." Her voice held a scratchy lilt. "Boy, do we have some great news! You won't believe where we just came from."

Jeremiah nudged Lainey's arm. "Get in the car and call Brooke. Just tell her to stay on the line." The Jeep's lights flashed as he pressed the unlock button on his key chain. "You'll need these in the car for it to start. Press the break and push the start button," he said. He dropped the keys in her hand without taking his eyes off Mrs. Forman.

Lainey hopped in then cracked the window so she could hear. Lastly, she called Brooke like Jeremiah had instructed.

Jeremiah crossed his arms and planted his feet shoulder-width apart. "Where's Deena?"

Pam dusted stray pieces of concrete from the third step and plopped down. Her flower-patterned, cotton skirt covered two steps. "Don't you worry about my daughter, Mr. Traynor. She's no longer your concern. In fact, she never was, was she?"

"The court gave me custody."

"You and I both know that's a lie."

"What have you done?"

With a tilt of the head, Pam Forman motioned her husband to go inside. He obeyed without a word. "Turn the porch light on!" she yelled to him.

After Lorne closed the front door, a dim yellow bulb lighted the front steps. Pam glared back at Jeremiah. "Deena came to see me this afternoon with that same old silly story incriminating my husband. Once she calmed down, we had a real good chat." She smoothed the wrinkles in her skirt with both palms. The hem dangled onto the crumbling concrete. "We reminded her that she ran away from home. She's finally confessed to lying about her stepfather."

"I don't believe you."

Pam folded her hands primly in her lap and forced a crooked grin. "She flat out admitted it was that Joey character who beat her up. Naturally, we went directly to the police station—pressed charges on him and then kindly informed them regarding who helped Deena run away from home. That would be you, Mr. Traynor, in case you have forgotten. Some might even call that kidnapping."

"Uh-uh." Jeremiah shook his head. "Deena wouldn't do that."

"Oh, Mr. Traynor. Jeremiah, is it? I tried to warn you—my daughter's a low-down, no good liar. Deceitful and rebellious, just like her father. Couldn't control him, but I'll be damned if I let her go without a fight. One quick anonymous phone call to social services to let them in on your proclivity for drinking, and you could lose your own children too. Don't mess with me."

Her wrist flicked toward the street, as if calling for a taxi or a waiter. The back door of her Monte Carlo creaked open. Deena stepped out, staring at the sidewalk, clutching the door handle as if it were the front bar on a roller coaster.

"Come on. Get moving," called Pam. "Tell Mr. Traynor your good news."

As Deena approached, chin glued to her chest, Lainey jumped out of the Jeep. "What are you doing?" she screamed.

Deena rounded on her. "Leave me alone."

"I will not." Lainey pointed to the house. "After everything my parents did, you go and lie for that disgusting…pig?" She shoved her shoulder.

"Don't touch me," Deena gritted out through clenched teeth, staggering back.

Lainey lunged farther and shoved again. "It's better with us. You said so yourself! Even had me convinced it was better."

Deena balled up her fists. "Just back off! And take off my jacket."

Lainey's face and ears blotched. "What's wrong with you?" Her words came out like shrieks from a monkey.

Jeremiah stepped between them just as Deena slumped to the sidewalk in a heap.

"I lied about Lorne. To protect Joey." Her voice had turned soft and quiet.

Deena peered up, eyes empty of emotion. "I really am sorry, Mr. T. But … I was scared of what … You were so nice …" She lowered her face. "Please don't hate me."

He stared at her a moment then grabbed Lainey's shoulders, steering her back to the Jeep.

Lainey ripped the jacket off her shoulders and threw it at Deena's feet.

Jeremiah helped her buckle the seatbelt, then picked up the cell she'd dropped on the mat by her feet. "I thought this was my chance to make it up to your mother for not protecting her that night. I can't get anything right," he said, shifting his gaze to the front steps. Pam smiled, waving a friendly goodbye. He clamped his lips tight, got in the driver's seat, then peeled out.

❧

BEFORE HEADING TO BED, Jeremiah told Lainey she could sleep in rather than go to school. "You won't be able to focus anyway, and I really don't want Brooke alone."

"Mrs. Forman said you helped Deena run away."

"Deena ran to us for help; her mom's just trying to twist the truth to scare us."

"Why did Deena change her story?" Lainey's eyelids felt too thick and heavy as she sat on the top step of the staircase.

Jeremiah sat down two steps below her. "She's a troubled girl, honey." He reached back to hold her hand.

Lainey yanked back in reflex. "I'm going to bed."

In her room, she kicked off her shoes without untying the laces but slept in her jeans and t-shirt. Once under the covers, she heard Jeremiah's car door slam shut. She was too tired to wonder where he was going.

She drifted in and out of sleep all night, replaying the fight with Deena. In the dreams, her former friend wasn't slumped on the ground. She was wearing the jacket and pounding Lainey's face and neck. Lainey tried to punch back but could never reach her. Her own punches were slow-motioned, weak jabs, and her arms felt like rubber when she swung. Then they turned to lead when dropped to her side. She woke up sweating and crying.

The next morning Lainey stayed curled up in bed, resting her eyes and listening to the silence of the empty room. At nine, the doorbell jolted the quiet, ringing out like the call to a church—another Fakemom purchase.

Minutes later, Brooke burst in, mumbling under her breath. "In bed with a hangover and now this. All the time and money. Love even. Ungrateful little liar."

Lainey sat up. Fakemom was in one of her cleaning furies, a large, black trash bag in hand. "Who has a hangover?"

Brooke stopped fussing with the bag. "Your father had a rough night. He won't be much help this morning."

Lainey rolled her eyes at the weakness of her father. "Will Jeremiah get in trouble for taking Deena to Virginia?"

Brooke shook her head but would not look at Lainey. "He was a bit misguided on that decision, but I don't think Mrs. Forman really wants to take Jeremiah down."

"What does she want?" Lainey couldn't comprehend the whole situation.

"Control, maybe? All I know is there was a courier at the door just now with a court order. We have till five to get all Deena's crap delivered to the Forman's. Get up and help me pack. *Everything.* School books, underwear, shoes. We're dumping every stitch on their rotten front steps."

Lainey threw her blanket aside and jumped up to yank on socks. "Let's just burn it all."

"Stop." Brooke dropped the half-full bag. She plopped onto the bed; her shoulders slumped. "I don't know whether to scream, cry, or pity the wretched girl. Grrrrrr. I'm just so pissed off! And I hope you can hear me, Jeremiah."

Brooke picked up one bag and shoved in dark-wash jeans with such force, she punched a hole in the plastic.

"Hey! Those are mine." Lainey fished her pants out and turned to Brooke. "Did you really just say 'Grrrrrr'?"

"Yes. Yes, I did. Did you sleep in those clothes from yesterday?"

Lainey gave a slight nod.

"Aren't we a pair? Come on. I'll let myself stay angry at the whole mess while we do this, then try to be mature later." She locked her elbow with a stern point toward Lainey's chest. "Don't you dare fold anything."

"Your big punishment for a lying traitor is not folding her underwear?"

Brooke shrugged. "I feel so stupid being played like that. When I think about my own foster parents, and how we tried to help ... grrrrrr." She snarled at Lainey. "And I mean it!"

Lainey raised her hands in surrender. "Growl all you want. At least you don't have to see her every day at school." She was getting good now at packing things up, having done it more in the last year than the whole rest of her life. She piled five textbooks on the desk: literature, science, math, health, American History.

"Knowing Deena, she probably won't show up much anyway," Brooke said. As she cleaned out the top drawer of the dresser, she picked up Lainey's claddagh, propped in between a picture frame and perfume bottle. "You took your ring off!"

"I thought maybe putting it next to that picture of my mother would bring us luck with Deena when we were going to look for her. So much for that."

"How sweet." Brooke cradled the ring in one palm then held it out. "I'm worried about you. Look at those dark circles under your eyes."

Lainey stuffed the ring into her jeans pocket. "Deena only has a few things hanging up. I can finish this and bring the stuff down. Plus, you are folding."

"Grrrrrr!" Brooke dropped the shirt she was holding and stomped out.

Lainey walked into the closet, shutting the door behind her. Darkness made her feel invisible. She crawled to the back corner, sat, and pulled her knees to her chest. The turquoise hem of the bridesmaid dress tickled her face. She reached into her pocket for the ring and held it out. There wasn't enough light to see, so she twisted it in circles in front of her face.

A salty wetness trickled over her lips as she raised her eyes to the ceiling. "Mama? You probably know Grandma Tessie took real good care of me. I don't really remember you—just the stories she told me. Why does everybody leave? You did. Grandpa Jude's gonna leave soon, Grandma Tessie said so. Jeremiah left me at the farm. And he's not much better now. My friend Corinne—she forgot all about me. Now Deena. That girl's so messed up, Mama. Why would she lie and ruin everything like that?"

Lainey shoved shoes out of the way to lay on her stomach, holding the claddagh up to the faint strip of light seeping under the door. "Love. Friendship. Loyalty. Mama, I can't help but think it's all a big load of crap."

She dropped the ring into an old tennis shoe, laid her head on the carpet, closed her eyes, and rested for a moment. Deena's things could wait a bit.

Chapter 13

A MONTH LATER, Tessie woke to her ring tone—a bird chirping—at three a.m. She sat up, adjusted her blanket, smoothing the satin to lie wrinkle-free over her waist.

"Hel—" Phlegm blocked the last syllable. "This is she."

A nurse from Heritage Manor was speaking in a very soft tone.

Tessie cleared her throat and pushed the speaker phone button. "Sorry? Still half asleep."

"It's your husband. I'm so sorry to tell you this, but Mr. Weston has passed away. Peacefully, in his sleep, half an hour ago."

Tessie couldn't feel her arms or legs, but her scalp itched fiercely.

"Mrs. Weston, we're deeply sorry for your loss. He was a fine man. We need to start preparing—"

"Thank you for calling," was all she could muster. Tessie pushed END on the phone and tossed it to the side of the bed. The one Jude used to sleep on. Fifty-two years.

She scratched her head, but the itch wouldn't stop. It traveled into her ears. Throwing back the covers and stepping into slippers, she turned in slow circles not knowing which way to walk. The phone chirped again, but she let it go to voice mail.

Cold. She took five brisk steps toward the closet.

When she flipped on the light, her forest green robe with deep pockets was right there on its hook. Like it should be. Right next to Jude's. Like it should be. Navy plaid, soft like lamb's wool. The man never used a towel after showering, only threw on the robe. He said it felt brisk; woke him up.

The one thing she hadn't done when Jude went into the home was put away his clothes, figuring she might need to take more to the facility when his wore out. And it felt disloyal.

Tessie calmly wrapped herself in his monstrous robe, tying the belt tight around her waist. Then she yanked out three dresser drawers and stacked them in the center of the room. The top one was full of socks: thick wool, white athletic, gray hunting, black dress.

Seeing three gaping holes in the dresser made her palms sweat. She looked away. Next, the closet. Making a pile of discarded hangers, she draped each dress shirt over her left arm. Then the button-down work shirts. She piled the burden on top of the wooden drawers. Next, sweaters and two suits. She kicked fallen hangers to one side to avoid tripping.

Hats. Ties. Belts. Shoes. She bent over at the waist, leaning her butt against the closet wall. She breathed deep. *Keep it moving, Tessie.*

White tennis shoes with grass stains on the toes. She placed them at the base of the pile, toes pointed out. *Breathe.* Black steel-toed boots for farm work. She set them two feet left of the tennis shoes, toes out. Deep brown, leather loafers for Sunday. Not one scuff because he'd refused to go to church at the end. Moccasins next. His shoes were framing the mound nicely.

Three pairs of cowboy boots. They smelled like old leather and stale sweat. She used them to complete the circular edging. Itching and numbness turned to tears. For an hour Tessie lay surrounded by Jude's possessions. The robe came untied.

Deplete of tears, she took a long, hot shower. She curled her hair then 'painted her face' as Jude called it. She dressed in her autumn, errand-running uniform: Fading black polyester pants with elastic waist, a black sweater embroidered with brown and tan squirrels playing with pine cones pulled over a brown cotton top. Black slip-on Thom Mcan's bought at J C Penney ten years prior. Her ankles looked unseasonably tanned thanks to knee-high nylons.

Rather than numb, her legs and arms felt limp now. Tessie rested on the edge of the old cedar hope chest, waiting for a decent hour to start making calls. She and her mother had filled that chest with her bridal trousseau. By the time she'd married Jude in the early sixties, the chest held a quilt, hand stitched by Tessie's grandmother for her own wedding in 1912. Plus, a collection of fine linen handkerchiefs, a complete china set with coordinating silver, and five silk nighties.

Now the chest was used for storing extra blankets. The quilt had worn out by the late eighties. The china was stacked in the dining room hutch. The nighties had gone out of style by 1969. Jude tried to use them as rags in the barn but said the slippery feel distracted him and snagged on his callouses. She still used the embroidered handkerchiefs—they just don't make some things like they used to.

Six a.m. Tessie didn't want to wake anyone so early. Her hands felt icy as she sat stick-straight on the wooden box, making mental notes of whom to call, what to say: Pastor Tim. Her daughters. Jeremiah. The funeral director—or would the home call him? They'd already planned both their funerals, less stress for the kids that way. Back when dying wasn't real. Cremation. Matching marble boxes instead of ornate urns, one plot for both.

At seven Tessie decided it best to call Madeline first; she could be there by eight-thirty. Then she'd head to Heritage Manor to set the whole burial process in motion.

She looked around their room; she looked out the window toward the tobacco fields. The home she and Jude had made.

She was alone.

&a.

TESSIE CALLED JEREMIAH while he was on his way to work.

"Hey, Ma," he answered.

"Jude's gone." Her voice sounded like a hollow echo.

"Where are you?"

"Driving to the home."

"Are you okay?"

"The Lord will bless and keep me." She paused to gather her thoughts. "I feel unprepared, Jeremiah, even though I've been expecting this for a long time."

"Yeah, it's so final."

"Yes, it is." She could feel thick tears clogging her throat.

"What do you need? Just ask, and I'll—"

"Everything's set. Most likely the service will be Monday afternoon."

"When do you want us to come?"

"Soon as you can. Madeline's meeting me at the home. Beth and Faith are flying in later this evening." *Dear Lord*, Tessie thought, *back we go to the church. The cemetery.* With the crisp cuff of her shirt, Tessie wiped a tear escaping down the side of her nose.

"Do you want to tell Lainey? I think she took her cell phone to school."

"This one's all yours, son. I just don't have the strength right now."

"She's on the bus already, so I'll change course and meet her at the school. Ma? Jude was a blessed man. If I can be half the husband and father he was ..." His voiced dropped off.

Tessie didn't respond.

"I have a ways to go, don't I?"

She heard a faint goodbye. Then only the empty silence of a dropped call.

❧

WHEN LAINEY HEARD her name announced over the classroom phone at the end of first period, her first thought was Deena got me in trouble again. Strange reaction since they hadn't spoken since Deena moved back with her mother a month ago. Plus, Deena only decided to show up for school about three times a week to hang by her locker or smoke in the bathroom. Today wasn't one of those days, and Lainey felt relief every day her former friend wasn't around.

English was almost over, so Lainey started packing up her bag. The teacher was discussing what she referred to as "the nuances of romantic love" from Shakespeare's *Romeo and Juliet*. Normally, Lainey liked literature, but those love-sick morons really irked her. How stupid could two people be to kill themselves because of love? And what was even worse, Ms. Reagan had made her play Juliet during the balcony scene. With Tommy Harris.

An echoing tinny voice repeated over the phone's weak speaker. "Lainey Traynor, please come to the school office. Lainey Traynor."

"Lainey, I think you better get a move on," Ms. Reagan said.

"Yes, Ms. Reagan. Sorry." She scooped up her backpack and walked to the front door. She could tell everyone's eyes were on her back, watching.

As she approached the glassed-in box of the administration offices, Lainey recognized Jeremiah's big head through the window. His hair was black, but she noticed splashes of gray had started to grow in.

She walked through the door. "Did I forget my lunch made with love again?"

Jeremiah's eyes looked watery. Deep lines creased his forehead. He didn't respond.

She snapped her fingers in front of his eyes. "Jeremiah."

Nothing.

She poked his shoulder. "Dad. What are you doing here?"

He blinked and looked up. He stared at her, making her very nervous. "Your eyes sparkle just like Genevieve's," Jeremiah said, standing up in slow motion.

She lifted her upper lip on the right side. One afternoon, when Deena was still staying with them, they'd spent four hours practicing snarls and rolling their tongues. Lainey could only curl the right side. Deena could do both.

"Okay. Now you're just acting weird." She crossed her arms. "Why are you here?"

"I've already signed you out," he whispered. "I don't know the best way to tell you."

Her father stood there rocking from foot to foot. He opened his arms like he wanted a hug.

A funny feeling started rushing to her heart. The day she'd feared since she had moved to Baltimore. "Is it Grandpa?"

He stepped toward her and gathered her in his arms. His grip was so tight, she could barely breathe.

"Yes, honey. Grandpa Jude's gone."

She felt her head swimming and clutched at Jeremiah's waist, her skinny, long arms reaching all the way around. Her tears streamed down her cheeks, staining Jeremiah's blue silk tie. She let him stroke her hair until she could control the hiccups. When she realized how long they'd held onto each other, she pushed him back and used her sleeve to wipe her face. "I need to see Grandma."

"Let's get you packed," he said. "Tessie is waiting for us at the farm."

&.

THE MEMORIAL SERVICE was set for ten on Monday morning at Hopewell Evangelical Presbyterian. Tessie had chosen Jude's three favorite hymns. As for people getting up and jawing on about all the memories—Tessie believed everyone should experience that in life rather than waiting for death to say it. Dead people just plain missed out on hearing the good stuff.

She'd refused to have a viewing before the cremation process. "Remember Jude as lively as he always was," she'd told them. Vibrant, tall, rugged, caring. Memory could feed her grief enough. She didn't really want closure.

The interment of the urn was more somber. The finality of that square black hole, framed by bright green grass, made Tessie feel even more alone. As Pastor Tim prayed, she imagined Jude and Genevieve hanging out in heaven, watching from the porch swing of Jude's new mansion. He held an extra-large, sugary lemonade in one hand and his sweet daughter's hand in the other. Genevieve laid her head on daddy's shoulder and smiled.

That evening the extended family crowded into Tessie's kitchen and family room, the noise level a welcome distraction. Three daughters, four sons-in-law, seven grandchildren, Brooke and Caden, Pastor Tim's family, Amos, Evelyn. Lainey and Corinne were sitting next to each other on stools, but neither was talking. The big topic for the women in the kitchen was how much Jude would've loved all this attention. In the family room—how crazy the Weston women were. They didn't notice Tessie leaning on the door frame.

Jeremiah clinked his glass with a knife and glanced around the room at his brothers-in-law. "No, no—listen to me! It's all women, not just the Westons. My wife is just as crazy."

As the men sent up rousing cheers, Tessie stepped forward. "Don't mind my eavesdropping, boys."

The room went quiet.

Tessie smiled but would not say another word.

Jeremiah bolted up, the knife clattering onto a metal TV tray. He cleared his throat. "We're not afraid of you, Tessie, or any of the Weston females. That's why we're all still here."

She sighed. "And for that I'm more grateful than you'll ever know. Now, Jeremiah—can we talk?"

"You've done it now, son."

"Don't go, man."

"Get out while you still can!"

Tessie touched his elbow. "Ignore them and go grab us a couple jackets. Jude still has a few hanging by the door."

He returned wearing a red flannel coat over his white dress shirt. He handed her a blue flannel, same size and style. She could've wrapped it twice around her.

"I love wearing his old clothes," she said.

Jeremiah sat on the swing and waited.

Leaning against the railing, she turned the collar of the jacket up over her neck then stuffed her hands into the pockets. "All right, then. Here's the deal. Not sure if now's the best time to bring this up, but you need to be thinking, making some long-term plans."

His eyes narrowed. "What's going on?"

Tessie leaned harder against the rail and crossed her ankles. She still wore black leather pumps from the funeral, making her ankles look frail. "It's about the will." She shook the static out of her black rayon dress. "Absolutely no one else knows this information, mind you."

"Then, I don't think you should discuss it with me."

She held up a hand. "My daughters are all set. Husbands have done right by them, financially and otherwise. Few worries on that front. Jude and I never could believe how fortunate we've all been."

"Tessie, really. I—"

"It must've been right after he got the diabetes when we had a long talk about what to do with our assets. At that point, we weren't so sure about you. You know—your state of mind." Her eyebrows raised in friendly judgment. "Either way, we felt like we had to do something to provide for Lainey. By the way, I've gotta ask. The summer episode was the last episode, correct?"

"Of course, Ma. I've got too much to lose. Work's going well. I've got it all under control."

"That's what I want to hear." Tessie started pacing the length of the porch. One board on the far end squeaked under the pressure of her heels. "You see, my parents had some money, too. Jude and I kept it saved for a rainy day, but those days never came. We put in our wills for it to be split between Faith, Beth, and Madeline. They can use it for their own kids or whatever they decide is best. Of course, Genevieve was gone by the time we decided all that."

Jeremiah sat on the swing, arms crossed, frozen in place. "What are you trying to say?"

Tessie sat down next to him. "It's simple, really. We want Lainey to own the farm."

❧

BACK IN BALTIMORE the next evening, Brooke and Jeremiah were propped up in bed, discussing the news about Lainey.

"What's a little girl going to do with a farm?" she said, muting the volume of the local news—another fire on the west side of the city.

"Shhh. Not so loud. She doesn't have to take it over tomorrow. Tessie's alive and well. Still living there. Amos runs everything and has some great ideas on modernization. You know, we don't even have to tell her right now. We could wait until she's eighteen then let her decide where she wants to live."

Brooke fiddled with the volume knob of the baby monitor on her nightstand, holding the speaker to her ear. "What about college? She has to go. Experience life, find out who she is—"

"Agreed. But we can't hide the fact she owns a whole tobacco farm. The farm she grew up on." He adjusted the pillow behind his back and crossed his arms under his head.

"It'll really tick her off if we don't tell her now. I just know it." Brooke squeezed a thick glob of sweet pea scented lotion into one palm and briskly rubbed it on both elbows. "You know it, too."

"Maybe we could just wait till Tessie passes away. Lainey doesn't need to decide anything till then, anyway. Besides, we're making progress with her. When I went to tell her about Jude, she called me Dad."

Brooke reached over and removed his glasses, leaning across to set them on his nightstand. She felt like a lightweight wrestler trying to pin her heavyweight opponent. From that position, she set his alarm for six a.m.

"That's great news, babe," she said, "but Tessie could live another twenty years. Or more. That woman is too stubborn to die. We can't sit on this information until our daughter's thirty-five. We risk alienating Lainey for good if that happens."

After she stopped fussing and rested her head on his chest, Jeremiah twisted a lock of her hair around his finger. "I know you're right, but what if she decides she wants to go live with Tessie now?" He wrapped his arms around her and squeezed.

"We should table the inheritance bombshell until after the holidays, at least. She just lost Jude," Brooke said.

He let go his strong embrace and lifted her chin. "First things first. She's turning thirteen in a week. A teenager. Since we didn't get a chance to plan anything, that's the next priority. Nothing big or fancy. Make it exactly what she would want. Take yours and her mind off the rest of this mess for a while. To be honest, I'm a bit jealous of her. Lainey has the rest of her life made now."

Brooke nodded and scooted back to her own pillow. She didn't care about the farm or having it made. All she wanted was to keep her new family together.

LATER THAT WEEK, Lainey tried to do homework at her desk. She wanted to get her makeup work over with, even if it was a Friday night. While she was gone, they had finished *Romeo and Juliet*, and Ms. Reagan assigned the students to research Shakespeare's time period. Lainey chose plagues and diseases, but it was hard to concentrate right now on festering boils or people who never, ever bathed—not with her so-called 'party' the next day. She wasn't really in the mood to celebrate or do homework. She'd rather just sit and think about how she'd never get to be with Grandpa on the farm again.

She went to her closet and fished along the back wall to grab the old tennis shoe. Her claddagh was still in there. Between losing Deena, Grandpa dying, and another trip to the farm for his funeral, Lainey had forgotten where she'd put the thing. The stupid symbol of love. She shoved the ring in a pocket and went back to the desk.

Brooke had arranged for Lainey to invite friends from school to go roller-skating tomorrow. "Maybe some boys, too!"

Friends. Not really. Lainey just found people to sit with at lunch, but these new girls were just as boy-crazy as Deena and Fakemom. After she'd invited Meagan and Holland to her so-called party, they'd both run directly to the corner table in the lunchroom where Tommy, Brad, and Ryan always ate. Without even asking her if it was okay, they'd invited the boys to come along to the rink. Worse than the girls' inviting them, they'd said yes.

She really missed Deena, but Deena was a rotten liar, and Lainey would never speak to her again. Although she sort of tried once. Lainey had gone to the office to order a new shirt for PE, and there Deena was, sitting on the floor, right next to a perfectly good chair. Her legs were spread as she bounced a pink super ball on the carpet. She'd broken at least five different dress code rules that day. Lainey felt anger bubble in her stomach. "Nice outfit, Deena. Maybe for Halloween, you can dress like a princess."

"Shove it, you little priss. Just doing my damn best to get kicked out of this place."

The principal spoke in staccato over the speaker phone behind the secretary's desk, "I am ready for her, please get her mother on the phone."

With eyebrows raised, the secretary nodded sideways toward Deena. "You're next, Miss Forman." Then she shook her head in what could only mean disapproval. Mrs. Smith knew everything Deena had ever pulled within the walls of that institution.

As Deena sauntered down the hall to face her judgment, she turned and flipped off everyone in the room with both middle fingers.

Lainey scrunched her face and yelled, "Right on track there, Deena!" That day, her ex-friend was dismissed from her free school lottery privileges.

Now that Lainey was less than twenty-four hours away from having to skate with an actual boy, she wished for some of the confidence Deena used to give her. That girl wasn't afraid of anything or anybody. *Deena's a liar.* She had to keep reminding herself. *I can't trust her.*

Still ignoring her homework, Lainey dug into her pocket for the ring and tried to spin it on the desk like a top. The lopsided design wouldn't let it keep true. She slammed it flat with one palm and looked around. On the wall directly in front of her hung the horse painting Grandma Tessie had wrapped and sent along when she'd first moved to Baltimore. She took it down and turned it over to see the Christmas picture taped on the back. Genevieve, Jeremiah, her.

She leaned her head back and spoke to the ceiling, "Mama? It's me again. I'm starting to see it. He loved you. Still does. And he loves Brooke for some strange reason. And Caden, of course. I think he misses Deena." She closed her eyes to gather courage.

"I don't trust him, Mama."

She opened her eyes and slid the claddagh back on the ring finger of her right hand, facing toward her. *Tell the world I'm trying to love someone.* She turned to check the time and noticed the fancy clothes once again.

Crap. The party tomorrow. She rested her forehead on the encyclopedia still open to the Elizabethan Age. What if Tommy asked her to skate couples? Meagan told Holland he planned to. She'd never held a boy's hand before. What if her hand got sweaty? What if Tommy wanted to skate backwards, and she tripped?

She heard a light knock and lifted her head. "Yeah?"

"May I come in?" Brooke opened the door, Caden propped on one hip. "Supper's almost ready, so I need you to come down to set the table." Her eyes darted to the clothes laid out on the bed. "Oh, look how pretty that shirt is!" She rushed over and stroked the sequins with her free hand. "The boys will flip when they see you. Now, what are their names again? Brad and—"

Lainey quietly got up and left the room. She left Fakemom talking a mile a minute to baby Caden. Right now, setting the table seemed much more appealing.

Chapter 14

SATURDAY AFTERNOON, the strobe lights pulsated balloon-sized blue, red, and green dots on the hardwood floor. "All-skate" was ending with Def Leppard's *Pour Some Sugar on Me*. Lainey leaned on the cement wall and glanced toward the arcade. Meagan and Holland insisted on skating every song and kept dragging her out to the center of the wooden floor. Lainey wasn't the greatest out on the rink; it was hard to control her long, skinny legs. At least she was starting to get the hang of stopping without having to slam into the concrete wall. The boys were having fun, too.

"We're going to the arcade," Ryan said. "There's a new racing game!"

"But you all promised to skate with us." Holland pouted.

Brad rolled over and laid an arm around her shoulders. His pudgy hand dangled half an inch from her flat chest. "Fine. When we hear the music change to a slow song, we'll get Tommy out here to skate with the birthday girl."

Tommy shoved him with both hands, forcing Holland to roll right into Meagan. Both girls toppled to the floor in a pile of tight jeans and neon pink.

Holland laughed, but Meagan looked like she wanted to cry. "You boys are lame. Go play your game." She held onto her left wrist and grimaced as they rolled away. "But don't forget the slow song," she called after them through closed teeth.

Megan turned to Lainey. "Unless you're scared of Tommy. Then I'll skate with him myself."

"You'll just fall over again." Lainey laughed and sped off, digging the tan wheels into the shiny flooring. She didn't want Meagan to notice how scared she really was. What if she embarrassed herself? As she skated past the arcade, she recognized Tommy's straw-colored hair and sweaty forehead through the clear partition. It bobbed up and down as he raced a life-sized plastic motorcycle.

Lainey rolled past the exit sign just as Brooke walked in through the double doors. The curve of her neck was tight, and her eyes squinted in deep focus. The weight of baby Caden's car seat made her lean left, as her head swiveled like an oscillating fan stuck on high speed.

Brooke was ten feet away when they made eye contact. Lainey took one more glance toward the arcade. There Tommy was, coming out alone. He stopped by the soda machines when Brooke shouted Lainey's name over the music.

She turned to see Fakemom huffing and puffing as she marched toward her. "Lainey! Why didn't you answer your phone?"

"You told me to leave it in a locker."

"Well, turn in your skates. We have to leave."

Lainey felt her hands clench into tight fists. She glanced toward Tommy, who was scrunching his forehead, staring. Ten feet to his left, Meagan and Holland huddled with their heads together. "You want me to leave my own birthday party?"

"I don't have time for this."

Lainey turned back toward Fakemom. "No."

"Excuse me?" Brooke's voice rose, emphasizing every syllable. Her eyes were red. They looked about to pop out of the sockets and roll away.

"You're three hours early," Lainey said.

"This is not the time to pick a fight." Brooke propped her free hand on one hip and leaned right to ease the weight of Caden's dangling car seat.

This couldn't be happening. It had been Brooke's idea to have this stupid party, and now she was ruining it. Lainey knew she'd be in deep trouble, but she was too embarrassed to care. "I'm not leaving."

Brooke set the baby down on the floor then placed her face three inches from Lainey's nose. "Deena's in trouble. We have to get to her."

Lainey felt her heart stutter. She squelched any emotion deep into her stomach. "Trouble follows Deena left and right. She deserves what she gets."

"What a horrible thing to say, Lainey." Brooke stood, grabbed her by the elbow and dragged her toward the skate rental counter. "Now, I'm the mother here, and I say get moving."

"You're the what?" Lainey's ears burned red hot.

"Move it!" Brooke's voice rose at the end to a pitch only dogs could hear, right when the music stopped for the announcement of Couple's Skate. Bystanders glanced over then looked away. Through the corner of one eye, Lainey noticed Tommy backing away, toward the others.

Brooke lowered her voice to a whisper. "You've got five minutes to get your stuff and change your attitude." She whipped around and left the rink in the same hurricane huff she'd flown in on.

Lainey's eyes felt like someone had blown black pepper into them. She didn't dare look toward the arcade, not again. As Lainey changed back to tennis shoes, Meagan waved goodbye with two fingers then skated toward the snack shop. She made it to the car with thirty seconds to spare, throwing unopened presents onto the floor behind Brooke's seat. She buckled up next to Caden, on the side as far away from Fakemom as possible.

The ride was deathly quiet, beltway traffic flying by in a haze. Brooke kept straight on the Northside Parkway.

"Where are we going?"

"The hospital." Brooke sniffed snot back up a nostril, still gripping the steering wheel with both fists. "Hand me a tissue from the diaper bag."

"Why are you crying?" Lainey waved a Kleenex toward Brooke's face. She should've been an actress. This woman could produce any amount of tears on demand. Deena had been in trouble more times than Jeremiah or Brooke even knew about. She would be fine, just like she always was.

Fakemom wiped her face and tried to blow her nose with one hand, while white-knuckling the wheel with the other. Tears relentlessly streamed down her cheeks. "I can't believe we let her go back." She rummaged through her bag for the cell. "Call your father and tell him we're on our way." She handed the phone over the seat.

"I have my own phone, remember?"

"Whatever, smart ass. Just call." Brooke dumped the phone back into her bag along with the soggy tissue.

Jeremiah answered Lainey's call just as Brooke was pulling into the Mount Sinai Hospital parking lot. He gave no greeting. "Meet me in the front lobby," he snapped. Then he hung up.

Lainey stared at the screen.

When Brooke and Lainey entered the building, Jeremiah rushed through the sliding electric door and grabbed Caden's car seat. "ICU, but they are allowing two visitors at a time if they are family." He gave Brooke a quick peck on the cheek.

"What's ICU?" Lainey asked.

Brooke's sobbing started again. She wiped her face on a cloth diaper.

Jeremiah led them to a sitting area the size of half a gymnasium. On the center wall, an electric fireplace was lit, a lame attempt to make visitors feel at home. The chairs looked comfortable, but the airy cushions flattened straight to a hard-wood base when anyone sat down.

Lainey moved from chair to chair.

"Pick a seat, would ya?"

Lainey felt like her veins could pop out of her temples any minute. She could hear Jeremiah take a deep breath.

"Lainey, seriously. Get over here and sit still."

If she kept moving, she wouldn't feel anything. The smell of hospital, a concoction of musty sickness and strong, cheap disinfectant, burned her nose and gurgled in her stomach. She could sense Jeremiah's staring eyes as she plopped into a lavender, upholstered seat ten feet away. "You'd think a hospital would have nicer furniture," she said.

"I've just about had enough of your crap, Lainey." Brooke gave another swipe of cloth diaper over her swollen eyes and rocked Caden's car seat with the toe of her flats.

"I can't believe you made me leave my own freaking party. I've never been so embarrassed—"

Jeremiah grabbed Brooke's arm. "Don't make a scene."

"No, Jeremiah. It's time someone was firm with her. I'm going all Tessie on her." Brooke shrugged his arm away and walked toward Lainey with a finger pointed straight toward her. "ICU means Intensive Care Unit. Your friend might die. If you could just shut up about your stupid party and show some compassion already—"

"Brooke," Jeremiah said.

Lainey felt tears warming her face. Deena wasn't going to die. She was too tough for that.

Jeremiah patted the chair next to him, but Lainey shook her head, refusing to give him any satisfaction.

He kept talking. "It's so much worse this time. You can't even tell it's Deena. Her face is all distorted. He broke her cheekbone and at least one arm." Jeremiah covered his face with his hands, elbows resting on his knees. Lainey watched his hands shaking against his face.

Lainey planted her feet on the gray carpet. With a pattern shaped in twelve-by-twelve squares, she was able to fit both feet into one square. It took all her energy not to glance back Jeremiah's way as she pictured Deena with her face all swollen worse than last time.

"Right after you left for the rink, I got a call from the police station. She was alert enough to call 911 and then she tried to call me. I answered but she didn't say anything, so I hung up figuring she pocket dialed me." Jeremiah let out another cry.

Brooke reached over to touch his shoulder. "They followed up on the calls she was trying to make and that's why they called your father. They have solid proof this time that it was her step dad."

Lainey tapped her toe against the carpet square. "Why are you so worried? She'll be okay. Deena's always okay."

"We should've fought harder for her, Jeremiah." Brooke's waterworks resumed as she picked up Caden and held him close to her chest. A dark puddle on Caden's light blue onesie grew the size of a grapefruit from her tears.

Jeremiah crossed to Brooke's chair then knelt in front of it. "We can't think like that right now. We can fix this. We just need her to pull through so we'll have a second chance to make it right." He laid his head on her knee.

Lainey watched as they whispered together. They weren't listening to her. Deena was going to be fine. How could they feel guilty? Deena didn't want their help. Anger boiled like a beaker in Lainey's chest. Had Jeremiah felt this much guilt when he left her with Grandma Tessie?

Lainey gritted her teeth but couldn't hold back any longer. She stomped across the carpet and stared directly into her father's eyes. "How can you sit there crying over someone who made you look like a fool?"

Jeremiah set his jaw.

Lainey could see his Adam's apple jumping as he swallowed.

"Deena's step dad beat her with a pipe out in the alley behind their house only months after his first attack. He left her in a bloody puddle on the street."

Lainey didn't want to hear any of this. "Why won't you listen to me?" They hadn't heard half of Deena's stories, getting in tight spots. She always got out. Always.

Jeremiah helped Brooke buckle the baby back into his seat. "Not this time, Alaina. 'Touch and go' the nurse said. That means she could die any minute." He leaned down, an inch from her face.

"Your breath smells like hand sanitizer. Nice time to start drinking again." Lainey started tapping her toe.

"Brooke and I are meeting with a social worker to fix the damage Mrs. Forman did last time. We have to convince them that we are fit to be an emergency foster family. If Deena lives through this, I will make sure she comes back to live with us." He walked toward the hallway and turned back to Lainey. "I suggest you help us by visiting her. They are making exceptions because she has no family around. If she doesn't make it, you'll regret the spectacle you just put on. Room 256. Second floor."

Tears burned her eyelids. Deena was too young. Only old people and mothers died.

"Get moving," he snapped. "Your friend is waiting."

As she walked alone down the second-floor hallway, she could hear people gasping for air. Machines were beeping everywhere at once. She focused her eyes on the teal green, rectangle signs outside every room ... 264 ... 262 ... 260 ... 258 ...

Deena wouldn't really die. She'd been hurt plenty of times and she always came out okay, even if Jeremiah hadn't been able to recognize her.

Lainey stopped and stared. There it was ... 256.

She pushed at the middle of the double wide, wood-grain door. It gave a cranky squeak. The jagged plastic flaps on the bottom fluttered. A deep scratch was etched in a perfect arc on the cold linoleum tiles.

She shoved harder with her shoulder. Tough like the barn door back in Virginia. Bracing her legs, she pushed inward.

The first thing she saw was a stark white bed. Next, a small thin body with skin the color of a paper grocery bag. Eyes closed and very puffy. Her right arm poked straight in the air, sheathed in a tube of white plaster. The sheet puddled on the floor, exposing blue-splotched legs with thick yellow socks on her feet.

The hospital gown was a dingy white and green pattern. Thin clear tubes poked out of her mouth and left arm. Liquid dripped every couple seconds from plastic lines hanging from a squishy bag on a pole. Lainey counted eight drops before venturing all the way inside.

She moved toward the TV stand. Two matching chairs were lined up perfectly against the wall, exactly like the ones from the lobby. She wanted to say something to break the silence, but what? It'd been different visiting Grandpa Jude. He looked at you. He smiled. He could talk, even if it did sound crazy sometimes.

Jeremiah was right. This didn't look like Deena at all. Her face puffed out like a blow fish with no hint of cheekbones.

The door flew wide open. A nurse in blue scrubs printed with yellow rubber duckies hurried in and fussed with the machines and tubes. "Don't just stand there, hon. Get over here and talk to her. She can hear, you know."

Lainey lifted the end of her ponytail and laid the tip on her tongue.

"Gracious, girl. Don't suck on your hair!" The nurse continued marking numbers on the chart at the end of the bed.

Geez. She sounded just like Grandma Tessie. Lainey pushed out her tongue and let the hair fall. One strand stuck, so she spit to dislodge it, then shoved a pinky nail between her teeth and chomped down.

"Hon, you're too pretty to chew your nails like that. I'm Nurse Violet. Sure you should be here all by yourself?"

Lainey dropped both hands and wiped the wet pinky on her faded black jeans. "My parents are talking to social services." She nodded toward the still body. "She's my foster sister. My friend."

The nurse nodded, changing bags on the metal pole. Then she covered Deena with the fallen sheet. When she pulled the curtain back from the window, the sun was so bright Lainey's eyes watered. Nurse Violet placed a hand firmly on the small of her back and steered her toward the bed. "Go ahead. Say hi. Do the poor thing some good to hear a familiar voice."

Lainey shuffled to the edge of the bed as the door closed behind the departing nurse. Alone again. The silly yellow socks showed through the thin white sheet. With her left pointer finger, she reached out and pushed down on the mattress. It was squishy and regained its shape in slow motion. She pushed the corner in deeper with two fingers. It rose back to normal, and Lainey's shoulders relaxed. If Deena could see what she was doing, she'd have called her a real weirdo. Once again, Lainey reached out to make a bigger indent. As her fist hovered over the sheet, Deena's big toe jerked.

Lainey crossed the room and dragged one of the chairs over to the bed. The low scrape of fake wood on linoleum didn't seem to bother the still, silent body. The large bed made her look small, less tough.

She planted herself right next to Deena's face. "I'm still mad, you know."

No response.

Leaning back, Lainey propped her feet on the mattress. "You lied, Deena. And really, which one was the lie, anyway? Loser Lorne or Joey?" A hot tear dripped to her chin. "Jeremiah and Brooke were helping you. Everything was turning out okay until you went and ruined it."

She gave a small kick to the bed frame. "How could you go back to your stupid mother? Or that slimy man. How could you do that?"

"She thought she had to."

Lainey whipped her feet off the mattress and turned toward the voice. "Jeremiah!" She clamped a hand over her chest, sucking in air. "My heart's beating so fast."

"Sorry." He brought the other chair over then propped his feet on the bed. Lainey resumed her original position, too. Her feet were six inches shorter than his size thirteen boats.

"It's not Deena's fault, Lainey."

"Whatever. She didn't have to lie. Not to me, anyway."

He laid his head back and closed his eyes. "Of course she didn't. No one has to do anything. Life just isn't as black and white as you make it out to be."

Lainey shrugged and chewed a nail.

"Bottom line is, you're going to have to find a way to forgive both her and me. If we can get into the system, she's coming home with us."

Lainey spit a piece of nail onto the floor so hard, saliva flew onto her sleeve.

"I'm done giving options." Jeremiah propped his hands behind his head. "I was too passive with Deena and look what happened. So now I'm laying down some laws. You've been with us almost a year and a half. It's time to accept facts—we're your family."

"And what a family it is!" She curled her lip. "A liar for a foster sister. A pink witch for a step mom. And a drunk father who cares about everyone in the world except his real daughter. Lucky me!" She dropped her feet to the floor and stood up.

Jeremiah reached over, eyes still closed, and clamped a hand over her wrist. "Sit. Back. Down. Mrs. Forman threatened to turn me into the police unless Deena took back her accusations against Lorne. She felt she had to lie."

Lainey slumped back down in the chair under the light pressure of his thick hand. She stared straight ahead. "She went back to her mom to protect you?"

Jeremiah nodded his head.

"You two deserve each other." Lainey couldn't figure out where the lies stopped and the truth began.

"You just refuse to give anyone a second chance, don't you?"

"Why should I?" She yanked her arm out of his grip. "Deena's just gonna lie again. You've got your precious new family. And if they don't work out for you, you always have the booze."

Jeremiah sat up straight, planting his feet flat on the floor. "You aren't the only one that's been hurt, here. Your friend's been beaten within an inch of her life, but still you only think of yourself. Genevieve would never have treated people the way you do. When are you going to grow up?"

She bit her lower lip and blinked back tears. "And she'd be so thrilled at how you've treated me?"

As he turned with his mouth open, rubber flaps scraped on the linoleum. He clamped his mouth shut.

Brooke knocked lightly on the half-open door. "May I come in?"

Lainey stood again and yanked the creases out of her jean legs so the frayed hems covered her tennis shoes. "Just take my chair. Then y'all can talk to your new daughter. She can *hear*, you know." Nurse Violet's words flashed hot meanness through her blood. It tickled her toes as she released them.

Brooke unpacked Caden from his seat once more. "Then where will you sit?"

Lainey snapped her white puffy coat shut and shoved her hands deep in the pockets. "Nowhere, Captain Clueless. I'm taking the bus home."

Brooke handed Caden over to Jeremiah and turned to her. "You can't just leave Deena like this—"

"Let her go," Jeremiah said. "It's not worth the fight."

Lainey yanked the door open so hard the handle slammed into the wall. She could hear the flimsy closet doors shaking from the impact. This time down the hallway, she couldn't see any room numbers.

Genevieve would never have treated people the way you do.

She pushed through big metal doors to the stairwell and sank onto the top step of the landing, hugging her knees. Her thoughts felt like a tornado blowing in her head. Everybody just expected her to forget all the bad things they'd done: Ditch her like Jeremiah, Grandma basically let them kidnap her, lie to her like Deena, aggravate her nonstop like Brooke. Then *poof!* Lainey has to forgive them all. *Poof!* She loves you. *Poof!* She's mature now. Well, it doesn't work that way.

As she twisted the claddagh around her ring finger, her mind floated back to the day Jeremiah and Brooke came home from their honeymoon, when Grandma Tessie had told her she'd gotten the order of things wrong. "You can't love right away," she'd said. "You have to try to be friends first."

What made her even angrier was the fact that Jeremiah was right. Deena didn't deserve this, and Genevieve would have wanted her to try harder to fit into the family. Her biggest desire had been to be just like her mother, but it turns out she just couldn't do it. Using the hem of her gray and pink striped scarf, she wiped her face dry and walked into the cold Baltimore air. Like Jeremiah said, Lainey wasn't worth the fight.

MOUNT SINAI HOSPITAL wasn't too far from the Traynor house. It took Lainey fifteen minutes to walk to the stop, ten for the bus to arrive, then a two-minute ride back to her neighborhood. From there she walked at a snail's pace, attempting to plan out her next move, but nothing feasible would come.

Because the streets in Mount Washington weren't laid out at ninety-degree angles, most of the arched intersections had triangular plots of grass right smack in the middle. The median on Ken Oak Road had a white pergola with a wooden park bench. A small bed of dirt sat waiting for spring planting. To the left was a bronze dedication plaque cemented into the ground. It honored Lieutenant Almond, a fallen firefighter who'd graced the community with protection, duty, and love for twenty years.

Instead of going straight home, Lainey tightened her scarf under her chin and sat on the bench under Lt. Almond's pergola, wishing she'd brought a pair of gloves. From that angle she could see the green, latticed frames covering the side windows of the house, the rounded hedges lining their corner lot. JT loved to bury things in that section of the yard. She'd have to leave him behind this time, since she didn't even know how she'd take care of herself. She couldn't neatly plan out a route like she had for the Sisters Tour. She wasn't crazy enough to try driving off in the car, like at the beach.

Lainey looked over at the plaque in the cement. She glanced left and right to see if anyone would notice if she started speaking. "Lt. Almond, I'm going to talk to you because I have no one else," she whispered. "I'm mad at the world, and no doubt my Mama's not so thrilled about that right now. What they expect me to do is ignore the truth. That's what they really want. Jeremiah acts like he wants me around, but he doesn't mean it. I remind him of Genevieve.

"It doesn't matter where I go this time, but I'm done. My own father doesn't love me enough to fight for me, even though he protects everyone else. He was fine for eight years without me." Saying the words aloud lightened the boiling anger to a light simmer. "And where would I go?"

She slid off the bench and knelt in front of the brave man's plaque. "If I tried to go to the farm, Grandma would just make me come right back. My aunts wouldn't be much help either. They'd never go against Grandma Tessie."

With one finger, she traced the reverent words engraved in bronze, praising the selfless man. "You sacrificed yourself. I probably would've felt safe with you around. If only Jeremiah was more like you, Lt. Almond. He said it himself. 'I'm not worth the fight.'"

"Yes, you are."

She tried to leap up but fell flat on her butt. "Crap, Jeremiah, you keep sneaking up on me," she cried. "I'm gonna have a heart attack before I turn fourteen."

Lainey stayed on the cold concrete slab and linked her hands under her bent knees. The chilly cement cut right through the thin denim. "How long have you been standing there?"

Jeremiah sat down draping one arm over the back of the bench and resting one leg on the other knee. "Long enough to hear what you think of me."

"Oh yeah?" She didn't feel bad. "What're you doing here?"

"Wanted to make sure you got home safely. Contrary to what you believe, I have paid close enough attention to know that you have a tendency to run when things get prickly." He pointed across the block. "I parked over there to keep an eye on the bus stop. Saw you come over this way, so I followed."

"Shouldn't you be with your new foster daughter? Your loving wife? Your precious baby boy?"

Jeremiah blew hot air into cupped hands. "Yes. I should also be with my first child. We should all be together at the hospital because a member of the family is fighting for her life, but it seems like one of us is always running away." He blew into his hands again.

"You planned to marry Brooke and start a new family, and the only reason you came and got me was cause Grandpa Jude got sick. You chose to drink your sadness away and never thought about my sadness. You choose everyone else in the world but me." Hard as she tried, she could not stop the tear from dripping down her cheek. She lowered her eyes so Jeremiah wouldn't see.

"You're not completely off track, Lainey. I am a selfish man. But when it comes to marrying Brooke, you got it all wrong."

"I'm not stupid. You were engaged before you ever came down to the farm." Out of the corner of her eye, she watched his chest rise up and down like he was holding a laugh inside. "What's so funny?"

"Can you keep a secret?"

"Yeah."

"It's not really a secret, but more of a sore-spot-so-we-should-never-mention-it-again kind of thing."

"Adults are crazy."

"Yes, we are, but I want to be completely honest with you or we won't ever get past all this."

"What's the secret?"

"You were the main reason I proposed to Brooke in the first place."

She raised her eyes and squeezed her eyebrows together.

"I was in such a panic of having to face Grandma Tessie alone, so I jumped the gun a little and asked her two days before we came down to Virginia."

"Would you have married Brooke if I wasn't around?"

"Not as quickly, but I definitely would marry her again." Jeremiah cleared his throat.

"Where's your coat? Your ears look sunburned."

"That would be the start of frostbite. I left my coat at the hospital." He covered them with his hands. "You know, we own a nice warm house just fifty feet away. We could take this conversation inside, then I wouldn't need to amputate my earlobes." He nodded toward the plaque. "It'll have to be without good old Lt. Almond."

Lainey hid her grin by laying her forehead on both knees. Her butt felt frozen from the concrete. "I don't want to go back to the hospital," she whispered.

"I'm not so thrilled at the prospect either. Being responsible wears me out and seeing Deena like that makes me want another drink. But in a family, we do what we have to in order to help each other." He stood and offered both hands. "Right?"

Lainey reluctantly put both skinny hands into his meaty ones. Despite the frozen air, his hands felt warm and moist. And scratchy. When he pulled, she flew up light as a dollar bill in the wind. He put an arm around her shoulders as they went up the stone walkway to their front door. She resisted the urge to pull away.

"We need to settle a few things," Jeremiah said. "Together. Just me and you."

The boiling she felt back at the hospital turned to butterflies. "I'm glad you came for me."

He nodded and held the screen door open for her. "That's good to hear."

In the kitchen, Jeremiah heated milk for hot chocolate. He stood in front of the stove, stirring, while Lainey sat holding JT at the breakfast counter burying her face in fur.

"Here's how it's going to work," he said. "We'll warm up now, because I froze off my gonad—" He cleared his throat. "I'm really cold. We also need to hash a few things out. Like this tendency to bolt whenever things get uncomfortable."

"Maybe it's hereditary." She raised her eyebrows.

"Hmm." He paused, raising his own eyebrows in response. "We're both done running?"

She nodded.

"Like it or not, we are stuck with each other, and I am far from perfect. I'm going to anger you at least once a week whether it be saying the wrong word, saying no to extra allowance, or making you obey Brooke."

She nodded again.

"Good. After hot chocolate, I have to get back to the hospital. If Pam Forman shows up, I don't want Brooke to have to deal with her alone. Especially since Caden's there. Understood?"

"Yes." Lainey cozied her nose and cheeks back into JT's fur. It smelled like he'd just eaten a bacon treat.

Her father kept clinking his mug with a spoon. "Now, let me explain the 'it's not worth the fight' comment."

She stuffed her nose deeper, until the nylon collar scratched her cheek. She felt a warm tear leak out.

"I'm sorry I hurt your feelings."

She closed her eyes.

"What I meant was, the situation wasn't worth arguing over. Ever hear the phrase 'pick your battles'? That's what I was trying to do. I wasn't saying I didn't want you around." He slid a blue china mug across the counter. "Understand?"

She opened her eyes to reach for the cup then blew at the rising steam. There was something else pressing on her heart even more. "You really think Genevieve is angry at me for treating people bad?"

"Yes, I do. And at me for leaving you behind. For drinking like a sieve. On top of that, I know she would've done better by Deena. I had a bad feeling and didn't do anything because I was too afraid of Mrs. Forman's threats. When I imagine someone hurting you like that, I … Deena didn't have anyone who cared enough to get angry for her." Jeremiah closed his eyes. "If Genevieve were here, things wouldn't be so messed up. That's for sure."

Lainey tilted her head, staring at his closed eyes, his sad expression. "Are you still mad at God for taking her away?"

"Yes. I'm working on that, too." He reached over the counter to nudge her shoulder.

She licked a drip of chocolate from the side of her mug.

"I made a lot of promises to your mother that I want to follow through on. That's why helping Deena is so important to me."

"I felt closer to Mama when I lived on the farm. Grandma and Grandpa told me so many stories; it always felt like she was going to come back at any moment. I try to read those stories now, the ones I wrote down. I even started talking to her, but it just doesn't feel the same as when I lived on the farm."

"Your mother was my best friend, and I have ten years of stories. It still hurts to tell them. Not quite fair to you, is it?" Jeremiah moved around the island to sit on the stool by her side. "I guess we both have to try harder to remember her."

Lainey reached out a hand to cover his. "She'd be really mad that I call you by your first name."

"She was forgiving, too. She always forgave me whenever I messed up." He laid his free hand on top of hers, like a stack of pancakes.

"I owe Brooke an apology for the way I've been treating her." Lainey lowered her eyes.

"You're right."

"I'm not a very nice person, am I?"

"I think you are a smart and passionate girl that likes things a certain way. You will learn how to love people the more you practice."

"I just get so annoyed!" Lainey rolled her eyes.

Jeremiah smiled. "Back to business, now. One more thing we need to discuss before I go back to Mount Sinai."

"Yeah?"

"You brought up the farm ..."

She glanced up when his voice drifted off. Was he going to send her back until Deena got better? Send her away again?

"Yeees?" she responded, a little louder.

"You own it."

"What?"

Jeremiah took a deep breath. "After the funeral, Tessie told me they want you to have the farm. You own it now. It's all yours."

"I just turned thirteen!"

"Until you're eighteen you'll need a guardian to conduct business. Sign contracts. That could mean Tessie, me, or even a lawyer. Just not that slimy crook who came with Mrs. Forman." Jeremiah laughed at his own joke. "Technically though, the Weston family tobacco farm in Waverly, Virginia is now owned by one Alaina Rose Traynor," he added. "It's in your name already."

She jumped off the stool, knocking her mug over on the counter. A thin stream of chocolate backwash trickled out. "Does that mean I have to go live there?"

"What it means is, you have choices to make."

She paced from fridge to sink, chewing on what was left of her thumb nail. "Like—what choices?"

"I know how much you want to be back there, but I don't want you to go. Mostly this will matter when you're older, and Tessie is gone. You'll always have a place to settle down if you want. Or to sell. Or you could even change things around like people have wanted Grandpa Jude to do for years. You'd be set for life, then. What I'm saying is, you have options."

Lainey stared at her father. Just an hour ago she'd wanted more than anything to run back to the farm, even though she knew it was impossible. Now he was sitting there telling her she could go if she wanted. Anytime. The knot in her stomach felt like she'd eaten a bucket of Lincoln Logs. "What should I do?"

"I think you should stay with your family." He took a deep breath in through his nose and exhaled. "Besides, if you aren't around, Brooke will smother poor Deena. You have to stay to protect your best friend."

"Ha!" Lainey leaped up to sit on the counter, drumming the cabinet doors with her heels. Deena really was her best friend. "What about Grandma Tessie? Does she want me to come back now?"

"That's something you two have to discuss. All I know is, we need you here, Lainey." He reached over the sink and tousled her curls. "There's one last thing I need to show you. Wait here." He disappeared down the basement steps.

He returned, holding three small, black books. The bindings were cracked from light use, and they smelled like mildew and dust.

"You should have these." He laid them on the counter.

Lainey reached out to wipe a powdery film off the leather. She had known about the books from when she'd eavesdropped on their fight, but she had never wanted to read Jeremiah's words. Now she was changing her mind.

"You and I have more in common than you might think." He tapped the books two times. "These are my Genevieve memories."

She looked up at him.

"The whole first year after the accident, I was a mess. Shocker, I know," he joked. "I couldn't eat, sleep, work. I started writing every memory from the day we met. All the way up to the pineapple pizza she made me eat that last night, before …"

Lainey wrinkled her nose. "I hate pineapple on pizza."

"I know, right? But I would have done anything for Genevieve."

After setting the mugs in the sink, he slid the two other notebooks closer. "These are yours now. New details about your mother to absorb in your memory. Ones you may not have heard."

He picked up his car keys.

Lainey noticed his hands shaking like they had been earlier in the waiting room.

"You don't need to come," Jeremiah said, "but I have to get back to the hospital."

"Can I have a hug?" It was the biggest emotional risk she'd ever taken.

Jeremiah stared at her with a look of fear in his eyes. She'd finally shocked him senseless. "Of course, come here." Father and daughter held a true embrace for the first time in almost ten years.

Lainey pulled back first, not wanting to cry in front of him. "Thanks, I sort of needed that."

"Me too, Lainey. I better go see what Phil wants."

Lainey nodded. "Don't forget a coat this time," she said. "And no stops at the state store!" She raised her eyebrows at her father as he gave her two thumbs up.

Lainey watched from the kitchen window as her father crossed the street. Jeremiah turned, spotted her in the window then mouthed, "I love you, Lainey."

She waved then opened one cover of his journals to caress the soft paper. More memories of Genevieve. And her father had come after her. He did love her; he just really sucked at it. She twirled her claddagh ring in slow circles, slipped it off and placed it on her left hand. "I love you, too, Dad," she whispered.

§

BACK IN HER BEDROOM, Lainey cuddled with JT in the dormer window seat. Jeremiah's memories lay side by side in chronological order on the comforter of her bed. She leaned herself on throw pillows then laid her sleeping pillow on her lap, turning it over to hide the drool stains.

She flipped through the pages, reading from how her parents met all the way to how Gen dropped everything the moment his parents had passed away. She was by his side for the rest of her life. Lainey sniffed back tears. She reached over to the desk to pick up her favorite gel pen. Three blank pages were left in the notebook. Once again, she started writing:

Dear Mama,

I think I completely understand now. You loved Jeremiah with all your heart, so you took care of him every chance you got. Grandma and Grandpa tried to tell me. I was just too stubborn to listen. They call me headstrong, and it's true. But I'm gonna do better. I forgive Jeremiah for being so sad when you died. That's really why he left me with Grandma Tessie. I've gotta try to love him better. And I'm even gonna be nicer to Brooke. She really does try (too hard). I sometimes wonder if you'd like her. From what everyone tells me, you probably would have. I'm not nice like you, not as much as I should be.

They're gonna help Deena, so I'll have a foster sister. And I have a brother, too. His fuzzy hair sticks straight up, and he has blue eyes just like me. I haven't told Brooke how much I love him yet, but I will. She probably thinks I hate Caden. She thinks I hate her, too. I don't. Not anymore. Right now, I could even say I like her—when she's not being a pain. I'm almost glad Jeremiah married her. You're helping me already; I just know it.

I need more help deciding what to do. The farm's all mine, Mama. Jeremiah says that everyone else already does the work, but wouldn't it be wonderful to be back in Virginia? The sweet smell of pink tobacco flowers, my room in the barn, the tiny orchard for JT to run in. Even though tobacco might not be the right thing to grow anymore, I don't think I'm strong enough to make any changes. I want it to be just like it was when you were there and Grandpa, too.

I've started making friends here, although who knows if I'll have any left after my disaster of a birthday party today. What's worse, Deena's real bad off. If she dies, I don't know what I'll do. I hated her for lying to me. <u>Hated</u> her. I'll tell her I'm sorry as soon as I see her.

Are you with God, Mama? I'm afraid to talk to Him anymore, and Grandma Tessie's not happy about that. I just don't know what to say. I've been mad for so long.

Grandma Tessie once said I'd know I loved someone when I was willing to be loyal. Well, I'm gonna be loyal to our family, I promise. And respect Brooke and love Caden. I'll be kind to Deena and love ~~Jeremi~~, I mean Dad.

One more thing: Could you please ask God to let Deena live? I'd really, really appreciate it.
I miss you, Mama.

Love, your daughter,
Alaina Rose

She closed the book softly. Then, with thoughts less jumbled, jogged up the street to the bus stop. She was going back to the hospital to be with her family.

Chapter 15

LAINEY FELT A LUMP growing in her throat as she walked down the long hallway to Deena's room again. Apologizing had never been her favorite thing in the world, but Deena would be easy. Apologizing to Brooke would be a new level of humility. At the end of the hall, she noticed Nurse Violet waving at her behind the counter. Lainey smiled, but fear gripped her stomach with a dull pain. Once again, she stopped at room 256 then pushed the door, opening a crack to see who was in there.

At the squeak and scrape of rubber flaps, Brooke turned and leaped out of her chair. "Hey there, Lainey."

Lainey took a good look at Brooke. Deep down she knew all her attention and actions came from a deep love. Lainey realized she could probably take some pointers from her stepmom.

"I tried to call you and Jeremiah, but you guys didn't answer your phones. Deena opened her eyes an hour ago. The doctor believes she should be able to make a full recovery with a little time." Brooke pointed toward Deena's bed.

"Jeremiah's not back yet?" Lainey asked.

"He texted me when he left the house that he had an errand to run and then he'd be back. I'll go call him again."

"Wait." Lainey held up her arm to stop Brooke. "I need to say something first."

"Okay." Brooke picked up Caden from his car seat and placed his head on her shoulder.

"Jeremiah told me about the farm."

"Oh good. I'm so excited for you, honey." Brooke bounced a slow rhythm for Caden's benefit.

Lainey swallowed. "I need to apologize for the way I've treated you all this time. I was a brat and never gave you a chance."

"I forgive you, Lainey."

"You're a good mom to Caden and a good stepmom to me." Lainey could feel a burden lifting from her shoulders. Forgiveness felt good.

Brooke teared up at the compliment.

"And I need some advice." Lainey could see Brooke pull her head back in surprise. She felt the same shock at her new feelings. "After Deena gets better, I'd like to hear your opinion about what I should do with the farm."

Brooke let out a guttural mixture of a laugh and sigh. "We don't have to wait till she wakes up. Don't go back to the farm. We need you with us. We love you." Brooke took hold of Lainey's shoulders and pushed her closer to the bed. "Go on. We can finish this when your father gets back. Your best friend needs you."

Deena hadn't visibly improved much in just a few hours. The swelling was everywhere, broken arm stabbing straight into the air. Deena's eyes opened to slits.

"Look who decided to show up," Deena mumbled through puffy lips and clenched teeth, the words strained and faint.

Lainey sat down in Brooke's chair. "Hi."

Deena blinked and sucked in a quick, deep breath. "Hey."

"Sorry I got so mad outside your mom's house."

"I would've been pissed at me, too."

"It wasn't your fault."

Deena tried to smile, then winced. "Shouldn't … have lied. I had no idea Jeremiah didn't have permission to keep me until Mom threatened to get him arrested."

Brooke took a deep breath and opened the hospital room door. "I'm going to call Jeremiah again. To see what's keeping him." The rubber flap squeaked faintly behind her and Caden when she closed the door.

Lainey turned back toward the hospital bed and propped her feet on the footboard. "So, you're gonna be stuck with us if Jeremiah can get everything straightened out."

Deena gritted out a shaky grin. "That's what Brooke said."

"I guess your stepdad is in jail."

"I sort of wish I had died just so he'd have to pay out the wazoo for this."

Lainey sighed in relief. Deena still had her sick sense of humor. That had to be a good sign. "So, Deena," Lainey said, "I have to warn you—we have the craziest step/foster mom ever."

"She's tried to clean this bathroom twice since I woke up."
Deena's jaw popped and clicked whenever she opened her mouth.
"Oww. The wires hurt."

"Stop talking then. I guarantee you, though, I can't ever call
her Mama. Not to be mean or anything, it's just—that's reserved for
Genevieve. We'll have to think of something more fitting." Lainey
tucked the sheet under Deena's good leg. "How about Mamooke?
You know, a mix between Mama and Brooke."

Deena winced again. "It hurts to laugh."

"Remember the first time Lorne did this a couple months ago,
and you came to the farm in Virginia? You liked it there, right?"

"Uh huh."

"What would you think about living there for good?"

Deena furrowed her eyebrows.

"My Grandma left me the whole freaking farm. I can move
there anytime I want."

Deena let out a groan. "You're leaving me after all this?"

Lainey leaned closer to Deena's ear. "No. I'm done running
away. Jeremiah said it was my choice to live on the farm or not."

"What are you saying?"

"I miss the farm, and I miss Grandma Tessie."

"You'd really go?"

"What if I could convince Jeremiah to let us all go?"

"Can I smoke the tobacco?" Deena joked as her eyelids
fluttered. She was struggling to stay awake now.

"I'll disown you."

"Wouldn't want that. I think I need to rest." Her eyelids closed
again. She was breathing shallowly through her mouth.

Lainey closed her own eyes to daydream about being in
Virginia, but no clear visions would come. She couldn't see
Grandpa standing by his tractor or Evelyn cooking in the kitchen
anymore. Even her loft was blurry. She couldn't remember which
horse painting was leaning on the wall directly under the porthole
window. The green luscious tobacco leaves would all dry out and
cause harm. What she really needed was to talk to Grandma Tessie.
She'd know better than anyone what Lainey should do.

She fished out her cell phone from her back pocket and moved
by the window as she dialed. All she could see of Baltimore was a
massive parking lot full of cars.

Grandma answered on the second ring. "Hello, sweets. How's
Deena? Brooke called me an hour ago to ask for prayer."

"She looks pretty bad but she's finally awake."

"I promise you, she'll heal real quick. She's tough, that one."

"Jeremiah and I finally had a conversation. I'm starting to let everything go. He also told me about the farm. Grandma? I'm scared to make the wrong decision."

"Let me be very clear, Lainey. There is only one decision to make."

Lainey knew it. The daydreams of living on the farm were just that. Daydreams. She had to live here with her new family. "I feel guilty when I think of you without Grandpa or Aunt Faith, and Beth, and Madeline."

"I love you for that, Lainey, but you have to realize I was only a substitute for Genevieve. And a poor one at that. You have to live your life with your father, and I am getting back to living mine. I have a great grandchild on the way, you know. When it's a better time for you to make decisions about the farm, your whole family can help you make the right ones. Me included."

"Am I your favorite grandchild?"

"You know better than to ask that. But I will admit, you were more than a granddaughter. You were a daughter for eight years."

Lainey glanced at Deena's cast. The fingers jutting out from the white plaster were all pink and purple and swollen. "It's probably not a good time to ask them to follow me to the farm, is it?"

"No."

"It feels like this whole family needs a little taste of Grandma Tessie. We're a mess."

"I am not a miracle worker, Lainey girl. That's God's department. When it's the right time, He'll bring you all back here. Don't fight the growth, Lainey. Embrace your new role."

"We'll take long vacations to the farm in the summer. For months at a time."

"That sounds like a good plan."

"Grandma?"

"Yes?"

"You were the best substitute I could ever have asked for."

"Thank you, my dear girl. I want constant updates on Deena, now. Hear me?"

Lainey hung up the phone, then slid the gold claddagh off her left hand. Grandpa had given it to Grandma Tessie because he loved her, and Grandma had given it to her for the same reason. Friendship, loyalty, and love.

"I don't think I need this as a reminder anymore," she said. She slipped the ring halfway onto Deena's swollen pinky with a steady hand and looked up at the white speckled ceiling tiles. "Mama, say hi to Grandpa—"

Lainey heard the door open. Turning to see Brooke, Caden, and Jeremiah, she finished her thought in a whisper. "And tell God I think we're going to be okay down here."

"Is she asleep?" Brooke asked.

Lainey got up to allow Brooke to take her seat. She stood next to her father.

"Guess what? Phil just offered Jeremiah a bonus," Brooke said. Her eyes were shining as she smiled with pride. Her glance went back toward Deena. "Hey, you put your ring on her finger. You're going to lose it if you leave it half on like that."

"I just wanted her to know we are true friends forever. Maybe even sisters someday. Do you think it's really a possibility?" Lainey glanced again at Jeremiah while taking the ring off Deena's pinky.

Jeremiah nodded again.

Lainey wondered what was making him so quiet. "I apologized to Deena for my anger toward her. And to Brooke for how I've treated her."

"That's really good, Lainey. I'm proud of you," Jeremiah said.

"We should take a selfie together. All of us with Deena while she's sleeping. That'll make her so mad but secretly she'll love it." Lainey directed them to put their heads next to Deena's and gave Jeremiah the phone since his arms were longest. Deena didn't wake up once during the commotion.

"Dad, I need a few selfies of just you and me."

"And why is that?"

"I guess this is the last of my confessions today. The summer before I came to live with you, I had made it my mission to black out your eyes in every picture in the house. I started with the photo albums so Grandma Tessie wouldn't find out right away." Lainey looked at the floor.

Jeremiah chuckled. "Then come over here, daughter, and let's take a few pictures together."

≈

Two weeks later, Deena was sitting up in her hospital bed wearing sweatpants and a t-shirt. The nurses allowed her to put on real clothes in anticipation of going home this afternoon. If the physical therapy department liked her progress getting herself up the stairs, she would be released. Her test was in less than an hour.

Lainey had set up a game of war on the rolling bedside tray. Deena had beaten her three times in a row already. "I should have just gone to school today. It's clear I will never get into college on a card playing scholarship," Lainey said.

Deena mimed a mic drop with her one good hand. "While I head to Vegas for the poker championships. I'll remember you in my will when I become a millionaire."

"I don't think your luck at war is going to help you learn poker."

"What a doubter. So where are the parental units? If I have to stay here one more night because they don't show up, I'll..."

"Just chill. Brooke went to see the head nurse about dietary restrictions for when you come home. Jeremiah disappeared early this morning and didn't tell anyone where he was going. Maybe he bought us a bigger house and wants to surprise us."

"I didn't really appreciate living with you all before. Not like I should have. But I am going to like having two attentive parents. And siblings. I won't take anything for granted. I even promise to keep my side of the room clean," Deena said.

"NO!," a voice shouted from the hallway.

Deena and Lainey jumped at the scream. A rush of premonition steamed through Lainey's blood. Something was wrong. She rushed toward the door and pulled it open. "You better stay here, Deena," Lainey instructed.

Right outside Deena's room, a large group had gathered; she pushed her way past adults twice her size. She could hear Brooke yelling. "Stop it! Jeremiah, let go!"

"Excuse me." Lainey shoved a man in purple scrubs to her right.

"I have to get up there." She shoved a woman with pearl-rimmed sunglasses on her head.

"Let me through; that's my mom." With one last shove, Lainey stopped short at the front of the small crowd face to face with Jeremiah, ripping Caden out of Brooke's arms. "I just want to hold my son for a second," he said with a slur.

Brooke tried swatting Jeremiah's hand away from her arm, but he was too strong for her. She switched Caden to her right hip and turned her body to shield him from Jeremiah's reach.

"Everybody out of the hallway!" Nurse Violet barked the orders to which all bystanders listened. In thirty seconds, the family was alone with two security guards sneaking up behind Jeremiah, looking ready to pounce.

Then Jeremiah saw his daughter. "I screwed everything up, Lainey."

She could smell booze fouling the air.

"I just want to give my son a hug," he said turning back toward Brooke.

Looking like she would hyperventilate, Brooke glanced over at Lainey. "He lost his job and didn't tell anyone. Which means we've lost Deena."

Lainey was confused, but she felt an innate desire to take control. The adults in her life certainly weren't going to. "Brooke, take Caden to Deena's room." Lainey set her jaw. "Now!"

A heat rushed through Lainey's veins as Brooke squeezed passed her with Caden's head crushed to her chest. Lainey couldn't hear a word anyone was saying; the pressure in her ears felt like it could explode. All she wanted to do was cry.

Instead, Jeremiah started to weep. When the security guard grabbed his arm, Jeremiah didn't even fight.

"Arrest him." Lainey heard her voice say the words but didn't know where the strength was coming from at first. Then she remembered she was Tessie Weston's granddaughter. She was Genevieve's daughter.

The guards both took hold of Jeremiah, the shorter one cuffing him from behind. "He can sleep this off in our office downstairs. He'll be home by—"

"No." Lainey shook her head with a little more force than necessary.

The guards stared at the skinny thirteen-year-old making demands of them. Her hair was flying in all directions, but her face was calm.

"Arrest him. Call the police to come get him. He's disturbing everyone in the hospital and he's a danger when he's like this. I watched him shove a pregnant lady once. Let him sleep it off in jail." Lainey felt her mind clear of all distractions yet full of fear.

Jeremiah lowered his head and sobbed, his arms cuffed behind him.

"Come on, Dad, stop crying," she whispered in his ear.

Jeremiah looked up and into Lainey's eyes. "I let Genevieve down." He flipped his chin toward the security guards who carted him down the hallway.

Shaking from toes to scalp, Lainey went to find Brooke and Deena.

❧

Jeremiah was released by 8:30 that night, but he did not come home. He answered one text to assure them he was alive. All day Thursday Brooke was ready to call a divorce lawyer, but Lainey convinced her to wait until Grandma Tessie could get there Friday morning. The hospital wasn't able to release Deena to Jeremiah and Brooke, so she was waiting for a new foster family to pick her up.

Now, Brooke was making breakfast to pass time until Grandma Tessie arrived. "I'm proud of you, Lainey. I could see something wash over your face as you analyzed the situation." Brooke reached over the counter to push Lainey's hair behind her ear.

Lainey didn't swat Brooke's hand away like she would have even a week ago.

"I also heard you call me mom. Didn't you, Lainey?"

She rolled her eyes. "Yes, Brooke, I called you mom. And I called Jeremiah dad. Can we not rehash this? I was shell-shocked, and I won't let it happen again." She smiled at Brooke to show her she was teasing. It felt good to be rid of the weight of anger she had been carrying for two years. If she could only get rid of the worry about her father and Deena, then life could maybe get back to normal. Adulting was not fun at all.

Brooke laid a plate of waffles on the table while Lainey got the forks and knives. "You have to go to school this afternoon to take that math test. Focus on that. I have to look for Jeremiah once Tessie is here and can watch Caden."

"I should help you. How can I think about Algebra?"

Brooke shook her head. "This is the best time to think about Algebra. Distract yourself. You need to go back to being a kid."

"I'm going straight to the hospital after school," Lainey said. "I want to sit with Deena until she gets a family. Nurse Violet told me she'd let me in."

"I can get on board with that."

"Deena cried when I told her what Jeremiah did, and Deena never cries. It was horrible, Brooke. I can't stop thinking about ways we could still take her in. Maybe you could be the foster parent. Leave Jeremiah out of it completely."

"It doesn't work that way, Lainey. We're married and that's all they will see on paper. While we know he wants to make good on his promises to Genevieve by adopting Deena, good intentions mean very little to social services unless you are the biological family."

"Maybe we could get Grandma Tessie to adopt her." Lainey was never too stressed to eat, so she dug into the waffle.

"That's a great idea, Lainey." The voice came from the dining room.

Brooke and Lainey turned to see Jeremiah standing in the doorway, disheveled, but alive.

"Jeremiah!" Brooke jumped up from her chair but sat right back down. She was holding back tears and sniffling. Lainey dropped her fork onto the plate.

"I know I forfeited my rights to an opinion here, but for what it's worth, I think that's a very good plan for you all," Jeremiah said.

After a few seconds of silence, Brooke stood back up. "What do you mean, you all?"

"What he means," Lainey interjected, "is he's ditching us. So much for a fresh start, huh Jeremiah?" She stood next to Brooke and stared at him. "I thought you said we were done running. Not coming home is mega running."

"I'm weak, Lainey." Jeremiah wouldn't look her in the eye.

"Your promises and words mean nothing." She turned to Brooke. "I'm going to get dressed. I don't want to be late for my math test."

Jeremiah gave way as she brushed past him and through the doorway. "And then there were two," Jeremiah said then followed it with a half-hearted chuckle as he sat at the table where Lainey had been.

"You're a mess, Jeremiah."

"I am."

"And a drunk." Brooke refused to look him in the eyes.

"And a liar, a lousy father, a wretched husband," Jeremiah added to his list of sins.

"Where have you been?"

Jeremiah sat down and grabbed her hand. "I can't handle the pressure, Brooke. Ever since Genevieve died, I kid myself that if I do this or make that change, then it will all come together. It does for a hot second and then I fall again."

"You didn't answer my question."

"I slept in my car outside of a bar."

"You stayed in your car for thirty-six hours rather than coming home to fix this?"

"But, I did not go into the bar, which is a miracle. I'd say you have to believe me, but as you heard, my word means nothing."

"Jeremiah, cut the crap and just tell me what's going on."

"I've ruined everything. Without my job, I just think it would be best if you and the kids went to Virginia to live with Tessie."

"We can't go without you. We're a family."

Jeremiah covered his face with his hands. "I didn't just lose my job, Brooke. I lost the house, too. We've got nothing. Phil had dropped me back to office manager, so I've been using the small savings I had originally set aside for Lainey's college to cover our bills. That nest egg ran out three months ago. As did Phil's patience. When Deena was first attacked, that's when Phil finally fired me with a little severance pay. I've been out of work all this time and when it came time to take Deena home, I panicked because I couldn't hide anything anymore. You know the rest."

"Why lie about the bonus? Why not tell us the truth? I could've gone back to work or something."

"I can't face you with any more mistakes, Brooke. I can't look myself in the mirror. I should be able to function by now. Ten years since she died and look at me."

Lainey came back into the kitchen wearing her plaid uniform skirt with a navy-blue cardigan. "Can I say something?"

Jeremiah looked up with tears in his eyes and stood up to face her. "Of course."

"Jeremiah, we don't need you."

"Lainey!" Brooke said.

"Hear me out." Lainey turned toward her father. "We have people that can take care of us. Grandma Tessie's on her way here so if you don't get it together, we'll still be okay. Like I said, we don't really need you. What we do need is for you to stop being so self-centered. When I watched you walking away in handcuffs, I got a scary sensation that you and I are alike, and not in a good way. We make everything about ourselves. Look where that's got us. I am a spoiled nightmare to anyone in my way, and you are a drunk."

"She's right," Brooke spoke up. "You both are self-absorbed and hard to live with. I want to strangle you for not coming home, Jeremiah. For not trusting us to help you. Caden and I deserve better, so unless you figure out how to get some help, we can't be a family." Brooke left the room crying.

Lainey bit her thumb nail. "I have to catch the bus. If you wait around, Grandma Tessie should be here soon. Maybe she can smack some sense into you." With those words, she left her father sitting at the kitchen table, not sure if he would be there when she returned.

😋

That evening Tessie walked up to Brooke's bedroom to convince her to come talk things out. "Leave the baby in his playpen. Grab the monitor." She knocked on Lainey's door. "Downstairs in five." She then went to the den where Jeremiah was hiding. The lights were out, and he was pretending to sleep on the couch.

Tessie flipped the light switch on. "Jeremiah, I left you to your own devices once before and I think we've all learned our lesson the hard way. Join us so we can figure this out."

Jeremiah opened his mouth.

"Don't bother, son. There is no argument to be made. You are part of this family, and we are having a family meeting."

They gathered with Tessie in the living room. Jeremiah had showered earlier at least, and Brooke looked like she'd been crying for days.

"Tessie, I've already told Jeremiah that if he doesn't get help, we can't be together. I'm uncomfortable with his being here."

"I don't believe that, Brooke. You're angry with good reason, so I have no intention of convincing you otherwise. But he's here because he needs our help. We all need each other right now."

Brooke sat in the oversized couch and put her hands in her lap. Jeremiah sat on the piano bench, and Lainey plopped on the soft carpet in front of Brooke.

"Okay, Tessie, let's just get this over," Jeremiah said. "I've got to find a place to live."

"I was heading here this morning, and then an inspiration hit me," Tessie began. "Finding foster homes can be very difficult for older children, so I changed my GPS to the Baltimore Social Service office and convinced them to consider me for emergency custody of Deena. She's old enough to get a say in the matter, so I'm just waiting for the final call to say it's a done deal. She'll be able to leave the hospital as soon as we get the go ahead."

"I told Brooke this morning that you should adopt Deena. How creepy to have the exact same idea without me saying anything?"

"It's not a coincidence, Lainey. Neither is it creepy. God put it on both our hearts."

Brooke furrowed her brow. "You're going to take Deena and Lainey back to the farm with you?"

Tessie grinned. "No, dear. I'm going to take all of you back to the farm with me."

Brooked started to shake her head no, but Tessie held up her hand. "I've felt lost since Jude and Lainey went away. Been praying for a project or something that would give me purpose again. What better than to keep a family together?"

"Jeremiah needs more help than we can give him," Lainey said with a quiet voice.

"You're absolutely right, Lainey, but we will get him that help. He'll get a job and finally get into counseling for his grief and addiction which should have happened long ago. The farm is dry, so the only way for him to fall off the wagon would be to go with Evelyn on Friday nights. I think we can help him avoid Jillie's, don't you all?"

"How about I hire him?" Lainey stood up and went to sit next to Jeremiah on the bench.

"What do you mean, sweets?" Tessie asked.

"I own the farm, so I can hire the help, right? I'll hire Jeremiah as Amos's assistant, and we can figure out a different main crop to plant on the farm." Lainey rested her hand on Jeremiah's shoulder. "How about it, Dad? Want me for a boss?"

"I don't deserve your help." Jeremiah was holding back tears.

"Well, we don't deserve to be without you," Brooke left the couch to stand on Jeremiah's other side, placing her hand on his other shoulder. "We're family, Jeremiah. We have to try to figure this out. Together," Brooke continued.

Jeremiah turned to Lainey. "Are you sure?"

Lainey nodded.

Jeremiah smiled. "I used to love visiting the farm. Jude and I would shoot rusty coffee cans off tree stumps in the orchard. The best time to go was when Jude prepared the tobacco seedlings by burning mounds of brush. The fires needed stoking all night, so some years it turned into a week-long camp out. The smell of burnt ashes was something Genevieve missed dreadfully once we moved." He went silent for a moment like he was lost in his memory. "I would love to have you as my boss, Lainey. We could switch to livestock or make soybeans the main crop."

"The burnt ashes are my favorite smell, too," Lainey said. "Just like my mother's."

"But, Jeremiah, you can't do all this for the wrong reasons anymore," Tessie said. "No more guilt about Genevieve. There are no promises you have to keep other than being a father to your kids and husband to Brooke."

"I hear you, Tessie."

"Then start the healing by asking forgiveness of your wife and daughter." She pointed to the girls.

Jeremiah started crying again; a gasp escaped from his throat. "I was too ashamed to face you when things started going south again. I'm sorry for lying. I'm sorry for not being strong enough. I'm so sorry for everything." He placed a fist on each eye like he was trying to keep the tears from flowing.

Brooke squeezed his shoulder. "We forgive you, Jeremiah," she whispered.

"I forgive you, Dad."

Tessie hit the wall lightly with her hand. "Okay, now that this family is getting back on track, we have some planning to do. Lainey, go catch up on your homework and what all you missed this morning. We can't have you going into high school next fall as a dummy. From what I can tell you have missed a lot of school this year. Jeremiah, call the mortgage company to see how much time we have to sell the house without going under. Brooke, you and I can make plans on how to get your little family some personal space in that big house."

Jeremiah stood up. "Wait."

The women all turned to listen.

"I need to apologize to one more person." Jeremiah turned to his mother-in-law. "Tessie, I'm so sorry that I dumped all my grief onto you. Forgive me for not holding up my end of the bargain for Genevieve and Lainey. Please help me do better by my family."

Brooke grabbed him in a hug.

Lainey went to her grandmother's side and hugged her tightly around the waist as well. "We finally get to be together on the farm again, Grandma."

Tessie patted Lainey's shoulder and smiled at Brooke and Jeremiah.

Lainey lifted her head. "So, Grandma, since you're going to be divvying out spaces, I'm thinking we should have a talk about moving bedrooms around so I can have the master. I got used to having my own bathroom here in Baltimore."

"Oh, did you now?" Tessie laughed. Her cell phone chirped in her handbag.

The family watched as Tessie nodded to everything being said on the other side of the line. She hung up and closed her eyes for ten seconds. "Amen," she said.

"Are you going to fill us in, Tessie?" Brooke asked.

"Well, Brooke, you and I have a bigger task ahead. We have to find a place for Deena to sleep as well. She's being released from the hospital, and I will be her new guardian. We can pick her up in the morning!"

"So, Deena's going to get to be a Weston and I have to stay a Traynor?" Lainey asked with a smile.

"Hey, your mother happily chose to be a Traynor," Jeremiah said.

Lainey hugged Jeremiah. "We're going to make Genevieve proud and make sure you're okay, Dad."

Jeremiah hugged her back. "As long as you are with me, I will be."

THE END

About the Author

RACHEL MENIN earned her MFA in creative writing from Wilkes University and her M.Ed. from Clarks Summit University. In her free time Rachel edits her writer-friends' novels, watches (and sometimes cries over) Philadelphia EAGLES football, and amuses her husband every day with silliness and shenanigans. *After Genevieve* is her first novel.

CPSIA information can be obtained
at www.ICGtesting.com
Printed in the USA
LVHW011204190522
719131LV00003B/3